Straightening her shoulders, Nikita swallowed against the tears clogging her throat. "I–I love you, Michael. I have for a long time," she said breathlessly. "Before I introduced you to Chenelle I thought..."

"Do you know what I see when I look at you now?" he snapped. "I see you and me and all the things we did in bed and in the shower. I can't forget that."

Those images played in her mind. Nikita's knees shook. Her voice quivered a little when she stood up to him. "Is that such a bad thing? You like sex."

Michael exploded with fury. "You've got that right. The difference between us is that I don't pretend it's love."

Indigo Sensuous Love Stories

Genesis Press, Inc.
315 Third Avenue North
Columbus, MS 39701

ISBN: 1-58571-069-5
Manufactured in the United States of America

First Edition

Everything but Love

by

Natalie Dunbar

Genesis Press, Inc

ACKNOWLEDGEMENTS

I thank God for providing the talent and making a way for me to write this book and get it published. I want to thank my family for their love and understanding while I spent valuable time writing. I thank my critique group partners, Angela Patrick-Wynn and Karen White-Owens for their suggestions and support. I thank my editor, Betty Caldwell, and Sharon Morgan at Genesis Press for helping me focus this book.

Chapter 1

"I don't know why I'm so nervous! It's not as if I'm all starry eyed at the thought of marrying Michael."

Nikita Daniels swallowed back a rush of pure envy and took a good look at her best friend who was frowning at herself in the mirror as she tugged at her gown. In the background she could hear the boisterous sounds of the bridesmaids in the next room laughing and talking in various stages of dress, and she knew that on the other side of the church, Michael and his friends were getting ready for the walk down the aisle. "Girl, please!" Nikita said with a touch of humor that she really didn't feel. No matter how hard she tried to conceal it, the fact remained that she desperately wanted to be the one who was marrying Michael Matheson. "Plenty of women would love to be in your shoes because the man has got it going on in all departments. The way you two have been carrying on, it's got to be love."

Chenelle grinned then, her green eyes sparkling mischievously in her golden brown face. "We've been going at it because that man knows his way around a bed and he comes with some awesome equipment!" She laughed. "That's definitely going to be a big plus after we're married."

"Chenelle!" Niki fought back images of Michael making love to her. Clamping down on those thoughts, she reminded herself that he obviously didn't know of or share her feelings. Neither did Chenelle. After today Niki might still love him, but she would have to give up her dream of some day being the object of his love.

On chic satin pumps, Chenelle turned in the mirror to reveal a side view of the creamy satin and lace covering her voluptuous curves. One finger traced the pearl-encrusted lace along the revealing neckline.

"You know you love him," Nikita chided.

Chenelle's expression hardened, her eyes going flat. "Huh! I don't believe in love anymore, Niki. I've been hurt too much in the name of love."

Niki blinked in surprise, clenching her fist. Chenelle's words hit her like a slap in the face. "Not Michael?"

"No girl. You know how many times I've gone round and round with Lance Coltrane."

Niki nodded. "So why are you marrying

Michael?" Her voice broke a little, but Chenelle didn't seem to notice.

"Why not? He's good looking, intelligent, and sexy. Like you said, what more could a woman want?"

"Love?" Niki couldn't help pressing the issue. Michael was everything she wanted in a man too, but unlike Chenelle, she loved him. She loved him so much she knew she'd never get over it.

Chenelle laughed and Niki felt anger building inside of her. "Me and Michael have an arrangement. We're going to travel and have fun. He's even agreed to invest in my five year plan."

Shaking her head in amazement, Niki found herself muttering under her breath. "What a waste."

"No, it's not." Chenelle put her hands on Niki's shoulders. "We're both adults, Niki, and we know what we want."

"And you really think that will make it work?" Niki swallowed again, angry tears burning her eyes. I'm not going to cry!

"Of course I do. I wouldn't marry him otherwise."

Chenelle turned and gave her friend a quick hug. "I know you're only thinking of what's best for me and I appreciate that thought, but don't be negative about this."

Returning the hug, Nikita struggled to hide her shock. If Chenelle wasn't her best friend, she knew she'd be in the groom's area of the church, trying to convince Michael not to marry her. How would she ever maintain her friendship with the two of them after the wedding?

Three years ago, she'd met Michael at the toy manufacturing company where they are both employed and work on a number of projects together. She had fallen in love with his sharp intellect, good looks, and warm heart, and they'd quickly become good friends. It seemed like she'd loved Michael forever. She'd hoped he'd see that their friendship was the basis for a lasting love.

After working late one night they'd grabbed a quick dinner and run into Chenelle. Michael hadn't been able to take his eyes off her, and Chenelle had sparkled like a rare diamond. Sitting between them, Nikita felt their sizzling attraction firsthand. After that, they'd been inseparable.

She'd hoped and prayed that the relationship between her friends was simply a physical attraction that would quickly fade. No such luck!

Nikita felt the tips of her freshly manicured nails cut into the palms of her hands. This isn't about you, she reminded herself.

In a rustle of satin, Chenelle sank down on the cushioned loveseat. One hand smoothed at the pinned-up mass of curls on her head. "I'm really fond of Michael. He's a nice guy and like I said, everything I've ever wanted in a man."

"Not quite," Nikita interrupted, remembering the only man she'd ever known to throw Chenelle for a loop.

Chenelle blushed, her chest heaving slightly. "I know what you're thinking, but what I felt for Lance was more like a sickness. Thank God I've gotten over that."

"Maybe you haven't." Nikita bit her lip, suspicion growing within her. The people who upset you most are the people you care most about. Is Chenelle still in love with Lance?

"Yes, I have. I'm marrying Michael today." A proud note crept into Chenelle's voice as she continued. "We make a great couple. With our combined salaries, investments, and my financial plan, we'll be secure within the next five years."

Swallowing back an exclamation of disgust, Nikita groaned under her breath. Then she bent over and kicked off the fancy shoes. Rubbing one aching foot absently, she suspected that the real issue with Chenelle was dollars and cents. Her friend had been working on that big plan for financial success for several years now, and Michael wasn't the first man with whom she'd tried to implement it. Nikita's expression turned skeptical.

Several sharp raps at the door interrupted her thoughts. A querulous voice spoke in good-natured but imperious tones, "All right, ladies, get it together in there. Chenelle, I told your mother I was coming back here to light a fire under you'all. Everyone that matters is here. Let's get this show on the road! You've got ten minutes."

Chenelle winked. Grinning mischievously, she yelled, "Thanks, Aunt Doris!"

It was an inside joke in Chenelle's family. Her spinster aunt, Doris, was always in charge of everything, and she took her duties seriously.

Aunt Doris grumbled on, but they couldn't catch the words because of a growing commotion outside the door. Raised voices thundered back and forth.

Nikita stood up and stepped back into her shoes. "Let me see what's going on out there." Aunt Doris was arguing with someone. When Nikita opened the door and saw just who it was, she nearly rocked back on her heels in surprise.

Aunt Doris' tone was heating up. "Nikita, will you tell this young man that he's no longer welcome at any of the Crestwood family functions?"

Nikita stood with her hands on the door, her body filling the narrow opening. "Hello, Lance." She heard Chenelle groan softly in the background.

His Tommy Hilfiger jeans and shirt contrasted sharply with Aunt Doris' pale blue tea dress. Tense fingers clawed through the roots of his dreadlocks. Red lines of misery scored the whites of his onyx eyes as he tried to insert the towering bulk of his muscular six-foot-three-inch frame between the furious Aunt Doris and the door.

Lips tightening, Doris moved to block his path as he tried to step around her. All the while she stared him down, as if he were some kind of bug.

Looking over her head, he called to Nikita, "Where's Chenelle?"

"Getting ready to be married."

"No! She can't do that!"

"Why not?"

"Because she's in love with me!"

"Lance, she doesn't even want to see you."

"Yes she does! Ask her." With firm hands, he held Doris still, then moved around her.

Furious, Doris wagged a finger. "Young man, if you don't leave now, I'm calling the police."

"Ms. Crestwood, I'm sorry, but I have to talk to Chenelle."

Aunt Doris stomped closer, her voice gaining volume. "You are the last person Chenelle wants to see."

Feeling somewhat sorry for Lance, Nikita broke in. "Aunt Doris, let me handle this, please?"

Aunt Doris deliberated for a moment. "All right, Nikita, but you girls have five minutes, ten minutes tops, to get out here."

Nikita controlled her tongue. "We'll be out in a

few minutes."

Aunt Doris nodded. "Then I'll go make sure everything else is ready." After a few steps, she wheeled and said to Lance, "I'll expect you to be gone, young man," and started towards the chapel.

"Lance, are you still in love with Chenelle?" Nikita asked.

He glared at her. "I never loved anyone else. Why do you think I'm here, letting Aunt Doris browbeat me?"

"Do you want to get married?"

"Yes. No. Hell, I don't know. I just know that I can't let her marry someone else." He shifted his feet and put a hand on her shoulder. "Come on, Nikita, have a heart. Let me talk to her. You know how she feels about me." That was for sure, Nikita thought. But did Chenelle realize it?

With a swish of satin, Chenelle approached the door. Her eyes glistened with tears. "I'll talk to him," she said quietly. "Just make sure you come back and get me in ten minutes."

"Sure." Nikita widened the opening to let Lance in.

Chenelle turned to Lance, her face full of hope.

Lance's eyes lit up. "Chenelle!" he cried hoarsely, then pulled her roughly, almost violently to him. His lips covered hers hungrily.

Carefully, Nikita shut the door. Neither of them

even noticed. She was certain that Chenelle still loved Lance. Hopefully, her friend would back out of marrying Michael. Time to go see what's going on in the chapel. Nikita headed towards the front of the church.

Stumbling around in a white tux, Earl, the best man, caught up with her. He virtually reeked of alcohol. Slurring his words just a bit, he said, "I've been looking for you, Nikita. Have you got an aspirin? My head is killing me." Nikita had a flash of sympathy for him. Still hung over from last night's bachelor party, he could barely walk. How was he going to make his stand at the front of the church? She fished in the little cutesy purse that went with her outfit and gave him two aspirin.

"Hey, thanks. I'm forever in your debt. Now all I need is the water fountain."

"Right outside the groom's area," she said helpfully.

"Yeah. Thanks." He started to stumble away, then turned. "Ah—Michael wants to talk to you."

"Is there something wrong?" she asked, wondering if he knew what was going on in the bride's camp right now.

"I don't know. He says it's urgent. He begged me to come out here and find you."

Nikita sighed. "All right. I'll go, but we've only got a few minutes."

She walked back to the section of the church reserved for the wedding party. What would she say to Michael? Her thoughts dwelled on the things she couldn't say, such as the big convincing speech on why he should call the whole thing off. Don't marry Chenelle. She doesn't love you! I do! Much as she wanted to, it wasn't her job to tell Michael about the scene between Chenelle and Lance. The wedding would probably go on as planned. Lance had given up a chance to marry Chenelle in the past, and chances were, he still didn't have the guts to do it now. So where did that leave Nikita?

A heady blend of male cologne and after-shave mixed with musk assailed her as she entered the rooms reserved for the groom and his men. As she knocked at the groom's closed door, a couple of the guys in the outer room called out compliments at the sight her. Somebody whistled and yelled, "Hey Nikita, you're looking hot!" Flattered, Nikita grinned and murmured her thanks. She'd spent so much of her life trying to be one of the guys that she hardly knew how to act when men appreciated her female attributes.

Michael opened the door on a whiff of Perry Ellis cologne, looking deliciously handsome in his tux. The suit hugged the lines of his tall, lean-muscled body, the white color contrasting perfectly with his curling black hair and smoldering brown eyes.

Mama mia! If she had ever wondered what people meant by 'eye candy,' Nikita thought this had to be it, every bit as good as double chocolate with the nuts on top.

He gazed at her appreciatively. "You look good, Nikita. You should wear dresses more often," he rasped in that husky voice of his. A thrill of excitement shook her and her heart contracted. Only someone who knew him well could catch the slight slurring of his words. Earlier, one of his buddies told her that the bachelor party had gone on till four o'clock in the morning. Was it any wonder that half the guys were either still drunk, or hung over?

Nikita breathed in the scent of him, her heart fluttering. "You're looking good too," she said a little breathlessly. "Just think, you and Chenelle are only minutes from going down the aisle."

"That's why I've got to talk to you. Come on in." His warm fingers caught her arm and drew her into the room with an unconscious intimacy that made her yearn for more. She glanced around quickly.

"There's no one else in here," he mumbled, closing the door. "You should have been the best man." He seemed a little off balance as he dragged a wooden chair forward and motioned for her to sit down. "Make that 'best person,' because I can talk to you better than anybody else." Hauling another chair for himself, he sat on it backwards.

"What's this about?" Nikita held her breath.

He thrust a hand through his dark hair. "I couldn't sleep last night, and I've been nervous all morning. After waiting all these years to get married, the thought of going down the aisle has me shaking in my boots. I feel strange. It's all I can do not to light up, and you know I quit smoking years ago."

Her pulse doubled, seeds of hope sprouting within her. What was that saying? 'It's not over till it's over.' You're wrong to feel such joy. They'll get married and live happily ever after. Carefully, she asked, "Why, Michael? What's the matter?"

"Nothing that I can put my finger on, but it's like a dark cloud's hanging over my head. You know, I thought of getting married, when I was a lot younger, but we could never quite work it out. It took a while to figure it out, but when I scrutinized the successful marriages in my family, and gave it some thought, I realized that I was looking for the wrong things. That's how I know that Chenelle is special. I'm not looking for love, but we're friends. I respect her, and she's one gorgeous lady. We're real compatible. I'd be fool to call it off, wouldn't I?"

"I wouldn't say that." Nikita bit down on the inside of her lip in an attempt to squelch what she knew she must not say. "What if you could marry someone who really loved you? Wouldn't that be better?"

Michael tossed her a cynical glance. "Mmmph! I know exactly what I'm getting with Chenelle."

Nikita pulled her lips into a smile, despite the little pain piercing her heart.

"Half the guys are jealous as hell." Leaning forward, he rested his head on the back of the chair. "It's time I got married, Nikita. I'm thirty-two years old. I want to change my life, maybe even start a family."

"I can see that." Nikita leaned forward and pushed back the soft lock of hair that had fallen in his face. She let herself have that much. "Do you love Chenelle?"

"Love, my friend, is a dream somebody made up. I'm marrying Chenelle with my eyes wide open."

"Oh, Michael!" she said disparagingly. "How can you marry without love? If I can't have love, I'm not getting married."

Michael rubbed her shoulder gently, and the tingling warmth beneath his fingers spread within her. "I know, and I hope you find it. You'll make some guy real happy. Chenelle and I are different. We don't have stars in our eyes, but we care about each other. We're happy. I'm not looking for love."

"I'm sure she'll be grateful."

"Hey, I caught that. Just because I'm nervous and about to sign my life away doesn't mean I can't tell when you're being sarcastic." He tapped her nose.

Nikita gripped the edge of the chair. "What do you want me to do?"

"Just talk to me a little more. You have a calming effect on me, Nikita."

"Yeah, I put guys to sleep all the time."

He chuckled. "That's a good one. Does that mean you wear them out?"

"What do you think?" she shot back.

Michael pulled two miniature bottles of Martell from the pocket of his suit. "I think we should have a toast to the future."

Nikita shook her head negatively. "I don't believe you're doing this! Remember the agreement? No alcohol in the church?"

Michael merely stared at her, stubbornly extending the bottle until she accepted it and reluctantly twisted it open. "Yeah, I think Reverend Adler would be quite upset if he knew. What he doesn't know won't hurt him." He opened his bottle and touched it to hers. "To the future, whatever it brings."

She nodded bleakly. Without Michael, the prospect was downright depressing. As Nikita watched, he chugged the cognac down with a few gulps. Resolutely repeating his toast, she followed suit with her own. "Got an extra one for Chenelle?"

"Anything for my future bride." He produced

another, placing it in her palm.

Nikita checked her watch. It was time to go. Impulsively, she leaned forward to quickly hug Michael and kiss his cheek. "I hope everything works out for the best."

He touched his forehead to hers. "Thanks. Is it time?"

"Yes." Opening her purse, she found some Altoids mints. "Here," she said, giving him one and popping the other into her mouth. "No sense getting the reverend all upset."

After chewing and swallowing the mint, he opened his arms wide, a vulnerable expression in his eyes. "How about another hug for good-luck?"

"You've got it," she said, stepping into them and folding her arms about his waist. She rested her head on his shoulder, experienced the warm, virile, strength of him, and felt herself connect with him on an emotional level they'd never reached before. And you're welcome to anything else you want, she added silently, hugging him tightly with all the love within her. Despite his disparaging comments about love, when he returned the pressure of her embrace, she felt loved.

"That was a good one," he said as they slowly drew away from each other.

Nikita gave him an affectionate smile. "Yes it was. See you out front." She opened the door. The groomsmen stood in a group just outside. "I'm going to get Chenelle."

Within the bridal rooms, the door to the inner room was ajar. When Nikita pushed it open, she saw Chenelle sitting alone. "Are you still marrying Michael?"

"Nothing's changed." Chenelle blinked back tears. "Especially not Lance Coltrane. How could I let him play with my emotions like that?"

"Michael sent you this." Nikita pressed the small bottle of cognac into her palm.

"The man has good taste." Chenelle twisted the bottle open and swallowed the contents. "I needed that. Got any mints?"

Nikita pressed a mint into Chenelle's hands. "We'd better get going. Where are the bridesmaids?"

"I asked them to wait by the chapel door."

Nikita lifted the rose and blue circlet of flowers with its cloud of chiffon from the box on the hassock. Together, they fitted it around the curls on Chenelle's head as an unchecked tear ran down her face.

Nikita hugged her. "Are you sure you want to do this?"

"Yes. I made a decision, and I'm going to get on with my life."

Sighing, Nikita retrieved the bouquet of ice blue flowers from the other florist box. Dusty rose ribbons trimmed in silver trailed as she placed it in Chenelle's trembling hands.

In a flurry of activity, they made it to the chapel door. On cue, the wedding march began. Chenelle's little sister, Nina, was a little princess in her white lace dress as she went down the aisle tossing rose petals. Her friend Paige's little boy followed with the ring.

This is it, Nikita thought as the bridesmaids began to pair with the groomsmen. Michael and Chenelle would be married in minutes. Still, she couldn't shake the conviction that she should have said or done something to let him know how she felt. But what good would it have done? And how could she have put herself in the picture anyway, without hurting Chenelle? Her knees trembled with nervous excitement.

She peered into the church and saw Chenelle's mother looking young enough to be her sister in a pale pink designer creation. With a lace hanky, she daintily dabbed at her eyes.

Nikita's mom sat behind the Crestwoods, in the tawny rose dress Nikita and Chenelle had chosen for her. Throwing Nikita an encouraging smile, she turned to make a comment to her friend, Kyle Eversole. Her dad sat at the end of the pew behind them. He smiled broadly, his face alight with warmth and welcome at the sight of her.

Michael's parents sat on the other side of the aisle. Lila Matheson caught Nikita's eye and nodded. She was a picture of elegance in an ice blue evening suit. Still, she didn't seem overjoyed. Michael Sr. sat beside her, with a comforting arm about her shoulders. He winked at Nikita and she grinned. Michael's parents were really friendly and supportive. She liked them a lot.

An air of unreality gripped her as the last of the bridesmaids walked the rose and blue-ribboned aisle with a groomsman. Earl took Nikita's arm, and they followed the same narrow path through the hushed crowd. At the altar, Michael waited, his expression intent.

Nikita's thoughts spun off into fantasyland. Instead of Earl, she imagined that her daddy, full of pride, escorted her down the aisle. He patted her hand encouragingly as she glided to the wedding march. Deliriously happy, and breathtakingly beautiful in her white lace gown, she approached Michael, her heart filled with love.

At the altar, he waited for her, his face animated with joy and adoration. This from the man who'd said he didn't believe in love? Just then, Earl released her arm and she awakened from her fantasy, just in time to veer away from the altar and take her place near the bridesmaids.

The pianist increased the volume as Chenelle

started down the aisle on her father's arm. Her green eyes were moist and luminous, her lips full and sensuous in a face that was serenely beautiful. A glow surrounded her as she floated past, her voluptuous figure lending a chaste, yet sensuous air to the elegant gown she wore.

She joined Michael at the altar and they stood together like the prince and princess in a storybook wedding.

The marriage ceremony began. Nikita's heart pounded so loudly that she couldn't hear most of the ceremony, but as she struggled to breathe, she heard her two friends, who didn't believe in love, promise to love one another forever. Her panic mounted as the ceremony progressed to that moment when Reverend Adler asked if anyone knew a reason why Chenelle and Michael should not be joined. Nikita prayed silently. Someone please say something!

Muffled footsteps echoed in the aisle. A booming voice split the air. "I do, Reverend. Chenelle can't marry this man because she's in love with me!" All eyes turned to Lance Coltrane, striding down the aisle like mean Joe Green on his way to sack a quarterback.

Pushing her veil to the side, Chenelle whirled to face him. Startled, Michael swung around too.

Nikita couldn't look away from Michael's face. Jaw locked, his gaze darted uneasily from Chenelle to Lance, and back again.

Lance's steps slowed as he reached Chenelle.

"Don't do this. Please." Chenelle's whisper echoed through the shocked silence of the church.

"I love you, Chenelle. I've never loved anyone else."

She backed up a little, her voice wavering. "It's too late."

"No. It isn't." He dropped to his knees in front of her. "Marry me, Chenelle."

"Get up, Lance. Please."

Lance hugged her about the legs, his face against her abdomen. "I'm not letting you go. Marry me, Chenelle."

Tears streamed down her face.

Nikita's insides knotted as she watched the drama. Hadn't she been wishing something like this would happen? Still, the reality was too painful for words. Both Michael and Chenelle were being torn apart.

"Chenelle?" Michael moved closer, as if to push Lance away.

"Don't hurt him, Michael." Chenelle's soft cry stopped him in his tracks.

"Chenelle, do you love this man?" Reverend Adler pointed to Lance.

"Yes," Chenelle admitted, crying harder. Her gaze locked on Lance's upturned face. She threw

Michael a fleeting glance. "I'm sorry, Michael!"

Rising, Lance gathered Chenelle into his arms. His lips covered hers in a gentle but passionate kiss. "Come with me, Chenelle. We can get married today."

She hesitated and turned to Michael. "I—I have to do this. I hope you can forgive me someday," she choked out. Then she lifted her train and Lance rushed her down the aisle and out of the church.

The low murmurs of surprise grew into a babble of voices as soon as the front door clanged shut. Dazed, Michael stood at the altar listening to Reverend Adler. After a moment, visibly pulling himself together, he walked over to the microphone.

The crowd quieted as he began to speak with a faint tremor in his rough voice. "I appreciate you all coming today." He scanned the room with obvious effort. "What can I say? I guess it wasn't meant for Chenelle and me to get married. I hope you'll all join me at the—the reception." His voice vibrated and broke and he lifted his head for just a moment and made eye contact with the crowd. Then jaw tightening, his facial expression hardened into a mask that gave nothing away. "I—I'm sure we can find something to celebrate."

With a stiff nod, he carefully replaced the microphone. Then with his head down and his shoulders hunched, he strode swiftly towards a side door. His parents followed close on his heels. Nikita hung back, wanting to go to him, but deciding to let his parents comfort their son in privacy.

"Nikita?" At the sound of the familiar voice, she turned to see Chenelle's mother. "You didn't know this was going to happen, did you?"

"No," she answered in surprise, but she felt guilty. She hadn't known, but hadn't she suspected that Lance might make another last minute plea? And she knew that Chenelle had rarely been able to resist him. "I didn't think she'd gotten over Lance, but she seemed determined to marry Michael."

"I've never been so embarrassed in my life!" Shelley Crestwood confessed in a typical statement. Everything always happened to her. Then, realizing the unsympathetic light her statement put her in, she quickly added, "And of course I feel terrible for Michael. He would have been good for her."

Nikita shivered at the thought. They'd come much too close to actually being married. Her voice hardened. "If she really loves Lance, then it's better that she didn't marry Michael."

"You're right, of course." Shelley Crestwood fumbled with her gloves and purse. "Are you going to the reception?"

The question penetrated the fog surrounding Nikita's brain like a sharp ray of sun. Was she? Michael and Chenelle had pooled their resources to pay for dinner and dancing at some swanky country club that both sets of parents belonged too. Now, it was going to be a fiasco. "I—I, yes. They had to pay for it in advance. Michael will be feeling pretty low."

"I imagine so. Well, I'm going to say a few words to Michael before I leave." Shelly Crestwood walked to the front of the church.

"Nikita."

She turned at the sound of her mother's voice.

"Honey, Kyle has an emergency surgery to do, so he's going to drop me off. Do you want me to stay?"

Nikita shook her head. "Mother, I'm fine. Michael's the one who's been dumped."

Her mother gave her a wise look laced with sympathy. "Give me a call when you get home."

"Okay." Nikita nodded. As her mother walked towards the entryway with her friend, Nikita saw her father hovering in the background, a strange expression on his face. "Do you want me to catch a cab back to the hotel, princess? I expect you want to take the time to comfort your friend."

"No daddy." She extended a hand and he caught it in a firm, comforting grasp. "I can take you back to the hotel. Do you mind waiting a few minutes while I talk to Michael?"

"No, of course not. The poor guy must be devastated."

Something in his tone made her turn her head to

meet his glance. She found him watching her intently. "Yes, I'm sure he is." Does he know how I feel about Michael?

He dropped her hand. "I'm going over to speak to Reverend Adler. I'll wait for you here."

The church was nearly empty when Nikita made it back to the groom's area. She found Michael zipping his tux into a bag. He'd already changed into a sweater and slacks.

"Michael, I'm sorry." The lie did not sit well on Nikita's tongue, but she knew that some lies could not be avoided. She couldn't launch into a happy dance in front of him when he looked so low and vulnerable. His handsome face was still flushed, his lips forming a grim line. She saw his fingers shake a little as she clutched at the edge of the door as if it were trying to get away from her.

Glassy-eyed, he rasped. "Nikita, I thought everything was fine. I never knew what hit me." Fine lines of fatigue framed his eyes and mouth. "And I'm still in shock. She never even gave me a hint that there was someone else. Did you know him?"

Nikita stepped into the room, her heart pumping like crazy. Swallowing the lump in her throat, she spoke as calmly as she could. "She was getting over him when the two of you met."

"Yeah? Well, it didn't work, did it?" He placed his tux on a chair. "We had an understanding. We weren't desperately in love with one another, but there were some pretty special feelings between us."

It hurt to see him like this. Nikita moved close and put her arms around him. His body was stiff and rigid, as if he were holding his emotions in. "Michael," she said in a low, aching voice.

He gasped, a faint tremor running through him. "How could she do this to me?"

She stroked the soft hair at the nape of his neck. "It wasn't planned. It just happened, Michael."

"Yeah." He ran a hand over his forehead. "I wish I had a plan. I'll probably spend the rest of the day on display as an object of pity and ridicule."

"Is there anything I can do?" She held her breath.

"Not right now, Nikita. The pain's too fresh. I can barely think, let alone talk about it. Now everything's changed. I'm facing a totally different future." Sticking a hand into his pocket, he produced another miniature bottle of Martell. "Last bottle," he mumbled, twisting off the cap.

"I'll see you later," Nikita said, watching him gulp down the contents.

"Hey, don't forget the reception," he called as she turned and started to leave the room. "Please."

Her gaze met his, something twisting inside of her. *I'll be there.*

As Nikita drove her father to the hotel, her

thoughts were with Michael and his pain. Things had happened for the best, hadn't they? For a man who wasn't in love, he'd seemed awfully hurt. Why, though, did she feel so guilty? Michael and Chenelle hadn't gotten married, but she couldn't help wishing that both her friends had agreed to call it off.

"Does Michael know how you feel about him?" her father asked, breaking in on her thoughts.

"No." She swiveled her head to face him. "How do you know?"

"It's in your eyes when you look at him and your voice when you say his name. Maybe I'm more sensitive to your feelings and emotions because you're my daughter, but I think he's a fool not to see it."

Keeping her eyes on the road, Nikita heaved a sigh. "He has no idea, and neither does Chenelle."

"Too lost in each other huh?"

"Mmmmph! Apparently not enough." Nikita stopped at a red light.

"Princess, why didn't you let him know how you felt before Chenelle got into the picture?"

"I wanted to, but no time ever seemed right, and then he met Chenelle and that was that." She lifted the hair away from her hot forehead.

"Looks like you'll get another chance."

"I hope so. I love him, Daddy."

"Then you've got to give it you best. No hesitating this time."

Nikita nodded her head in agreement. "What about you and Mama?"

"What about me and your mother? We divorced, and she moved on with her life."

"What about you? Did you ever go back and see that woman you were in love with before you met Mama?"

Clay Daniels stared out at the passing scenery for several moments before he spoke. "Yes, I did."

"And?" Nikita prompted.

"And nothing. Princess, the grass always looks greener. She was still beautiful, just not the loving, caring person I remembered. Maybe she never was. She was also looking for husband number three. I had no interest whatsoever."

"Maybe she really loved you and couldn't help comparing the men she met to her memory of you."

Her father chuckled. "And maybe that romantic heart of yours is filling in the blanks again. Is that how you feel about Michael?"

Nikita nodded. "Yes, but stop trying to change the subject. When you and Mama split up..."

"When your mother and I split up, I'd been feeling trapped and I thought I needed to be free."

"You thought?" Nikita shot him a quick glance before focusing back on the road. Was that regret she saw on her father's face?

He laughed. "You read me like a book. I'm older

and wiser than I was then, and I've learned that being single out here in these streets is not what it's cracked up to be. Some of the best years of my life were spent with you and your mother."

Digesting this new information with amazement, Nikita's thoughts raced ahead. "For what it's worth, I think Mama still loves you," she said carefully.

"Maybe, but I think I broke her heart and I don't think she'll ever forgive me for that." A note of sadness crept into his voice. "Some things said and done can never be taken back."

Nikita exited the freeway. "Do you still love Mama?"

"That goes without saying."

Anticipation sent adrenalin coursing through her. "Do you want her back?"

"Princess, I love you dearly, but I've said about all I'm going to on the subject of your mother and me. Give it a rest, okay?"

"Okay, Daddy. Tell me about that promotion you mentioned."

"If I accept, I'd head up the Midwest region, and have an office here. There'd be more work, but a lot less travel, and I could spend more time with you."

Nikita pulled up in front of the Hilton. "Oh, I hope you take it! When do you have to give your answer?"

"Next week. You'll be the first to know how it

goes." He released his seatbelt as the doorman stepped forward and opened the passenger door.

"Are you coming to the reception tonight?" she asked as he got out of the car.

"No, I've got an early flight in the morning. Besides, it doesn't sound like it'll be any fun."

"I have to go," she told him.

He leaned back in to hug her and kiss her cheek. "I know, Princess. Hang in there, okay?"

"Okay! Bye, Daddy."

Should I tell Mama about my conversation with Daddy? she wondered as she drove home. After wavering back and forth several times, she decided that she wouldn't. She wasn't going to meddle in her parents' relationship.

Chapter 2

Nikita slipped into the little black dress she'd bought for the reception, crossed the opening in front, and did the hidden snaps and hooks. Smiling, she rotated slowly in the mirror. Yes! The dress was everything she wanted it to be.

The clingy top crossed her breasts at an angle that attractively outlined their curve and created cleavage. The short, swingy length of its skirt made her waist look small and emphasized her long, athletic legs.

She applied a coat of wine-colored lipstick and was fluffing the front of her short pixie hair cut, when the doorbell rang. "Coming!" she called. Quickly, she snapped swirling black rhinestone disks into her ears, and stepped into matching black evening sandals.

The bell chimed for the third time as she opened the door. Reed Winston stood on the porch looking handsome and mysterious in an olive suit that caressed his big muscular frame. Obviously a product of racially-diverse parents, a few almost blond streaks stood out in the straight, sand-colored hair feathering back from his broad forehead. In his golden brown face, startling sea green eyes studied her from behind the lenses of his black-framed glasses.

Clark Kent! That's who he made her think of, with his quiet air of confidence and mystery. She sometimes suspected him of hiding behind those glasses. If he took them off, would he become Superman?

"Hello!" Reed stepped into the hallway, took her hand and twirled her around. "You're beautiful, Nikita. Definitely worth the wait."

Nikita smiled. "Thanks. I like your suit. Olive is your color. It really brings out your eyes."

He held on to her hand. "Are you ready to go?"

"Sure. Just let me get my purse." Nikita turned and headed for her room.

"Did you think I wasn't coming?" he called.

"No, but I would have understood if you hadn't, since I know your project is due day after tomorrow."

Reed, Michael, and Nikita were part of a team working on a domestic robot. Reed's first prototype for the control circuitry was due on Monday, so she hadn't been sure he'd be able to take her to the reception as planned. She found the glittering rectangle on her bed, checked the contents, and headed back to the front.

Reed filled the small hall. "Actually, I had a breakthrough. The circuit card worked a lot better when I shielded those components and did some of the tweaking you suggested. Thanks for the tip."

"You're welcome. We make a good team," Nikita said grinning. "Our project's right on schedule."

"Yes, it is." Reed stepped out on the porch while she locked the door. "Even if I hadn't solved the problem, I'd have taken you to the reception."

"Really? Why?" Nikita started down the steps with him.

"Because this is more or less our first date."

The thought startled her. Why hadn't she thought of that? Was she that wrapped up in Michael? "I guess you could say that," she answered, following him to the gold Corvette. "Nice car."

"Thanks. I figured I should have at least one thing I wanted." He opened Nikita's door.

Gracefully, she settled herself into the low seat. "What else do you want?"

"Oh, lots of things," he said, eyeing her speculatively before shutting her door.

Heat rushed to Nikita's face. She must have been walking around in a daze. She liked Reed, but she'd never actually thought about going out with him. "Did you hear that Chenelle left Michael at the altar?" she asked after Reed took his place beside her and started the car.

"No!" Reed turned to face her, concern filling his blue gaze. "What happened?!"

Nikita shook her head. "It was the classic scene where the reverend asks if anyone knows why the two people should not be married, speak now or forever hold your peace... Well, Chenelle's ex-fiancé showed up and spoke his piece. When it was all said and done, they left Michael standing at the altar."

"Wow! I can't quite believe that! The way the two of them have been acting, you would have thought it was a match made in heaven."

"Yeah, you'd have thought," she agreed. "Poor Michael's pretty hurt and depressed about the whole thing."

"Who wouldn't be?" Reed sighed dramatically. "She might as well have castrated him in public."

"I wouldn't know about that," Nikita lifted an eyebrow. "But I don't think I'd go that far in describing what happened."

"Poor guy. Is there still going to be a reception?"

"Yes. Everything's paid for and they can't get their money back. If you want to back out, I'll understand."

"You kidding?" Reed put the car into gear and took off. "I'm with you."

The parking lot for the Loflen Hills Country Club was half empty. Lively strains of music from a top forties band beckoned as they walked in past lush greenery and well-manicured lawns.

Michael stood near the door in a black suit with gold accents, talking to Earl. He'd slicked his hair back into dark waves. Ahead of them, his Aunt Mamie Lee folded him into a dramatic hug and spoke in a warm, southern accent, "My poor baby!" I come all the way from Georgia to see you get married and that girl takes off with the wrong man!"

Michael returned the hug.

She placed a plump hand along the side of his face. "I know she probably broke your heart, but I want you to know that there's plenty more girls where she came from. Plenty more! I'm sure there are several young ladies that would be glad to spend time with you when you're feeling better."

"That's okay, Aunty. I'm not looking for another fiancée. I think I'll just be by myself for a while." When he surreptitiously glanced around to see who might have heard their exchange, Nikita knew that in addition to being hurt, he was embarrassed. Michael had never had a problem getting girlfriends and getting dumped was a new experience for him.

Michael's Aunt Mamie Lee moved on to talk to his mother. Nikita and Reed approached.

The scent of Polo cologne filled her nostrils as he nodded, and then shook hands with Reed. "Nikita, Reed, glad you could make it."

Nikita glanced around the room. They'd dispensed with the wedding arch, congratulatory signs, and even the happy couple on the wedding cake. She knew there must be stacks of napkins and matches engraved with Michael and Chenelle in the back room. Among the white–covered tables, a small crowd of close friends and family socialized. A few couples danced on the huge dance floor near the perimeter of empty tables. It could almost have been a gathering of friends at a club, except the atmosphere was low-key. "Considering everything that's happened, you've got a nice crowd."

"Sure. Free food and drink, and a live band, who could pass that up? Of course no one on the bride's side has bothered to come." His words were light enough, but there was something poignant about him standing there, left to face the crowd alone.

Nikita said nothing. She didn't know how to view Michael's mood. Before the fiasco in the chapel, he'd been a little apprehensive about the loveless arrangement he'd made with Chenelle. Now, he gave every appearance of being the wronged bridegroom. She could look in his eyes and see that he was still hurting. Despite his comments to the contrary, he must have loved Chenelle. Is there any hope for me? Nikita wondered.

"Hey man, I'm sorry." Reed put a hand on Michael's shoulder. Nikita told me what happened. I'm really feeling you...," Reed said in a low voice.

Michael shrugged, his basic, good-natured personality taking over as he said in a rusty voice, "Thanks. I guess it just wasn't meant to be."

Listening to him, she wondered how many times tonight he'd had to repeat that phrase. "Where should we sit?" Nikita found her voice.

"As you can see, you've pretty much got your pick, but when we planned this, we reserved a table for you right next to me and..." Michael stopped in mid-sentence and regrouped. "Your table's on the right, near the stage. There's a reservation card with your names on it." He made a show of glancing at his watch. "Come on, I'll show you."

While Reed went to get their drinks, Michael went to the buffet table with Nikita. She saw a long smorgasbord of everything from cocktail shrimp and sauce, egg rolls, spareribs, crab cakes, crab salad, potato salad, hot wings, tossed salad, spinach salad, to fruit and vegetable trays. Most of it hadn't been touched. At the end of the table a chef stood carving prime rib and turkey. The food was beautiful, but Nikita could see most of it being thrown out at the end of the evening. There was simply too much. "You've got a lot food," she said inanely.

"Tell me about it," he rasped. "My mother has already called a few of the local shelters and they're coming to get most of it. At least it won't go to waste. I could do a lot worse than feeding the homeless."

"You should feed yourself too," Nikita quipped. "I bet you haven't eaten all day and you guys were out drinking most of last night."

"I couldn't eat a thing, even if I wanted to," he told her. "My stomach is burning."

"Sounds like you need to eat," Nikita said, grabbing a plate and putting some crackers, cheese, fruit, and a couple of cocktail shrimp on it. "Here, this should stop the burning." She thrust the plate at him.

"In case you haven't noticed," he said in a slightly irritated tone, "My mother's on the other side of the room."

"I noticed," she retorted, "But since she either hasn't gotten around to it or you refused to listen, I'll fill in for her."

They stared at each other for a moment, neither giving an inch until Michael decided to accept the plate.

"This doesn't mean I'll eat it," he said stubbornly.

"That's okay, ba-by!" Nikita laughed, surprised when he joined in. She saw a few people turn to look.

He looked more relaxed. "See, you're good for me, Nikita. This reception was like a funeral until you showed up."

Smiling, she placed shrimp, spinach salad, egg rolls, and fruit on her own plate.

"Hey, why don't you come on the cruise?" Michael

blurted out, a look of surprise on his face. "It would liven things up, and I know you would have a good time."

"Huh?" She froze in the act of selecting a fork and napkin. "What are you talking about?"

"Chenelle and I paid for a honeymoon cruise. Remember? Sixteen days on a cruise ship through the Panama Canal? Several Caribbean islands, Costa Rica, and some of the Mexican Rivera?"

She nodded. "Yes, now that the wedding's off, I thought maybe you'd get Earl to go with you."

"Earl?" He looked at her as if he thought she was crazy.

"Yes, Earl. Remember the best man? You could turn it into a buddy trip."

"Earl's my buddy, but I don't like him enough to sleep in the same bed with him."

Nikita harrumphed. "Well, I'm flattered that it means that you like me that much, but you know as well as I do that most of those cabins on cruises have twin beds."

"Oh yeah? We paid extra and got a nice room with a king-sized bed."

"Oops." A giggle escaped her lips at the picture forming in her mind of two macho males in a flowery honeymoon cabin with a king-sized bed. Her shoulders shook with such laughter that it took a few moments to stop. "I'm sorry, Michael. I know it's not funny."

"Then why are you trying so hard not to laugh?" he demanded roughly, but he laughed too.

"I keep imagining you and Earl and the king-sized bed in the honeymoon cabin! Champagne and flowers..."

Michael shot her a half-serious look full of daggers, but she could see that he thought it was funny too.

Suppressing a smile, Nikita straightened her shoulders. "You were saying?"

"We outdid ourselves on that one. I tried to give the trip to my parents, but Mom doesn't want to be on a ship that long and Dad insists that I need to get away."

"You do, at least until this thing blows over."

"Well, if I've got to go, why don't you come along and keep me company?" Despite his air of nonchalance, there was almost a pleading note in his rusty voice.

"What would people say? They'd probably swear that you'd been carrying on with me and Chenelle all along. It sounds like something out of a soap opera like 'Days in the Lives of the Sex-Crazed Engineers at Techno Toys and Gadgets. Will the engineers slink off for a torrid affair aboard the Passionate Love Boat? Tune in tomorrow folks! Da-da-da dom! ' "

"Quit fooling, Niki. I'm serious!" A hint of exasperation filled his tone.

"Really?" She scanned his face.

"Really. You haven't taken a vacation in a long time and you're always saying that you want to travel."

Her mind raced. Her heart threatened to leave her chest. Her? Alone in the honeymoon cabin with Michael? In the same bed? For more than two weeks? Why wasn't she jumping at the opportunity? Her gaze met Michael's. Pure unadulterated fear filled her. What if I let him know that I love him and he rejects me? "You're asking me to go on the honeymoon cruise with you?" Nikita asked incredulously.

"Yes. I wouldn't lay a hand on you, you know that."

"Yes, I do." He never had, and that bothered her. It wasn't something she wanted to brag about. As her first friend at the company he had always given Nikita her due as a fellow engineer, and treated her with the proper respect. He'd made her transition into the group easy. Michael had never so much as kissed her anywhere but on the forehead, and on the cheek.

As they returned to the table with the food, Nikita turned the idea over in her mind, trying to get used to it. Would she give herself away under closer circumstances? On the other hand, maybe it was time she told him how she felt.

"Think about it?" He squeezed her hand. "I have the tickets and everything's all taken care of. All you need is your clothes and your passport. Please?"

Nikita quivered inside. She wanted to go on that trip with Michael, but could she cope with the intimacy of a honeymoon without being a bride? Pulling her thoughts together, she saw that Michael still had that shell-shocked look in his eyes. Her gaze fell on his hand covering hers. It shook a little. "Sure, I'll think about it. When do you need an answer?"

"The plane leaves at seven tomorrow morning."

"Then I'll try to let you know before I leave tonight."

He released her hand. "Good."

Nikita glanced up. Reed was back and placing a Coke in front of her. "Thanks."

"I brought you a cognac." Reed set a glass of dark liquid in front of Michael, and then sat down beside Nikita with his own.

"Thanks." Michael gulped it down, then got to his feet. "I guess I should mingle. See you guys later."

"Poor guy," Reed mused when Michael walked away, "he's doing a lot better than I would be doing in his shoes."

Nikita sipped her Coke, pondering Michael's plea that she go on the cruise with him. If she did, at the least she could help him get over Chenelle's betrayal. And deep within her heart she hoped to find the courage to use the opportunity to confess her true feelings to Michael. Her mind was made up: She would go! Yes!

"Does seeing him hurt bother you enough to go on that honeymoon cruise with him?"

Reed's words mirrored some of her thoughts. Turning her startled gaze upon him she almost knocked her glass over. "What?"

"I heard his dad telling someone that he was stuck with the honeymoon cruise. Didn't he ask you to go with him?"

"Yes, but it's not the way you make it sound," Nikita said hotly, color rushing to her face. "We're just good friends."

Reed threw her a look of disbelief. "That's because he's too blind to notice that mile-high crush you've got on him."

"Reed!" Nikita tightened her lips in fear and embarrassment and she put her trembling hands beneath the table. Were her feelings so obvious to everyone?

"Don't worry, I'm not going to tell him." He leaned closer, lowering his voice. "I know how you feel."

"No way," she countered in a tough tone.

"Oh yes." Reed's voice softened. "How do you

think I feel about you? I've been trying to get your attention for months, yet the first time you'll go anywhere with me is when he's off the market."

"He's not," she corrected him, trying to keep the satisfaction out of her voice.

Reed grinned, a cynical look in his green eyes. "And you wish I'd just disappear."

"No. I don't." Nikita put her chin on an upturned palm. "I just want to do what's right for me."

"Don't go, Nikita."

"Why not?"

"Because he doesn't love you. He doesn't deserve you."

"And you do?"

"I care a lot about you, Nikita. It could be love."

"I'm flattered."

"You say that in the same tone you'd say, 'I'm cold'."

Nikita shook her head in exasperation. "What do you want?"

"You, any way I can get you."

She stared at him in amazement. Where had all this emotion come from? Reed had never talked to her this way. "At least you're honest," she murmured. He looked as if he could see clear through to her thoughts.

"What are my chances?"

"Not too good," she said candidly. She liked Reed

Winston, but no man had ever truly competed with Michael as far as she was concerned.

"Don't go, Nikita."

"You said you knew how I felt. If you were me, wouldn't you go?"

"In a heartbeat." Reed took her hand and pressed it to his lips. "You're everything I ever wanted."

"Then you should understand."

"I do, but I see my chance with you slipping away from me."

Nikita gently pulled her hand from Reed's. "I must have been blind."

"Not totally. I know how to behave myself at work. I wouldn't want to jeopardize our working relationship."

"So why change now?"

"I thought he was out of the picture, but I see you're getting ready for round two."

Nikita pursed her lips, blowing air in disgust. "I never had a round one."

"So you're going to make up for it?"

"I–I don't know," she stammered. Maybe she should pass on the trip. "Let's talk about something else."

"I've got a better idea." Reed extended a hand. "Let's dance."

He's really good, Nikita thought as she floated around the room with him. His moves were smooth and coordinated, and he never stepped on her feet. One hand rested politely at her waist, and the other clasped hers.

Like a magnet, Michael drew her attention as he circulated among the guests. They were about to begin their third dance when he cut in. "As the deserted groom, I'm claiming the right to one dance with each lady," he quipped. "Reed, do you mind?"

"How could I?" Reed stepped back smoothly. He caught Nikita's eye. "I'm going to say hello to the boss. See you back at the table."

"Just a couple more hours and I can go home," Michael remarked as their dance began.

She wanted to wrap her arms around him and dance all night, then go back to his place to lie with him until it was time to leave for the cruise. Instead, she said carefully, "Michael, you seem to be handling things so well."

"But I don't think I can keep this show going much longer," he grated out.

"Why don't you go now? No one would expect you to stay through the whole thing." She rubbed his shoulder, wanting to touch his face but lacking the nerve.

His steps slowed, relief easing his expression. "I think I will. Can you call and let me know what you've decided?"

She wanted to say yes right then, but she needed to talk to her boss and her mother first. "Yeah. You know I've got to talk to the boss anyway."

"Do you think it's a problem?"

Raising her eyebrows, she considered for a moment. "No. I've finished my scheduled part of the project, and I've got a couple of weeks coming."

"Then I'll talk to you later." He leaned close and kissed her forehead. "Hey, I really appreciate your sticking by me. You know, you're as close to a sister as I'll ever get."

Nikita stiffened, a fire growing within her. Sister? The words strengthened her resolve. She was going on that trip, and she was going to change his mind about her if it was the last thing she did.

As Michael said his good-byes, Nikita went back to sit with Reed. He shot her a questioning look and she shrugged.

"Do you want to leave?" he asked astutely.

"After the next dance." Nikita took his hand.

Before they left, she stopped to talk to her boss. A perceptive man, he was polite enough not to question her about her last minute opportunity to go on a cruise when she asked for the time off. He confirmed that she had no new work pending, that her files were accessible, and then wished her a Bon Voyage.

When she got home and called her mother to tell her that she was planning to go on the honeymoon cruise with Michael, Alita Daniels arrived at Nikita's apartment within minutes. Grasping her daughter's hand, she led her to the living room couch. "Honey, I really think you should reconsider this. You've never said, but do you really think I don't know that you're in love with Michael? I watched you suffer when he started going out with Chenelle. You were heartbroken! Nikita, he almost married your best friend!"

"I know Mother, I nearly lost him forever." Nikita watched her mother recoil. "He's completely demoralized over Chenelle's betrayal and he's stuck with the honeymoon cruise, so he asked me to come along as a friend. How can I pass on this opportunity to show him how much I care?"

Her mother's voice rose. "I care about you and I don't want you hurt! Nikita!" Her eyes grew shiny with tears. "You're setting yourself up for heartbreak. If you throw yourself at him, do you think he'll respect you for it? He's vulnerable right now, so he'll probably take anything you offer. Are you prepared to live with the consequences? Can you really go on that cruise and pretend to be his wife in every sense of the word?"

Nikita cringed at the nasty slant her mother put on things. She gasped, "It's not like that! I just want him to see me, love me, for a change."

Alita turned and gripped her daughter's shoulders hard. "Do you really think you can be in that room with only one bed and not sleep together?"

"I...I want to sleep with Michael—at least eventually. I love him."

"And when the cruise is over and he's ready for the next girl?"

"It won't happen," she said, shutting out the possibility.

"This is a small town. When you come back, everyone will know where you've been and what you've been doing."

"I don't care," Nikita said obstinately.

"Isn't there anything I can do to make you reconsider?"

Nikita met her mother's stare head on. "No."

"I bet you think I don't know how you feel." Alita's face crumpled. "When your dad started talking divorce, I did everything I could to make things work between us. For the entire year after you'd left for college, I lived on pins and needles. I wasn't sure he would stay with me. Then he told me the truth. He'd been on the rebound from another relationship when he met me and never had the depth of feeling for me that he should have had. After I got pregnant, he stayed all those years, waiting for you to grow up. I always knew that I loved him more than he loved me, but I never imagined that he didn't care at all. Niki, it's a terrible thing to give your heart to someone who rips it apart, then throws it away, someone who never really appreciated the gift."

Hugging her mother tightly, Nikita found herself crying. She'd never been able to understand or accept her parents' divorce during her first year of college. Still kind and generous, her father grew distant and moved away. Keeping to herself, her mother seemed lost and abandoned and had taken a couple of years to begin dating again.

Deciding it was time she grew up, Nikita had focused on her education, but she still missed her daddy and the special closeness they'd shared. Now she knew that her father still had feelings for her mother, but she couldn't bring herself to tell her. She was still too emotionally fragile.

When both women were calm, Alita kissed her daughter and wished her luck. "Do you have enough money for emergencies and extras?" she asked Nikita as she dug through her purse for another Kleenex.

"I've got my charge cards," Nikita told her, certain she wouldn't have time to stop by the anytime machine.

"Here, take this." Her mother pressed two Traveler's Check envelopes into her hand.

Nikita saw $500 printed in blue on each envelope. "Mama, this is too much. I don't need—"

Her mother spoke in a firm tone that brooked no

resistance. "Take it, Nikita! If you don't find a use for it, you can give it back after the cruise."

"Thank you, Mama!" Nikita hugged her hard.

Slowly, her mother pulled away. Sad eyed, she left quietly, asking Nikita to call before leaving.

When the phone rang, Nikita knew just who it was. Lifting the receiver, she summoned her confidence. "Hello Daddy," she said in a tone that implied there would be no argument.

"Your mother says you're going on a cruise with Michael," her father said carefully. "Do you want me to come over there so we can talk about it?"

"No daddy, I'm fine and I know what I'm doing. Mama's just upset because...because."

"Because of me," he finished for her. "She sees herself in you and she wants to stop you from making some of the same mistakes. There's nothing wrong with that, Princess."

"Except the fact that I've got to live my own life. I've been so busy waiting for the right moment and trying to break it to Michael just right, that he doesn't even know how I feel! This cruise is just the sort of opportunity I've been dreaming of. Daddy, if we don't connect the way I'm thinking we should on this cruise, we never will."

"Just so you realize that you're taking a big risk. The poor guy's been royally dumped and he was supposed to be married by now. You'll more or less be filling in for the bride, whether you realize it or not. Bottom line Princess, he's had all three years to choose you and he hasn't. How are you going to tackle that?"

Nikita gripped the phone so hard that her fingers numbed. "I've thought about it, Daddy, and I don't know what I'm going to do except love him, and show him that I really care about him. I'm hoping that when there's just the two of us, he'll see the real me and deal with it."

"And if he does finally see you and realize how you feel, but doesn't want to go any further with it?"

At the thought, she placed a knuckle between her teeth and knawed it. She wasn't going to think about that.

"Nikita?" her father prodded.

"He loves me, Daddy!" Her voice rose. "He just hasn't realized it yet."

"Nikita!" her father sighed, "Are you sure you're not projecting your hopes and dreams onto Michael?"

"Yes, I'm sure."

Her father sighed again. "Then I'm going to say good night."

"Good night, Daddy."

"Now I want you to call me when you get to the first port, okay?"

"Alright, Daddy."

"And I want you to be very careful and make sure

you've got your passport."

"I've got my passport right here," she told him, fingering the blue plastic cover, "And I'll be careful."

"I love you, Princess."

"I love you too, Daddy."

Soon after she hung up the phone, Nikita called Michael with her answer. His exhilaration lifted her spirits and she spent that night and the early hours of the morning packing for the trip.

Knowing that she always dressed too conservatively, Nikita boldly selected and packed her most provocative and daring clothes. Into the large rolling suitcase went the skimpy bikini Chenelle had given her for her birthday, which she'd never had the nerve to wear. Next came the more conservative black peek-a-boo swimsuit that covered more than it seemed. Then she added the beige and black cocktail dress, a slinky gold number, a navy sundress, and four pairs of shoes. Michael would want to kiss a lot more than her forehead when she got through!

She checked her watch. Four in the morning. In a tizzy, she grabbed a light jacket, sweats, exercise wear, shorts, and tops and added them to the case. A smile curved her lips. More than two glorious weeks with Michael! It didn't matter how it happened, did it? She was going to make the best of this opportunity.

Because Michael purchased seats in first class, they boarded before the regular passengers. Nikita settled into her seat on the aisle and crossed her legs. Then she noticed that her short jumpsuit rode up to expose quite a bit of thigh. Unable to tug it down, Nikita gave up with a sigh. Michael should be looking at my legs anyway. She glanced over to see that he was and felt her temperature rise.

"Need any help?"

She chuckled. "I think I can manage."

"Not from where I'm sitting. Besides, I was enjoying the view."

Flattered, Nikita smiled. "Thanks. Don't let me spoil your fun."

"I don't think you could. To think that I've known you all this time and never even suspected you had legs like that."

She threw him a teasing glance. "Well that's because your radar was primed for other targets. Now that you've readjusted, who knows what you'll see?"

He raised his brows. "I don't know, but I'm sure it's going to be interesting."

The whine of the warming engines and the rushing sound of the air conditioning filled her ears. Michael was still watching her.

He took her hand and leaned closer. "You saved my life. I can't tell you how glad I am that you decided to come along." His rusty voice was music to her ears.

She smiled and whispered back, "What are we going to tell people when they assume I'm Mrs. Matheson?"

"Would you mind not saying anything about it?" he asked, the harried expression coming back to his face. "At least until we get on the ship?"

Nikita considered it for a moment. "I can get into that fantasy," she said. "But where are my rings?"

"Oh crap! I never did get them from Earl."

"I did." Nikita opened her purse, pulled out Chenelle's flashy wedding rings, and offered them to Michael. She hated the gaudy design, but she was proud of herself for thinking ahead.

"Could you...could you wear them just for now?"

Nikita nodded, a pleasant warmth spreading within her as he slipped the rings on her finger. This was too close to her dreams and fantasies.

"Thanks." Michael settled back in his seat. "I haven't slept for a couple of days now. Once we take off, I'm going to sleep. You don't mind, do you?"

Nikita noticed the faint darkness of grocery bags beneath his eyes. "No, I don't mind. You don't have to entertain me, Michael. I'll read my book, or talk to some of the other passengers."

"Good morning! Mr. and Mrs. Matheson?" A pleasantly cheerful voice captured their attention.

At their nod, the perky, red-haired flight attendant continued. "Congratulations on your marriage! You make a beautiful couple."

"Thanks," Nikita said, smiling up at her.

The attendant's attention strayed to Michael. "As soon as we get underway, there'll be champagne for all the first class passengers in honor of you newlyweds."

"Great." Michael threw Nikita a glance full of double meaning.

"We'll have to toast our love and our future." Nikita quipped, settling into her role as Mrs. Matheson. She saw Michael wince.

The attendant continued, "Is there anything I can get for you in the meantime?"

Nikita extended her legs. "Magazines? Do you have Cosmopolitan, and Popular Electronics?"

"Sure, I'll get them right away."

"You're a cruel woman, Nikita Daniels with that crack about our future," Michael grated after the attendant bustled off.

Nikita smirked at him. "Are we going to toast our love?"

Mouth opening, he hesitated, then laughed. "That's as good a toast as any." "Good," she replied. It was time he started thinking of the future. Chenelle was gone. He needed to get used to that fact, and she was just the woman to help him do it.

"Honey, are you going to be a jealous husband?" she asked Michael in a light, teasing voice.

His eyes popped open. "Why? Are you going to leave me too?" Despite his snappy reply, and the smart aleck expression on his face, she sensed an unusual vulnerability in his response.

Nikita's heart contracted. She touched his arm. "No, Michael. It's just that I plan to make the best of this entire trip and I think you should too. I haven't had a vacation in a long time."

"Give me a couple of days for things to sink in, then I'll be fine, okay?"

"Okay." She pushed the curly hair out of his face. Staring blankly out the window, he didn't seem to notice.

That's okay for now, she thought, settling back into her seat and stretching her legs. This trip has just begun. Give yourself some time.

She forced thoughts of her mother's warnings out of her mind. Though she didn't think Michael would hurt her, her mother's tears and her words regarding her father's abandonment had not been lost on her. It's a terrible thing to give your heart to someone who rips it apart, then throws it away, never really appreciating the gift. Those words evoked a sense of foreboding that logic couldn't dispel. She shuddered and shifted in her seat just as the flight attendant brought her magazines. Nikita buried her nose in them, glad to lose herself in something else.

Later, while several other first class passengers hit their glasses with their spoons, Michael lifted his glass of champagne and touched it to hers. "To forever love."

Nikita swallowed hard. This was part of her dream. She knew that Michael was teasing, but he seemed so sincere. His brown eyes mesmerized her. Nikita repeated his toast in a breathless voice. Lifting the glass to her lips, she felt the slightly sweet liquid bubble on her tongue and down her throat.

Like a real bridegroom, he moved closer. Her pulse sped up, her heart nearly leaping from her chest when Michael leaned so close she knew he was going to kiss her. The question was in his eyes. She tilted her head in answer, giving him better access. His scent and his cologne made her a little dizzy as he clasped her arm, his warm lips lightly brushing hers in a kiss as sweet as warm honey.

Nikita trembled as he settled back into his seat. The kiss hadn't been overtly sensual, or sexy, but it had been their first. She would treasure it forever.

"Oh that was so romantic," a woman to her right sighed.

For Nikita it was just too much. The back of her eyelids stung. Turning to face the seat in front of her, Nikita blinked rapidly. She'd wanted this moment to be real, and in her mind, she'd suspended reality just enough to believe in the little fantasy they'd just played out.

Michael tapped her shoulder lightly. "Have you got something in your eye?"

The man was too observant. "Yes," she lied, "right eye, outer corner."

"Let me help." With gentle fingers, he held her face, to closely inspect her eye. I don't see anything."

"It's probably just an eyelash," she answered.

Carefully, he brushed at the area with the corner of a clean tissue. "Better?"

"Yes, thanks." She accepted another tissue and blew her nose.

"Then I'm going to catch up on a few Zs." In no time she heard the even breathing of his sleep.

For a while, she studied him. Being able to do this without the guys or other friends around to notice was another first for her. She liked the sensual curve of his lips and the way his long lashes curled against his caramel-colored skin. How innocent and vulnerable he seemed in his sleep. She yearned to take him in her arms. Instead, she leaned back in her seat and soon the events of the past 12 hours caught up with her. She fell asleep too.

From time to time she awakened and saw that Michael still slept, but he surprised Nikita when the plane went through a patch of rough turbulence and air pockets. She sat rigid in her seat, one hand clutching her stomach, and the other holding the arm of her seat in a death grip. As the plane dipped once more, her grip tightened. Then she felt a hand cover hers.

"Are you all right?" Michael asked, loosening her fingers and taking her hand in his.

"No," she moaned, clenching his hand. "I hate it when the plane drops."

Lifting the armrest between them, he pulled her closer. "Don't be afraid. We're not about to crash or anything."

"It's not that," she answered irritably. "All that uncontrolled up and down just makes me queasy. I don't like this roller coaster feeling."

"Want to play cards?" he asked, obviously trying to get her mind off the ride.

Once more, the plane dropped. "Not when it's like this," Nikita gasped.

"Then talk to me," he urged. "Tell me what you found last time you surfed the Internet."

Immediately, she relaxed a little as she remembered the new auction site where just about anything could be had. "You'll never believe this...," She began.

Chapter 3

At the airport in San Diego, cruise line personnel whisked them to the ship. In the warm, humid air, Niki's spirits soared at the sight of the smooth lines of the seventy-eight ton dream ship. Now she could hardly wait to share the cruise with Michael, dancing, swimming, the spa, nightclubs, and all the restaurants aboard. Yes!

After taking Chenelle's name off the paperwork and adding Niki's, they stood in line to board. Then, arm in arm, they posed for the photographer.

"Welcome aboard, Ms. Daniels, Mr. Matheson." The futuristic decor of the lobby area resembled a spaceship, Niki thought as they trekked in the wake of one of the crew. Openings in the atrium ceiling revealed a heavenly blue framed by a golden star design. Down cool, carpeted corridors they went until the crewman stopped, three doors from the end of a corridor on the Vista Deck, and ushered them into the room.

A large bouquet of exotic fresh flowers with splashes of red, yellow, peach, blue, and violet welcomed them from a table in the small sitting area. Niki's gaze touched on the king-sized bed and slid back to Michael. He still looked tired, but incredibly attractive in black jeans and a collared T-shirt. The crewman began showing him how to work the environmental control system. Michael caught her looking at him and smiled.

Niki stepped around Michael's suitcase resting on the carpet near the closet. Where was hers? It had to be somewhere in the room. Scanning the area, she didn't see it. As she took in the gorgeous window extending from the ceiling to the floor, all thoughts of the suitcase fled. Fascinated, she went to it.

For several moments, she silently admired the view of the sparkling blue water and the dock. There were even a couple of comfortable looking deck chairs out on the small verandah in front of it. She knew she'd spend some time out there. "Michael, this is great!"

"Glad you like it," he answered in an affectionate tone. Turning back to the crewman, he asked, "So where's the dining room?"

Trust a man to think of his stomach first. Smiling to herself, Niki gazed around the small room, noting the television and VCR, and the champagne in a container of ice on the dresser. She lifted the cold champagne from its bucket to read the label. It was Dom Perignon, 1992. Placing the bottle back into the bucket, she turned up the two flutes. As soon as the crewman left, she would propose a toast.

When she turned on the television set, she saw people milling about the lobby area on a closed circuit channel. A schedule on the side listed movies to be shown in the room. Switching it off, she moved across the thick blue carpet.

Niki pulled open the first of the bleached oak closet doors and saw there was plenty of room to store their clothing. Catching sight of herself in the full-length mirror, she decided that she didn't look too much the worse for wear. Her weariness didn't show on her face, and her outfit was still unwrinkled. Good choice, Niki! She listened to the soothing sound of Michael's voice as he talked to the crewman.

She pulled open the second set of doors and noted the large space for luggage. She scanned the room again. Where was her suitcase? It should have come with Michael's.

The crewman turned, pointing to Michael's suitcase. "Sir, do you have all your luggage now?"

Michael frowned, the lines marring the smooth skin on his forehead. "No. Niki had a large black Pullman on wheels. Has all the luggage been brought from the plane?"

"Yes it has. Hopefully, your wife's suitcase was simply delivered to the wrong room."

Niki bit her lip, too unhappy about her missing suitcase to react to the crewman's assumption. She thought of all the things that she'd packed to get Michael's attention and make herself comfortable. What was she going to do if they couldn't find her suitcase? "I need my things. When will you know for sure?"

"Sometime before dinner, ma'am. Don't worry, we'll find it, and if we don't, the cruise line will issue you a credit at the ship's boutique." He glanced at the congratulatory note gracing the champagne bucket in the corner and added, "You'll be fine."

"I hope so." Niki headed for the door near the foot of the bed. She'd heard that the bathrooms aboard a cruise ship were miniscule. Michael had paid for extras, but did that include a bathtub and room to dress? Prepared for the worst, she pulled open the door.

A sigh escaped her lips as she surveyed the sink, toilet, and shower. A mirrored medicine chest gleamed above the sink. The chrome and Plexiglas shower door hid a shower massage. The entire bath wasn't much smaller than a regular bathroom would have been. I could change clothes in here, she thought, at least until we're more comfortable with each other.

She felt a warmth at her back. Michael spoke from directly behind her. "You're always going home for a nice hot bath, so I know you like a bathtub. You're not too disappointed with the bathroom, are you?"

"No." Niki turned to face him, aware that they were now alone. "It's small, but I can deal with it."

"Smart lady," he rasped. "I don't think I could get another cabin at this late date."

The entire area suddenly seemed incredibly small. His proximity sent a chill coursing through her. She swallowed the sudden lump in her throat and focused on his shirt. That was a mistake. The hint of black hair sticking out of the top made her think of its likely trail down his naked chest to disappear below his waist. Her stomach curled. "You did good, Michael. We're going to have a great time."

He shot her a crooked grin. "I hope so. You want to freshen up?"

Niki lifted an eyebrow and ruthlessly shifted the direction of her thoughts. Reality check. "Actually, I'm a little tired. I'd like to kick off my shoes and take a little nap."

"Me too." He breathed a sigh of relief. "I was afraid you'd want to explore the ship immediately. " Giving her the thumbs up, Michael turned and headed for the bed. "We've got a couple of hours before the ship sails. We could both get a good nap."

And a little afternoon delight? That's what most of the real newlyweds were probably doing. Niki wondered if she'd ever get to do that with Michael.

Following him to the bed, she helped him remove the exotic print bedspread and pull back the sheets. There was something intensely intimate in their task. In all the years she'd known him, she'd never gotten this close. Suddenly it all seemed a little too intimate.

They stopped to look at one another and smile nervously. "This feels a little weird," Michael quipped, looking uncomfortable.

Niki chewed her lip. She felt an inner trembling and her hands were cold. "I agree. What are we going to do?"

"You take the bed, I'll take that loveseat over there."

Niki stared at the overstuffed loveseat. It wasn't big enough for her to sleep on, not to mention Michael. "It's your room. I think you should get the bed."

"Our room, and let's not argue about this," Michael snapped. He stepped away from the bed and barreled towards the loveseat.

Niki followed in his wake. "We're having a discussion. I couldn't sleep comfortably knowing you were stuck on the loveseat. It's much too small for you and it's not that comfortable." Her voice rose a bit.

"Then what do you want me to do?" Michael raised his voice to match hers. "We've both admitted to being uncomfortable with the idea of sleeping in the same bed right now."

Maneuvering around him, Niki blocked his path. She couldn't let him get away with this. "Listen to me! We're going to have to get past this sooner or later. We're both adults, and it's a king-sized bed. We don't even have to touch one another."

Michael put a hand on her shoulder. "I wouldn't mind if we touched, Niki." Stopping to shake his head, he continued, "What am I saying? What I meant was—"

"I know what you meant." Niki cut him off. "And I'm telling you right now, if you don't sleep on the bed, I won't either."

He threw up his hands. "All right. You win." Forcefully expelling the breath in his lungs, he pulled the champagne from the stand. "We'll give the bed a shot. Can we have a tired people's champagne toast to that?" Deftly removing the foil cap and untwisting the wires, he popped open the bottle.

"It might loosen us up a bit," she admitted. Tilting the bottle, he poured bubbling gold liquid into Niki's glass, and then filled his own.

"To the cruise of a lifetime." She touched her

glass to his.

"To a hell of a cruise."

Niki took a sip. "Mmmm." She smiled at Michael. Reality and fantasy were starting to converge, and this was only the beginning. How far was she prepared to go? The bed was a foregone conclusion, but would they do more than sleep?

His attention never left her as he swallowed his champagne and set the glass down. Niki saw something in his eyes that made her think of a little boy lost. Poor Michael. She wanted to take him in her arms and tell him that everything was going to be all right.

He hesitated for a moment. Then bending at the waist, he pulled off the collared T-shirt. Niki couldn't take her eyes off the smooth curving flesh of his arms and chest revealed by the muscle shirt underneath. With quick, efficient movements, Michael dropped down and took off his shoes. Then like a big exotic cat, he coolly stretched his magnificent body out on the bed. As if sensing her hesitation, he asked, "You okay?"

Niki took in the faint shadow of a beard and mustache beneath his teak complexion and the unconsciously sensual expression in his liquid brown eyes. He looked delicious.

"Sure," she croaked from the depths of a throat suddenly as dry as the desert. She forced herself to swallow a little more of the champagne.

This was what she wanted. Niki sat down to take off her sandals. If she'd been alone, she'd have stripped down to her underwear. For now, she lacked the courage. She saw that Michael had already turned on his side and closed his eyes. The man could sleep anytime, anywhere.

For several moments, she listened to his slow, even breathing. Then, too tired to resist, she lay down close to the edge on her side of the bed. Feeling cold and lonely, she inched as close as she dared to the welcoming warmth of his body.

She'd wondered if she'd be able to sleep with his stimulating presence so close, but her lids were heavy. In her dreams, he always held her while she slept. Would they get that comfortable with each other? Niki pulled the sheet up over both of them and drifted off to sleep.

Michael awakened to the low, steady throb of the ship's engines and realized he was on the cruise. For the first time in days he felt somewhat rested. The familiar, light floral scent of a woman's cologne filled his nostrils. Niki liked to wear that scent. He lay on his side, snuggled spoon fashion with a soft, warm bundle of woman. A firm, but rounded derriere pressed against his crotch. His hands lay on the soft globes of her breasts, his chin on the fluff of her short, black hair. Black hair? He'd asked Niki to go on the trip with him! Niki! Quickly, Michael peeled his hands from her breasts, praying she wouldn't wake up. She could still change her mind about coming along, and he really wanted her to stay. He didn't want her to think he was trying to put the moves on her. No, Niki was his buddy.

With some of the smoothest maneuvering of his life, he gently eased away from her shapely derriere and out of the warm bed. Standing by the side of the bed, Michael wiped the sweat from his forehead. He still could hear Niki's even breathing. Whew! That was close. Lifting a foot to slip into his shoes, he nearly fell over when the ship's horn blasted the silence.

Niki moaned and turned over. "Michael?"

"I'm here." His voice was rusty. He cleared his throat and tried to wipe the guilty look off his face. His thoughts ran rampant. She knows you've had your hands all over her and she's about to chew you out. What kind of friend are you? Didn't you promise to keep your hands to yourself?

He'd never seen her like this. She sat up in the bed, running a hand through her tousled curls and looking sexy as hell. Her skin was flushed, her lips full. What would it be like to really kiss Niki? he wondered. With the sheets pooling at her waist, the top of her shorts suit was askew, offering him a view of the provocative area where his hands had rested only moments ago. Michael tried to steady the sight with a vision of the usual Niki, cool as a cucumber as she raised the stakes at one of the weekly poker games, on her way to cleaning them out. She was a hell of a poker player. He'd never thought of Niki as sexy. He'd never even thought of her as someone he could get intimate with. Michael turned away to pull on his T-shirt. This was the wrong time to start.

"Is something wrong?" Her voice was a little breathless as she focused on him with clear gray eyes. She straightened the top of her outfit.

"No. Why do ask?"

"You look a little funny. Did I confess all my deepest, darkest secrets in my sleep?"

"No, but you can consider this your golden opportunity. I'm all ears." He stood by the bed, stepping into his shoes.

Niki jumped as the ship's horn blasted again. "Believe it or not, that was the train in my dream."

"Did you make it?"

"No. No matter how hard I ran, I just wasn't fast enough." Her gaze strayed to the large window. "The ship is getting ready to leave the port. We're going to have to hurry and get up on deck."

"I'm not the one lounging in bed," he chuckled.

"Mmmmph!" Tossing back the sheets, she treated him to a view of her long, shapely legs. The view got even better as she scooted out of the bed.

With effort, Michael turned away. Uh-oh, you're in deep doo-doo! Down boy!

In a matter of seconds, she'd stepped into her sandals, and was fluffing her hair. Then they each took a quick turn in the bathroom to freshen up. On the way to the door she asked, "Do I look okay?"

"You look fine," he said, tugging at one of her silky black curls, which had a mind of its own.

"Thanks. Let's get going."

On deck, the late afternoon sun dipped low on the horizon. The ship pulled away from shore with the rousing sounds of a mariachi band. Several passengers stood waving good-bye to people on the shore. Michael and Niki stood at the rail, enjoying the moment, until those left behind became miniscule dots and the shoreline disappeared.

A warm, sultry breeze caressed Michael's skin, and gently rearranged Niki's hair. "Want to take a tour of the ship?"

Dreamily, she gazed out over the horizon where the golden orange of the sun dipped into a darkening ocean. "This is the kind of stuff you remember when it's all over. Let's stay and watch the sunset."

He'd known she'd say that. Niki was such a romantic. She'd probably have him watching the sunset every night. Nodding in agreement, he took two complimentary rum punches from a passing waiter and gave one to Niki. Strains of Caribbean music drifted on the air. On both sides of them, couples kissed passionately. It made him think of Chenelle. He should have been here with Chenelle.

As if she sensed his change in mood, Niki turned to face him, a wise expression on her face. "Do you want to start the tour now?"

Michael sipped his rum punch. She saw right through him. Determined not to be selfish, he answered, "No, let's wait until the sun goes down." Her answering smile warmed him, making him strong inside. He was going to have to get past Chenelle and the sooner, the better.

Minutes after the ocean swallowed the sun, Niki took his hand. "Do you mind if we check out the jogging track and the fitness and aerobic center first?"

"No, we've got days to explore the ship," he answered, glad to move away from what was obviously a romantic spot. Heading aft, they took hold of the rail and began to climb. Three decks up, the wooden jogging track curved around an entire deck. A few stacks of chairs filled the area in the center. There wasn't much else on the deck, so it was pretty breezy.

Niki leaned against the rail, the warm wind blowing her short hair back. "You've got to come up here and jog with me sometime."

"Sure. But not every day. I'm not in that good a shape."

She turned to look at him, her gaze touching on the muscular arms and legs he worked hard to keep toned. He could see that she wasn't going to let him get away with that statement. "Yes you are. You're in excellent shape."

Her frank appreciation sent a ripple of excitement coursing through him. A silly grin took over his mouth.

Playfully, she punched his arm. "As much as you play basketball, I bet you could hold your own," she smirked, her eyes sparkling.

"Maybe. Maybe I can find some guys to play with. There's supposed to be a couple of hoops around here somewhere," he said, thinking it would be a good way to get rid of some tension.

In the background, they heard the announcement for the first seating for dinner.

Niki moved away from the rail, her hands in her pockets. "I'm glad we're not in the first seating for dinner. I want to shower and change first. Let's go back to the room."

Niki was holding up like a trooper, Michael thought as they headed to the cabin. He hoped her luggage was in the room, but he had an ominous feeling that she would not be seeing her suitcase anytime soon. She wasn't a clotheshorse like Chenelle, but she had to be tired of the short white jumpsuit.

Niki fell silent when they reached the room and there was still no sign of her suitcase. As her jaw tightened, he felt a rush of sympathy for her. "You're welcome to anything I've got to wear," he said, trying to keep things light.

"Gee, thanks." She dropped down into the nearest chair, her disappointment evident. "I'm sure they'll let me into the formal dining room dressed in a pair of your shorts."

Then Michael thought of the little boutiques they'd passed during their deck tour. "Hey, let's go buy a few things right now. Then you won't have to worry about it." She threw him a skeptical look, her head drooping towards the floor. "Come on!" he said, instantly hauling her to her feet.

"We're supposed to sit down to dinner in about an hour and a half," she protested half-heartedly. He could see that his idea was catching on.

Opening the door to their room, he stepped into the corridor, dragging Niki along. "We've got plenty of time."

It took a while, but they found an open clothing boutique on the main deck. Together, they went through the rack of dresses.

Michael took a casual look at his friend. At first glance, she seemed all slim lines and gentle curves, but beneath that short jumpsuit were surprisingly full breasts and one of the cutest butts he'd ever seen. Niki was always wearing those dark, conservative colors, he thought, as he selected a teal blue sundress, and a long red cotton tank dress with a slit up the side. A little color would probably look good on her.

"Try these," he suggested, placing the hangers on her fingers, along with the other clothing she'd selected.

Her gray eyes widened, her eyebrows lifting as she examined them. "These colors don't look good on me."

"Try them on. What have you got to lose?" he urged.

Giving in gracefully, she headed for the small dressing area. Moments later, when she stepped out of the curtained dressing room, he wanted to whistle. Unable to contain his appreciative smile, Michael stopped short of saying, 'I told you so.' The dress made her figure seem perfect and it made him think of Christmas and Niki as his present? He shook off the thought. "No arguments, you're buying that one," he insisted as she stared at her reflection in the mirror, a slightly self-conscious expression on her face.

"I'll buy it." Niki turned in the mirror. "I'm just surprised," she admitted. "I didn't know I could wear this color."

Again he assessed her figure, something he'd done all too often today. Her tiny waist, flaring hips and long legs were just made for a man's hands. He'd noticed in an offhand sort of way that she had a great figure, but given their working relationship, had never felt attracted until now. "You could wear anything you wanted, you've got the body for it."

"Thank you."

"Don't thank me. I'm just calling it as I see it. Now try on the blue one."

The blue sundress was another hit, and the kind of dress that managed to make her look fresh-faced and sexy at the same time. Suddenly dry-mouthed, Michael stared, at a loss for words. Niki was gorgeous.

She whirled in the mirror, an infectious smile on her face. "Well? What do you think? I like this one too."

"It's a go, Niki. Feeling better?"

"Yes. I like shopping with you. You have good taste." She carefully placed the dresses on the counter and looked around. "Now I need some tennis shoes, shorts and shirts, socks, and basic necessities."

While Niki selected shorts and a T-shirt, Michael focused on the basket full of sexy French underwear. The jewel tone colors of the tiny silk panties drew him. Before he really thought about it, he was fingering the soft lace. He liked his women in sexy underwear, and Chenelle had been more than happy to oblige. He looked up to find Niki's wise eyes staring at him.

"I'd prefer to pick my own underwear, thanks," she quipped, looking only slightly flushed in the face.

"You sure?" he asked, noting that the dainty silk panties in his hand would match the teal blue sundress perfectly. Come to think of it, there was a red pair to match the red tank dress too. He hadn't meant to pick underwear for Niki, but why be embarrassed about an item everyone had to wear?

"Yes, I'm sure!" Niki gave him a little push. "You've been a big help, but I think I can take it from here. Why don't you wait for me outside?"

Taking in the self-conscious expression on her face, Michael grinned, then apologized. "Hey, I'm sorry if I've made you uncomfortable. I was just checking out the selection." When she nodded and moved on to look for herself, he shrugged and stepped outside the boutique.

Instead of waiting outside the shop, Michael decided to investigate some of the other shops and businesses lining the hallway. Lively piano music drew him to a bar at the end of the hall.

Black and white pictures of old movie stars covered the walls and in several cushioned booths people sat and talked. Liking the atmosphere and resolving to come back, he took a seat at the bar near the entrance to keep an eye out for Niki while he sipped an orange juice.

Slapping his fist with one hand, Michael glanced around. So here he was on the honeymoon cruise without the bride, without Chenelle. He'd thought she was the one. All right, so he hadn't been in love with her, but he'd never cared so much for any other woman, or been as compatible. She'd been everything he'd wanted in a wife. Would he ever find another woman as good for him? Did he even want to try?

He signaled the bartender for another juice. It had taken him years to realize that he needed to settle down and get married, and where had it gotten him? He felt vulnerable. Too vulnerable. Why else would he be on a cruise with a woman who was just like one of his buddies and find himself suddenly unable to keep his mind off her physical assets? He liked Niki, but he'd never felt like making a pass at her. Now he was in danger of crossing the line big time!

He saw her come out of the boutique and waved. What a difference in her facial expression, he thought. Losing her suitcase had put her in the dumps, but a few purchases in the boutique, and she looked like her cheerful self again.

She glided towards him like a breath of fresh air,

her gray eyes sparkling. Michael stood and paid for his drinks. He wondered fleetingly whether Niki was hoping to snag a new boyfriend on this cruise. He couldn't expect her to spend all her free time with him.

"Nice place," she murmured as she reached him. Her eyes scanned the room.

"Yeah, we'll have to come back." He extended a hand for some of the bags she carried. After a moment's hesitation, she gave him half.

She glanced at her watch. "We've got forty-five minutes."

"Let's go back to the room," he suggested, knowing she wanted to change.

"Good idea." Niki turned and started walking back the way she'd come.

Chapter 4

After Nikita disappeared into the bathroom, Michael stood and went over to the closet to pull out his suitcase. Scanning the contents, he selected a lightweight sport coat with matching pants in an off white color. A beige and white print shirt completed his outfit. Adding his underwear, he dropped the clothing in a pile on the bed and sat down to scan the ship's brochure.

When Nikita opened the bathroom door twenty minutes later, the spicy aroma of her perfume rode the steamy air rushing out to caress his cheek. Michael closed his eyes, breathing in the pleasant scent. His mind filled with thoughts of warm summer breezes and dances in the moonlight.

"What do you think?" she asked in a sensual tone he'd never heard before.

He started his slow, leisurely assessment with the mid-heeled sandals. The straps seemed to caress her feet and emphasize her long shapely legs. The teal sundress hit her mid-thigh and wrapped her slim figure like another layer of skin. Nikita smiled tentatively as she tugged at the hemline. She looked luscious and as curvaceous as hell.

Inclining his head, he got an eyeful. He found himself wondering if she was wearing those teal silk panties. A slow, easy smile escaped him. "Damn, you look good."

"Thanks." She turned in a circle to give him the full effect, her face slightly flushed. "I've never heard you say that before."

"That's because you didn't look like this before." With little success, he tried not to stare. "I can't stop looking at you."

This time she did blush. "I'm glad you dragged me into that boutique. Whether they give me a full credit for the clothes or not, it was worth it."

"You've got that right." Michael took one last good look. What was wrong with him anyway? Nikita was not on the menu. "If you're going to look so delectable, I need to change into something more formal. Lord knows, I could use a shower."

Nikita moved away from the doorway. "It's all yours."

He grabbed the clothing from the bed and headed for the bathroom. He was feeling a little reckless and crazy.

Michael hung his clothes on a hook near the sink.

As he turned to close the door, Nikita asked, "Why don't I unpack your stuff while I wait?"

He liked the thought. Living out of a suitcase was tough. "Sure. Knock yourself out."

"I—I'll leave the underwear to you," she added quickly.

He grinned at the thought of Nikita handling his underwear. He knew she wasn't up to letting him handle hers. "Whatever you like," he chuckled. She could probably handle him, if she really wanted to. Michael's pants tightened, and the grin faded.

She was busy hanging his shirts in the closet when he shut the bathroom door. Down boy, he told his reflection in the mirror. This is better than crying in your beer over Chenelle, but there will be no sex with Nikita. Get that? No sex! Furthermore, you're going to stop drooling over her.

With rough hands, he ripped off his sport shirt. Visions of Nikita whirling around in the teal sundress danced in his head. Uncensored thoughts of her long, long legs, those nice breasts, and her clear gray eyes followed. What was the matter with him anyway? Nikita was not someone he could or would casually sleep with. In fact, he shouldn't be having thoughts of sleeping with her at all.

Michael shook his head in irritation and then bent to ease his zipper past his erection. You're acting like a teenager! Quickly he stepped out of the pants, and tossed them onto a hanger.

So he'd been royally dumped at the altar. The rejection still stung. He'd thought that what he had with Chenelle was special. He'd wanted to bury his head in the sand, to be anywhere but in the church in front of all his friends and family, but he'd lived through it. Was he still so raw and vulnerable inside that he needed to console himself with Nikita? Resolutely, he switched on the shower and made sure the water was cold.

As the bathroom door clicked shut, Nikita glanced at her reflection in the mirror. The steam in the bathroom hadn't frizzed her hair. She liked the way she looked and so did Michael. This was only the first day, and he was obviously already seeing at her as a desirable woman. Things were moving much faster than she'd imagined. Then a thought hit her like acid, threatening to burst her bubble of happiness: He could simply be on the rebound from being left at the altar.

Nikita carefully placed several pairs of pants on hangers. No, she told herself, it wouldn't do to go second-guessing Michael and his motives. She'd give herself an ulcer. If she could just get him to really turn to her during this cruise, she'd enjoy every precious minute of it. Then she'd make sure it became permanent.

As she put a stack of T-shirts in a drawer, she

realized that several were thick and large enough for her to sleep in. She hadn't bought a nightgown, but a filmy gray number in the boutique stuck in her mind. If things escalated between them, she'd go back and get it.

The boutique! In a flurry of activity, Nikita placed the undergarments she'd purchased in a drawer and her own new shorts and T-shirts on top of them. Darn if she'd tell him that she'd followed his recommendation and purchased the matching panties. If he happened to discover the fact while she had them on, well, that was different. In the meantime, she was going to act the way she usually did.

The bathroom door opened and as casually as she could, Nikita feasted her eyes on Michael. The faint shadow of his dark beard was gone. He'd shaved. He'd also shampooed and the still damp black hair waved gently back. Michael smiled, the corners of his brown eyes crinkling. The classic lines of his sport coat and matching pants enhanced his lean-muscled frame. He looked like a male model.

Nikita caught her breath and returned his smile. Waves of pure masculine virility and charm flooded her senses. She wanted to touch him, assure herself this moment was real, and that the look in his eye was for her. Her heart swelled with love and anticipation.

Suddenly aware of the long silence, Nikita broke the spell. "I like the way you look." That was an understatement. She'd been staring like he was the last piece in a box of Godiva chocolates. He nodded calmly, murmuring his thanks, and moved past her to put his discarded clothing in a corner of the closet.

Her throat felt dry. She swallowed, glad he hadn't noticed how goofy she'd been acting. After all, she'd seen Michael looking his best a number of times when he'd accompanied Chenelle to various affairs. Uncomfortable, and a little disgusted with herself, Nikita checked her watch. She hated being late for anything. "We should be heading for the dining room," she announced breathlessly.

They left the cabin and followed several other couples to the large, formal room. On the way to their table, he noticed that most of the people were wearing suits, sport coats and dresses.

After a few wrong turns, they found their table, a table for four, near the white curtained windows. An older, white-haired woman in a beige dress sat with an athletic-looking younger man. Michael sized him up, noting the strong physical resemblance, and concluded that they were mother and son. The man turned to face them, his sea green eyes warming at the sight of Nikita. They exchanged greetings and the man introduced himself as Tyson Ward, then introduced his mother, Alice.

"I'm Nikita and this is Michael," Her pleasant voice gave away as little personal information as possible.

Tyson Ward held Nikita's hand several seconds longer than necessary. "Are you two newlyweds?"

Tired of the easy lie he been telling all day, Michael decided to come clean. After all, it wasn't fair to Nikita. "No," he answered quickly, before she could reply. "We're good friends." He glanced quickly at her to gauge her reaction, but her expression revealed nothing.

"Then I hope we get a chance to know each other better, Nikita." Ward's eyes darkened, his lips smoothing into an extra special smile. Nodding politely, she returned the smile, and assertively retrieved her hand.

Michael groaned inwardly. Nikita didn't need his protection, but the expensively dressed Tyson Ward seemed all seasoned wolf. The way his eyes consumed her, she could easily have been a delicious cut of meat. Was he going to be able to stand it? This wolf was probably going to spend most of each meal drooling over Nikita. Could he blame him? No, Nikita looked beautiful. And she was also the most intelligent woman he knew.

Clamping down on his annoyance, Michael opened the menu and scanned the choices. The rich spicy scent of beef and chicken floated on the air, making his stomach growl. Near the bottom of the list of entrees he found the prime rib and relaxed. All he needed was prime rib, au gratin potatoes, a salad, and some of that French onion soup. Before he closed the menu, he saw coq au vin on the list of entrees. The chicken in wine sauce was one of Nikita's favorites, one he knew she couldn't resist.

He saw her mouth the words, and glance up to smile at him. "They've got coq au vin!"

"Thought you'd get a kick out of that." Michael flipped open the wine list. "Now all we've got to do is find the right wine to go with it." Since he didn't recognize many of the wines on the list, he waved the wine steward over to their table to make a recommendation.

The room buzzed with conversation. They were happily sipping a German wine when their waiter, an attractive, mahogany-skinned black man, appeared. In a lilting West Indian accent, he explained the menu options, took their orders, and then bustled off to fill them.

Obviously determined to monopolize Nikita, Ward prattled on and on about the fabulous show scheduled for the main lounge after dinner. Nikita turned to Michael, "Do you want to go after dinner?"

Michael observed the sleepy look about her eyes. She'd be lucky if she made it through the show without falling asleep. The wine hadn't helped. He didn't care if he went to the show or not, but if Nikita wanted to go, he'd sit through it. "Sure, we can do that."

He watched as she unconsciously wet her lips and continued. "Then maybe we could go back to that little piano bar you discovered."

Leaning towards her he enjoyed the proximity, still surprised that Nikita could affect him this way . "Tonight's your night, Nikita. We can do anything you want."

She glanced at him quickly, her eyes deep pools of gray as she bit her lip reflectively. She'd sensed the double meaning in his words. A questioning look lit her eyes.

He could drown in the depths of those eyes. Michael's pulse speeded up. The urge to touch her grew within him.

Tyson Ward broke the spell. "There's a live band in the Ten Four Jazz Club, if you looking for something good to do."

Glad for his thoughts to be interrupted, Michael sat back in his chair. He'd been drooling again. Clenching a fist beneath the table, he chastised himself.

"Oh, that sounds good. Somehow I don't think I'm up to the show and two night spots." Nikita laughed and sipped her wine. Her eyes sparkled.

"But there's always tomorrow."

Ward tapped his glass to hers. "A toast to tomorrow."

They all followed his lead then, toasting tomorrow and the vacation ahead. The waiter reappeared to serve the soup and appetizers.

Michael dug into his soup. "So what do you do?" he asked Ward between spoonfuls. Since Nikita seemed to like the guy, it wouldn't hurt to know more about him.

"I run the family business. We own a chain of restaurants in California. Ever hear of Longstreet's?"

"No, but I'll make sure I go next time I'm in the area." Swallowing the last of the soup, Michael set down the spoon and pushed the bowl away. He hadn't known he was so hungry. The waiter cleared away dishes.

"I've been there," Nikita chimed in, her wide smile showcasing the tooth that stuck out a little in front. "The food's great!"

Ward and Alice thanked her.

"So what do you do?" Ward asked Michael politely.

"We're both engineers for a Michigan toy manufacturer," Nikita answered.

"That's great." Ward's eyes filled with admiration. "Are you any good with computers?"

"It's my hobby. I like to surf the Internet. I can't believe I didn't bring my laptop." She looked a little wistful.

Michael saw the light bulb go on as Ward seized the moment. "I brought my laptop and you're welcome to use it."

"Really? What kind is it?" Nikita leaned forward in her excitement.

"It's a Compaq. I know they've got a Cyber Café on board and some LAN drops in the library. I figured I could try to download my email."

Her eyes lit up. "Great. I can take care of my email and check in with a couple of my favorite web sites."

"Be my guest."

Her soft lips curved into a smile. "Thanks. I've been planning to get a new one, so I'm looking forward to trying yours."

"So am I. I just got the darned thing and don't really know how to use it."

And the elevator forgets which way is up. Michael bit back his comment. He didn't believe the guy. Surely Nikita was too intelligent to miss Ward's setup.

"I'd be happy to show you what to do," Nikita offered, Miss America till the end. Michael worked hard to maintain his bland expression.

Ward moved to cinch the date. "Could you meet

me tomorrow in the library or out on deck?"

"Sure, in the library about two o'clock?"

Alice put a hand on her son's arm. "Tyson, let Nikita and Michael enjoy their vacation."

"Mother, stay out of this, will you?" Ward's tone seemed light enough, but Alice's expression hardened.

Nikita's eyes widened with concern. "Mrs. Ward, please don't worry," she said, in a gentle voice any mother would love. "I'm glad to be able to get my hand on a Palm VII. It's really not going to affect our vacation one way or another, is it, Michael?"

"No, it won't," he said firmly, ignoring the contradictory voice inside his head. She was supposed to be his friend and companion on this cruise, but what could he say? If Nikita wanted to go play with Ward tomorrow afternoon, she didn't really need his input or permission.

Making no further protest, Alice seemed to relax after that. From time to time she watched Nikita with a little smile, when she thought no one was looking. Michael knew the signs. Nikita had made another conquest. His parents loved her too. His own dad had asked him how he could contemplate marriage to someone like Chenelle with someone as special as Nikita around.

The waiter brought the main course and they stopped talking briefly to enjoy the meal. Michael's gaze flicked quickly over Ward. He didn't like him, and he couldn't quite figure out why. He knew he didn't like the way he alternately kissed up to Nikita, then tried to pique her interest. There was something sneaky about those green eyes he used to charm her.

Shifting in his chair, Michael gave himself a mental slap. He was thinking like a jealous boyfriend. All right, he'd picked the wrong fiancée. Maybe Nikita would have better luck. It wasn't as if she was his type. After all, he liked more voluptuous women, didn't he?

Discreetly scanning of the room, he saw nothing else worth looking at. Sipping his gourmet coffee, he decided that as long as he was circumspect, and kept his hands to himself, he could look at Nikita too.

Leisurely strolling out of the dining room after dinner, they wandered down to the Showcase Lounge. Michael scrutinized the room, then drew Nikita to seats close to front center. Tyson and Alice Ward followed.

Uncomfortably full from dinner, Nikita settled into her chair. She felt like a stuffed pig. Why had she eaten so much? Days of delicious food stretched ahead of her. And why was she still so tired? The little nap had just barely taken the edge off. A trip to Michael's little piano bar seemed unlikely, but she could enjoy the show. She refused a drink from the roving lounge attendant and saw Michael follow suit.

Still not quite believing she was on a cruise with him, Nikita stared at his profile as he read the elaborate program, her gaze lovingly tracing the lines of hooded brows divided by the narrow bridge of his nose that widened to an almost triangular shape. She wanted to stroke her fingers across the cleft in his chin beneath his thin but sculpted lips. What would those lips feel like?

The black fringe of his lashes lifted as he tilted his head and looked up from the program. Almond brown eyes captivated her, pulling her into their realm of influence. "I recognize some of the people performing tonight. The show should be great." He pointed to a couple of names. "These guys play for Deep VI." He indicated another name. "And this lady has a few CDs out."

Nikita nodded, opening her own program.

"Didn't I tell you the entertainment's fantastic aboard these ships?" Tyson spoke from the other side of Nikita.

"Yes, you did. I hope it's like this all week." Nikita focused on Tyson's sea green eyes. He was an attractive man. Hopefully she wouldn't be encouraging him too much with a few computer lessons in exchange for being able to surf the Internet.

No matter how much she wanted to be with

Michael, the prospect of following him around like a little puppy for the entire cruise, or dragging him in her wake, was unappealing. She had too much pride. They'd need some time apart, unless things went the way she hoped.

An irresistible metallic percussion beat began. Nikita found herself tapping her feet and the arms of her chair as the curtains on stage opened on a New York City setting with tall buildings and people standing on fire escapes. Several performers used drumsticks and spoons to play tunes on the pots and pans strapped to the front and back of their costumes. Then they combined it all with a street-wise tap dance. The audience went wild.

The first act ended with thunderous applause. Nikita curved her body towards Michael, propping her chin on a palm. Her lids felt heavy, but if the rest of the performances were as good, she'd make it.

In the second act, a sultry voiced, sensually dressed diva stepped on to a set resembling a New Orleans Jazz Club called Chantal's and belted out a few classic jazz and blues tunes.

"She's the one with the CDs out. I've got two of them," Michael whispered at one point.

Nikita lost herself in the music and the images it invoked and drifted off to sleep. The sound of applause jolted her awake. Her cheek rested against Michael's warm, beefy shoulder. She sat up straight in the semi-circle of his arm.

"You all right?" Michael steadied her with a warm hand.

"Yes." Nikita yawned sheepishly behind an open palm. "I think I'll head on back to the cabin."

"I'll come along and make sure you get there safely."

The thought bothered her. Although she enjoyed Michael's company, he didn't need to baby-sit. "No, I want you to stay and enjoy the show."

He rose quickly, taking her hand. "You know my mother raised me better than that. Now, come on."

It wasn't worth an argument, she decided, seeing his determination. Saying her goodnights, Nikita rose and walked out of the lounge with Michael before the third act began.

"Walking around the ship alone at night is not a good idea," he said as they got on the gold-mirrored elevator.

Nikita ground her teeth. "I'm a big girl, Michael." She pushed the button for their level and watched the doors close. "I can take care of myself."

"Nikita, you're not at home here. People drink and party late into the night. Lord knows, none of us have to get up and go to work in the morning. The thought of you wandering around in all that makes me worry. Promise me you won't wander the ship alone at night."

He had a point, she realized, but she hadn't been planning to hang out in the clubs alone. Hopefully, he'd spend each night with her. "All right, Michael, I promise." The elevator doors opened and they stepped out into the corridor.

When they got in the cabin, Michael closed the door. Concern filled his eyes as he turned to Nikita. "I guess you think I've been preaching at you."

"Not really. I think your heart's in the right place. I didn't want you to miss the show just because I'm sleepy."

"Nikita, you are not a burden to me, or someone I think needs baby-sitting. You're an intelligent adult, capable of taking care of yourself. I'm glad you came along on this cruise to help me pull myself out of the dumps. I care about you and don't want anything to happen to you. Okay?" He tugged playfully on a lock of her hair.

"Okay." Nikita caught his hand and moved it away from her hair.

She spotted a folded paper on the floor near the bottom of the door. Bending down, she picked it up and read the printed words with mounting disappointment. "They can't find my suitcase. It never came in from the airport. I'm supposed to follow up with the airline when we get to Cozumel. Could I borrow an extra large T-shirt to sleep in?"

"Sure." He opened a drawer and rummaged

through the contents.

Michael pressed a large blue T-shirt into her hands. "At least we hit Cozumel the day after tomorrow. I'm sorry, Nikita."

"So am I," she muttered, glancing down at the T-shirt in her hands. So much for getting Michael's attention with some of the clothing she'd packed. She was going to spend a lot of the next two days washing and wearing the clothing she'd bought in the ship's boutique. "Hey, it could be worse."

"True." Michael leaned up against the door. "It's not the end of the world, is it? I know that clothes are just not that important to you." His expression changed to one of astonished amusement. "Nikita, you're good for me. I haven't thought of Chenelle or the wedding fiasco for hours."

Warmth spread within her. Lightly, she massaged his arm. "I'm glad. And you're right, it's not the end of the world. Just inconvenient and frustrating. I'll just have to make the best of it."

"You always do. That's what I like about you. Instead of sucking on lemons, you're always sipping the lemonade."

Except when the man of my dreams was determined to marry my best friend. Michael Matheson, you wouldn't know what was good for you if it came up and bit you on the butt. Nikita kept her thoughts to herself.

Michael pushed up off the door. "I can't believe you're insulted."

"What makes you think that?"

"You've got the 'your ears should be burning because I'm royally roasting your butt in my thoughts' look."

"No." Sometimes Michael's ability to read her was uncanny. Recovering quickly, she glanced down at the shirt. "I was just wondering if this shirt is big enough."

The warmth in his almond brown eyes as they flicked over her quickly made her blush. "I think it'll cover the essentials. Are you really going to bed?"

"Yes, Michael. I guess I'm just boring."

"No, I can understand your being tired. I'm tired, but too keyed up to sleep. I'll wander around the ship for a couple of hours and then come back to crash." He hesitated for a moment as his glance held Nikita's, seeming almost reluctant to leave. Abruptly, he turned the handle and opened the door. "Good night, Nikita."

"Good night." He left so quickly that she might well have been talking to herself. She kicked off her sandals and went into the bathroom to wash her face. Stripping down to the teal silk panties, she slipped into his shirt. As she gathered her clothing and neatened the counter, she heard a knock on the outer room door. When she came out, she saw that the sheets had been turned back and chocolate mints placed on the pillows.

Slipping between the sheets, she turned out the light. The thought of Michael coming back to climb into bed with her made her tingle all over and want to stay awake. It was the sort of thing she dreamed about. She sank her head into a pillow still scented lightly with Polo cologne and smiled into the darkness. Today he'd looked at her and really seen her for the first time. He'd seemed to like what he saw. If she could just take things nice and easy, avoid talk about Chenelle and the wedding disaster, and concentrate on being herself, he'd see that they belonged together.

Chapter 5

Nikita awakened in the predawn hours of the morning to find herself alone in bed. Did Michael spend the night somewhere else? she wondered, suppressing the discordant thoughts reminding her that she didn't have the right to ask. She sat up in bed, huddling beneath the covers in the air-conditioned chill of the cabin and scanned the room.

Barely visible in the darkness, an uncomfortable looking figure huddled beneath a blanket on the loveseat. So much for togetherness! She knew it was silly, but she felt a little hurt because they'd both agreed to share the bed. The last thing she'd wanted was to kick him out of his own bed.

Throwing back the covers, she tiptoed on the cool carpet, grabbing the running gear she'd stacked on the table near the bed last night, and crept into the bathroom to dress. When she'd finished, she eased out of the cabin and headed up one of the outside stairwells to the sports deck.

It was just starting to get light. Niki paused to gaze at the small slice of orange sun peeking up from the edge of the glassy water. It reminded her of pictures she'd seen on postcards. She breathed in fresh morning air, determined to enjoy herself. Glancing at her watch, she hurried up the stairs and began her laps.

She covered the wooden deck in her twelfth lap, her breath hitching in her throat. The air had warmed considerably with the rising sun and a gorgeous blue sky heralded a beautiful day. Her outfit was so damp that she felt as if she'd already had a dip in the pool. Two more laps, she promised herself as she pushed herself forward.

· Her legs and feet throbbed as she walked back to the cabin. From time to time she paused to sip water from her bottle. At the cabin door she brushed a hand across her damp hair. She knew she looked a mess, but there was nothing she could do about it. Using her key, she carefully opened the door.

Michael was pulling on a shirt. Niki's breath caught in her throat at the sight of his smooth, brown, padded chest and his trim torso. He glanced up, his smile full of unconscious welcome and charm. "Did you have a good run?"

"Pretty good," she answered, "I'm huffing and puffing because I'm a little out of shape."

"Coulda fooled me." He dropped down on the

unmade bed to pull on a pair of sandals.

"Thanks." Smiling at the compliment, she went over to the chest of drawers and found a pair of navy shorts and a white T-shirt. Turning her back to Michael, she selected underwear.

"If I wanted to see which panties you bought I could just look in the drawer, you know." He chuckled.

Covering the underwear with her T-shirt, Nikita turned to face him. "Why are you pickin with me?"

"Because I think your reaction's kinda cute. I've never really seen this side of you."

She twisted her lips. "Keep it up and you may see something you'll wish you hadn't."

Michael laughed aloud. "Now that's the Niki I know and love."

She stared at him for a moment, wishing he meant he loved her the way she loved him. Then she took her pile of clothing and headed for the bathroom.

"Will you be ready in time to make our seating for breakfast?" he called as she turned to close the door.

She nodded.

"Then I'll come back in about fifteen minutes and we can go together."

"Sounds good." With that, she closed the door and turned on the shower. Stripping quickly, she stepped into the warm spray to wash her short hair with Michael's everyday shampoo. Afterward, she washed with the deodorant soap and dried herself with the large, white towel. She'd dressed, towel dried her hair, and applied a little of the curling gel she'd found in the ship's boutique when she heard the cabin door open.

"Ready for breakfast?" Michael's voice echoed in the room.

Nikita opened the bathroom door. "One minute."

"That was quite a transformation," Michael quipped, his eyes sparkling appreciatively.

"Thanks," Nikita said with a smile, "You're just full of compliments these days."

He answered in a teasing tone. "Maybe you've become more worthy of compliments."

"And maybe it's about time I kicked your butt at poker again. It would take the edge off some of your smart remarks," she snapped back.

Shifting his feet, he replied, "If you win, it would, but no one can win all the time."

Nikita sighed airily and walked out of the bathroom. "I can only point to my flawless record in my games with you."

"And I can only point out that maybe you're cheating and I just haven't figured out how." He harrumphed.

"Michael!" Nikita playfully punched his arm. "You know I don't cheat."

"Probably not." He led her out of the cabin. They barely felt the ship moving as they walked to the dining room.

There were considerably fewer people seated in the dreamy blue dining room than there had been at dinner. The curtains were open to reveal a heavenly sky dotted with fluffy white clouds floating above the jewel-colored water.

"Good morning. You're looking fresh and beautiful." Tyson greeted Nikita as he pulled out a chair and sat down at their table. He nodded politely at Michael.

"Thanks. How are you this morning?" she murmured as she placed her napkin in her lap. Accepting a menu from their waiter, she thanked him.

"Oh I'm fine, just fine." Tyson said. His green eyes, full of admiration, reminded her of a cat surveying a bowl of thick cream.

Nikita opened her menu and began to read. On her left, she heard Michael ordering steak and eggs with hash browns and coffee. When she saw strawberry crepes on the menu her mouth watered. She had to have them. Then she decided on smoked bacon, pineapple juice , fruit salad, and decaff coffee.

The waiter brought Michael's coffee and took her order. "Where is everyone?" she asked conversationally as the waiter bustled off with her order.

"In bed catching a few Zs or ordering room service, up on the Lido deck getting their own breakfast at the buffet, or out on deck getting a little of that early morning sun and exercise." Tyson flashed his pearly whites.

Nikita smiled. "I like having so many choices."

"That's the good thing about a cruise," Michael said, joining the conversation for the first time. "You get pampered and fed and you don't have to lift a finger if you don't want to."

"What are you doing after breakfast?" Tyson asked Nikita between bites of French toast.

She shrugged. "I hadn't really thought about it. She glanced at Michael who seemed kind of distant and watched him shrug. "What are you doing?" she asked Tyson.

"There's a Latin dance class in the Terraboca Lounge."

"Ooh, sounds like fun!" Nikita sat back as the waiter set the fruit salad, coffee and juice in front of her. "Michael, what do you think?"

Michael lifted his knife and fork and went to work his steak. "I—think I'll just spend some time on deck."

"I could go with you—"

"No, no. Go on down to the Latin dance session with Ward."

The firmness in his tone stung Nikita. She felt

certain he was trying to get rid of her. Was it because he was still hurting over Chenelle's betrayal? Of course he is, Stupid! she admonished herself.

Tyson shot Michael a glance. "You can call me Tyson."

"Sure thing Tyson," Michael said evenly, but his tone lacked warmth.

Nikita didn't know what to think as she ate the rest of her meal in relative silence. Tyson chattered on obliviously, asking questions to which she supplied one-syllable answers. Had she misread the interest she'd seen in Michael's eyes?

When they'd finished eating, Tyson stood up, full of enthusiasm. "Let's go on down now."

Nikita slanted Michael a glance. Sipping coffee, he didn't meet her gaze. Do you need him to spell it out for you? a little voice whispered at the back of her thoughts. "See you later, Michael," she said, turning to follow Tyson out of the dining room.

As soon as they stepped into the Terraboca Lounge, Nikita knew she was going to have a good time. Foot-tapping music filled the air and a tall, graceful woman with an infectious laugh introduced herself as Maria Rosa. She had an assorted group of people behind her trying to do a Latin Hustle. Taking an instant liking to Tyson and Nikita, she put them in the front of the group and demonstrated each new step with them first.

Pretty soon, Tyson and Nikita were twisting and shaking and moving their feet in an intricate hustle that included parts of the Mambo, Samba, Cha-Cha. and Salsa dances.

"Oh, you guys are so good!" Maria said, clapping her hands at the end of the session. "Keep this up and I'm going to put this class on the program for the passenger talent show! Would you all like that?"

The entire class applauded the idea.

"Great." Now give yourselves a round of applause," she said with a wave of a hand.

The applause was loud and enthusiastic.

"Can we all now give a round of applause for our great instructor?" Tyson called out.

The applause and cheers were so boisterous that it sounded like someone had made a winning sports play.

"Thank-you." Maria held open arms out to the class. "Same time tomorrow? Excellent!"

Nikita was breathless and thirsty as she exited the lounge with Tyson.

"Let's go have a drink in one of those bars on the Promenade," he suggested.

"I'd rather have something on deck." Nikita pushed open a door to an outside set of stairs.

"Fine." Tyson followed her persistently. "How about a Margarita or a Caribbean Punch?"

At the top of the stairs Nikita paused at the sight

of Michael stretched out in the shade in one of the deck chair loungers. She smiled and started towards him until she spotted the attractive woman at his side. Exposing several yards of smooth, nut-brown skin, she was dressed in a hot pink bikini top and short shorts. She was also laughing provocatively at something he'd said.

"Nikita?" Tyson pulled up short behind her.

"I'll—I'll have the Caribbean Punch," she said.

"Do you want to join Michael and his friend?"

"No," she answered quickly in as light a tone as possible. "Let's go back down to the pool area. There's a band playing there."

"Cool." Tyson led the way down the stairs, following the sound of a guitar band playing and singing Spanish love songs.

Nikita sat sipping her drink in one of deck chairs in the shaded area to the rear of the pool. It was too hot in the sun, so she simply stretched out in her chair and let the music and scenery set her mood. A sultry breeze teased her skin and the gentle motion of the ship lulled her into a dreamlike state.

When the band took a break, she realized that she been poolside for more than an hour. The combined aromas of hamburgers, hot dogs, and pizza filled the air and people were starting to line up at the various stands and serving areas. Over the PA system, the ship's announcer spoke of lunch in the dining room for the first seating.

Nikita's stomach growled. She wondered how she could be hungry after eating so much at breakfast. Turning in her chair, she found Tyson looking at her.

"Want to go down to the dining room for lunch or get something up here?" he asked.

She thought of Michael getting rid of her after breakfast this morning and then seeing him with the woman on deck later. She wanted to talk to him and coordinate her plans with him, but maybe it would be better if she stayed away a little longer. It would probably spare her from getting her feelings hurt, she decided. It had hurt to be sent off like a kid sister at breakfast and then see the man she loved having fun with another woman. "Let's get something up here," she told Tyson.

He stood, a look of triumph on his face. "Tell you what," he said dropping his daily event schedule into his chair, "Why don't I get the food while you hold down the chairs?"

"Sounds good. These are good seats and another band is going to start playing in about fifteen minutes." She tossed the summer sweater she used to combat the chill of the ship's air conditioning on top of his schedule. Then she told him what she wanted.

Tyson Ward was a nice man, but Nikita wanted to spend her time with Michael. By the time they'd eaten lunch and listened to the new band for a number of songs, Nikita had had enough of Tyson's company. Since she'd decided to give Michael some space, she wanted to go back to the cabin for a nap. Postponing their two o'clock meeting in the library for another day, she took off for the cabin.

Walking down the hall, as she approached the cabin, she couldn't help wondering what she would find inside. Would Michael be there asleep on the bed? Would he be there with another woman? She scratched that thought because she knew that although he could be wild, he had always treated her with respect.

Nikita opened the door and found the cabin cool and empty. Dragging back the spread, she took off her shoes and got under the covers. Except for muffled snatches of conversation and movement in the cabins surrounding her, it was very quiet. Fixing her eyes on miles and miles of ocean pictured in the window, she fell asleep.

Michael let himself into the cabin, glad to see Nikita stretched out in the bed. He'd been looking for her. It had taken quite a while to get rid of the woman who must have staked him out as her date for the cruise. She'd slipped into the chair beside him on deck, engaged him in conversation, and then followed him down to the dining room to sit with him and Alice Ward at their table. Tyson and Nikita had never showed up.

After lunch, with the woman determinedly sticking like glue, he'd gone to check the pool area, the mechanical horse races, and the casino to no avail. He told himself he was just making sure she was okay, but deep inside he knew he missed her. At the antique car bar, he'd finally gotten rid of the woman and spotted Tyson. When he asked about Nikita, Tyson gave him a smug grin and said, "She was a little tired after lunch, so she begged off the meeting in the library. Isn't she asleep in the cabin?"

Gently closing the door, he took a seat in the high backed chair facing the picture window. He divided his attention between the deep blue water that stretched on to forever, and Nikita's face, angelic, yet incredibly sexy in sleep. When she awakened, yawning and stretching, he was waiting.

"Hey," she mumbled at the sight of him. Then she smoothed the tips of her fingers over her eyelids.

"Hey, yourself," he said shifting in the chair. "How long have you been sleeping?"

Checking the condition of her short hair with her fingers, she sighed. "Oh, since about one-thirty, two o'clock. Did I miss anything?"

"Mechanical horse races, sun and shade on deck, poolside bands, and music in the piano bar, and four o'clock tea."

She sat up in the bed, the covers falling to reveal her rumpled shorts and T-shirt. "It'll all be there tomorrow."

"That's the truth," he acknowledged. "What do you want to do next?"

She was silent, but he saw a mischievous light animate her eyes and fade.

"What?" he asked, wondering what could make her look like that, certain it would be fun.

"Nothing," she answered a bit defensively. "We could do dinner in the dining room and hit the casino afterwards."

"And check out the comic in the Comedy Center after you lose your money," he added.

She folded her legs beneath her. "I'm not going to lose my money."

"Wanna bet?" He lifted an eyebrow. No one could win all the time and Nikita was definitely overdue for a loss.

"Okay smartass. I'm only going to play with about $75. I figured we could go in there for a couple of hours. You can time it. I figure that at least $25 of it should count as entertainment. If I lose more than that, you win the bet. Okay?"

"What do I win?" he asked. He could count the times he'd beaten Nikita in games of chance on one hand. If he won this one, he wanted to enjoy it.

The mischievous light sparkled in her gray eyes

once more. "The loser has to do what the winner wants them to do for one entire day."

Michael considered it. "We're pulling into the first port tomorrow. Won't that make it difficult to make good on the bet?"

"Hmmph! It should make it easier," she snapped back.

As he held his hand out to shake on their bet, Michael's thoughts spun ahead to imagine Nikita wearing a big T-shirt with loser printed on both sides or singing something stupid in the karaoke club. This might be a lot of fun. Could he try something more provocative? He imagined her in a string bikini and had to block the thought immediately. It was simply too exciting.

They shook hands on their bet and then took turns using the bathroom to get ready for dinner.

At dinner that night, Tyson dominated the conversation with talk of his plans to hire a car in the next port for a personal tour and to visit a popular restaurant. In her own little world, Nikita seemed oblivious. Finally, Tyson quit hinting around and asked her to join him.

Nikita's gray eyes focused on Tyson for the first time that evening. "I don't think so, but thanks for asking. I think I'll just do some shopping." She turned to Michael. "Are you getting off the boat tomorrow?"

He stared at her, knowing he was too damned attracted to her. He wanted to go ashore with her. Hell, better yet, his thoughts ran to staying aboard ship in bed with her, but she was one of those women who romanticized sex. She had to be in love with the man and expected marriage to follow. The fact that she was one of his closest friends didn't help the situation. It was driving him crazy keeping his hands off her and leaving her to Tyson's pursuit. "I hadn't really planned to go into Puerto Vallarta," he answered, deliberately ignoring the unspoken request in her eyes. "I thought I'd stay aboard the ship and relax."

"You're getting dull and boring in your old age!" she teased.

Michael smiled. "I promise to get off at the next port."

With a tap on Nikita's shoulder, Tyson seized the moment. "Hey, why don't I go shopping with you and you join me at the restaurant?"

"What about your mother?" Nikita asked, glancing at Alice.

"I'm going to sleep in." Alice set her fork on her plate. "If we're still in port when I get up, I'll go down to one of those stores near the dock. I don't need much."

Michael almost felt sorry for Tyson, who was trying hard to get Nikita's time and attention.

Reading the subtle nuances in her expression, he didn't think she wanted to bother with Tyson at all. This didn't make sense because she'd spent all morning and the greater part of the day in the man's company.

"Why don't you check with me in the morning on your way off the boat?" Nikita answered, lifting her spoon and dipping it into her cherries jubilee.

"Okay. I'll do that." Tyson's tone all but signaled his acceptance of defeat.

Later that night Michael sat at the poker table with Nikita and played. His pile of winnings went up and down until they finally disappeared as Nikita's pile grew steadily. A quick check of his watch verified that there was still an hour to go. Buddy, you're about to lose to Nikita Daniels again! With the smell of defeat in the air, he vacated his chair and slunk off in search of a nickel machine.

He'd found one and began plugging nickels into it and watching to see if the lines of fruit, trees, and animals would line up. He'd gone into automatic pilot and was merely pumping in the nickels and alternating between pulling the lever and pushing the spin button when the machine began to play a catchy little tune. His head snapped up in amazement as he recognized the "We're In the Money" tune.

Sure enough, he had a row of grinning monkeys! The number 5000 flashed on the win meter. He'd won $250 in nickels. "Yeeesss!" Michael's cheer filled the air. A few people wandered over to see how much he'd won and to congratulate him. Riding high on a rush of adrenalin, he felt as if he'd won the lottery.

One of the casino workers came over to clear the machine and pay him off. Nikita appeared at his elbow as the worker counted his money out with a bunch of fresh $50 bills.

"Okay, you win." She climbed onto the stool beside him.

"What about the big pile of chips you had at the poker table?" he asked, stuffing the money into a pocket.

"What about it?"

"Did you cash it all in?"

The room rang with the sound of coins dropping into machines and the corresponding video noise. In the background, there was a collective 'Oh', signaling a big winner at one of the tables. Nikita looked down at her lap where she was rubbing her hands together. "I lost it."

Michael stared at her, noting the subdued expression on her face. "You what?"

She nodded her head up and down. "I lost it. You won the bet."

"I don't believe it." Standing, he turned to face her. "You must have had at least a couple of hundred bucks."

She climbed off the stool to stand beside him, her facial expression downright frosty. "Yes, and— ?"

"Niki, I'm not trying to rub it in. I'm just amazed. I'm going to have to write this one down."

"Maybe you should," she said, leading him towards to exit. "And you might as well enjoy it because I don't plan to repeat this one anytime soon."

The comedy club was at the other end of the ship. There were a few other couples seated when Michael and Nikita walked in and found a table in a dark corner. Nikita asked for a glass of white wine and Michael ordered Martell.

As they sipped their drinks, the comic went through a round of relationship jokes. Michael chuckled as he recognized himself and several of his friends in the characters mimicked. As the routine reached its peak, he was laughing so hard his stomach ached. Glancing at Nikita, he saw her shoulders shaking. The guy was so hilarious, they loved him.

After the comedy show, they headed back to the cabin, mellow from a day of salt air, sun, and fun. She used the bathroom first and then climbed into bed, dressed in one of his T-shirts. When Michael came out of the bathroom clad in a pair of pajama bottoms, she was sitting up in bed, fighting the pull of sleep, but she wasn't too sleepy to notice the smooth caramel skin on his chest and his trim waist.

"I thought you'd be asleep," he muttered as he stepped over to the closet to place a folded stack of dirty clothing in the bottom.

"I thought I'd wait for you," she said, waiting to see what he'd do next.

He pulled a pillow, sheet, and comforter from the top shelf of the closet.

She watched him make a pallet on the couch. "Didn't we make an agreement to share this bed?"

He locked gazes with her and she saw the steel of determination in his. "Since I wasn't as comfortable as I thought I'd be, I changed my mind."

"Ha! Michael, you were asleep as soon as your head hit the pillow."

"Yeah?" Myriad expressions crossed his handsome face in rapid succession.

The last one caught Nikita by surprise. It wasn't guilt was it?

His jaw tightened. "Niki, trust me. This is not a good time to argue about our sleeping arrangements, and this is one argument you won't win tonight."

"Michael, I'm not comfortable sleeping in your bed while you sleep on that couch, so you will deal with it before this cruise is over, right?"

"Definitely." He climbed onto his pallet and tugged the covers up.

Nikita flipped the switch, plunging the room into darkness. Drifting off to sleep, she wondered why Michael was avoiding her. Maybe staying away for most of the day hadn't been such a good idea after all. Tomorrow she would convince him to come ashore with her.

It was already nine o'clock in the morning. Nikita had dressed and combed her hair in record time, but Michael lingered beneath the covers on the couch.

"Come on, Michael! You really need to get out and get some exercise," she said, for the third time. A low, unintelligible mumble was her answer. "Michael!" She tapped his shoulder lightly, but insistently.

Suddenly he snatched the covers from his face to glare at her with sleep-fogged eyes. "You couldn't let me sleep, huh?"

Even with the imprint of the pillow on his face and his tousled hair, he was gorgeous. Realizing her selfishness, she found her voice. "I'm sorry I bothered you, Michael. It's just that it's already nine o'clock and I was hoping you'd change your mind and come with me."

"Nope."

Amid a wave of acute disappointment, Nikita retrieved her purse from its spot by the bed. Hoisting it onto her shoulder, she took a few steps towards the door.

"Not so fast." His voice stopped her progress.

A shiver of anticipation ran through her as she turned to face him.

"There's going to be a penalty."

"What?"

"I said there's going to be a penalty for waking me up," he promised in a low voice. The last vestiges of sleep were fading from his eyes.

Nikita flicked her fingers at him. "Ha! I'd like to see you enforce that."

"I don't have to. I won that bet last night, remember?"

"Yeah," she said with a heartfelt sigh. "So what's the penalty?"

"Hmmmmh..." he hesitated for a moment. "Tell you what, if Tyson comes by and asks you to join him at the restaurant again, you go."

"I don't think so..."

"I do." Michael shifted beneath the covers. "Whatever happened to your word is your bond?"

"Awwl Michael, can't you think of something else? I don't want to encourage him."

A knock sounded on the door.

Michael chuckled. "I guess that settles it.

"Can't you think of something else for me to do?" she asked in a plea for mercy.

Eyes narrowing suggestively, he grinned. "Yeah, but I don't think you'd actually do it."

"Michael!" With a sigh of exasperation, she went to the door and opened it to meet Tyson's expectant smile.

****

Once Nikita got over her pique at being forced to go off with Tyson, she had a good time. A perfect gentleman, he accompanied her into several stores, waited patiently while she looked her fill of jewelry and clothing, and even offered his opinion when she couldn't decide what to buy. She had several bags when they climbed into a taxi and took off for Tyson's restaurant.

It took approximately 20 minutes to get to Café des Artistes, which was located in the foothills of Old Vallarta and considered one of the top restaurants of the world. Looking at the expansive, white building that included a turret-like structure, she listened as Tyson explained that the restaurant had started in a rejuvenated villa and expanded to the house next door with its one hundred-year old tropical garden, and then across the street, where it became an art gallery.

It was a good thing he'd thought to make reservations, because although the restaurant could hold up to two hundred people, a lot of people were waiting. The couple was seated at a semi-private table with a glorious view the Pacific Ocean. Inside, groups of people sat at delicate white tables and chairs amid walls covered with beautiful, impressionistic art. To one side of the restaurant, she glimpsed an exotic garden where a large group dined.

"We've got to be back to the ship in three hours, " Nikita reminded Tyson as she scanned the mouth-watering menu.

"We've got plenty of time," he assured her.

After much debate, she selected grilled swordfish and spicy crab with cactus, green tomato-avocado sauce, and left the choice of wine to Tyson. He ordered filet of red snapper wrapped in black olives, served with a tempura tomato stuffed with vegetables, and baked polenta.

The food was superb. Nikita closed her eyes to savor the tender, flavorful swordfish, complemented by the piquant crab and cactus. The green tomato-avocado sauce enhanced the combined flavors, topped off with the white wine Tyson had selected. She enjoyed herself so much she felt like singing.

Tyson seemed to be having a good time too. His food disappeared quickly and his smile was radiant. On a number of occasions he used his knowledge of Spanish to converse with the waiter and their host.

It was all exotic and fun.

They left the restaurant with an hour and a half to get back to the ship. When they couldn't find a taxi, Tyson asked the host to call them one, and half an hour later, they were settled in the cab and on their way to the port. For some reason, traffic was incredibly congested. Driving in the crowded streets reminded Nikita of running in place. Would they ever get to the port? She checked her watch, her stomach tightening. They had an hour before the ship left.

"We'll make it. We've got plenty of time," Tyson assured her as if he sensed her tension. At a light he spoke to the driver in Spanish, tapping his watch with a wad of bills to emphasize his words.

An opening appeared up ahead and the driver accelerated towards it suddenly. Another car speeded up, cut them off and forced them onto the edge of the sidewalk. The driver lost control and they crashed into a pole and part of a magazine stand. Nikita screamed as she and Tyson were violently thrown against the other side of the cab.

****

Michael paced back and forth in front of the cruise ship. It was due to depart in a few minutes. Where were Nikita and Tyson? He wondered. This was cutting things much too close. They were in danger of being left in Puerto Vallarta. An overwhelming thought was growing in his mind. Something's happened to them.

For the fiftieth time he stared down the roadway leading to the dock, willing them to appear. He saw no one. Overhead, the ship's horn blared a warning that the ship was about to take off.

Michael's hands fisted as he fought with himself. What if she never comes back? I should go after them, find them and bring Niki back! It's my fault she went off with that fool.

One of the crewmembers approached him. "Sir, you're going to have get back on board the ship. We're about to take up the gangway and set sail for the next port. I'm sorry your friends didn't make it."

"Could you give them just a few more minutes?"

The man shook his head negatively. "Sorry sir, but those are the rules. Your friends can find other transportation and meet us at the next port."

Adrenalin pumping the heart in his weighted chest, Michael checked the road once more, and this time he caught sight of a yellow taxi moving fast down the road. As it neared, he saw that it was battered and the damage looked fresh. He swallowed hard and prayed that Nikita and Tyson were in the car and all right.

As the crew urged him towards the gangway, the taxi sped down the dock and stopped in front of the ship. The doors opened and the couple got out, laden with bags.

Suddenly he could breathe again. "It's them!" Michael shouted, springing forward to help Nikita. "Are you okay?" he asked, taking her bags and rushing her to the gangway.

She nodded, her eyes strangely moist.

Then he noticed the limp and a puffy red swelling on her left leg and outer thigh. "You're hurt and you're limping!" he declared in amazement. "Let me carry you."

"No Michael, I can make it," she said, already starting up the vertical ramp.

As soon as they were inside, the crew disassembled the gangway and closed the doors.

On board, Michael grabbed Nikita and held her tight, pressing a kiss to her temple and her forehead as the ship's horn signaled departure. He felt her trembling. "I was so worried about you. I thought you weren't going to make it back. All sorts of crazy thoughts went through my mind," he said in a rush.

"I'm okay," she whispered, but Michael noticed that she didn't try to get out of his embrace.

"What happened?" Michael's voice grew short and curt as he confronted Tyson. "Why is Niki limping?"

"We had an accident on the way back from the restaurant." Tyson looked pale and sweaty. He wasn't moving very fast either. "We got thrown around in the back of the cab."

"Maybe you should have left earlier!" Michael wolfed. "You should have been back to the ship an hour ago."

"It wasn't that far, and we had plenty of time!" Tyson returned loudly. "We just had some bad luck."

Nikita's hand tightened on his arm. "It wasn't his fault, Michael..."

Michael glared at him, adrenalin and anger running high enough for him to punch Tyson out with the least provocation.

"Michael, I'm going to the room to lie down." Nikita's voice held none of its usual strength.

She started towards their room and Michael followed her, determined to see that she was all right.

Back in the cabin Nikita lay down on the bed while Michael retrieved the first aid kit . Then he applied ice to the swelling. "Do you want to see the ship's doctor?"

Nikita's head sank into the pillow. "No, I'm just exhausted. I'm going to take a nap. The swelling will go down." Her eyelids drooped and closed.

"Can I get you anything?" he asked, feeling useless.

"Mmmmph...," she murmured, already beginning to fall asleep.

He couldn't make himself move, so he sat on the

side of the bed holding her hand and wondering what had caused the change in their friendship. He'd begun to dwell much too much on her eyes, her smile, her soft, shapely body. If it had been anyone but Nikita, he'd have taken her to bed and gotten it out of his system on the very first day. Because of their friendship, their working relationship, and her views on love, this was not an option.

Nudging her towards Tyson had been a bad idea. His meddling had almost caused her to miss the boat. He'd have to find another way to keep his mind and his hands off Nikita.

Hours passed as they both slept.

Nikita awakened to persistent throbbing in her legs. The ice pack Michael had placed on the swelling has stopped working long ago. Shifting carefully in the bed, she found that he had fallen asleep beside her on the bed. For several moments she simply stared at him, memorizing and appreciating the male beauty of his thick, dark, lashes against his smooth skin, the planes and angles of his face, and the sculptured softness of his lips. A wave of love left her shivering in its wake. She'd gotten her wish. Too bad she was in too much pain to enjoy it.

She swallowed a couple of aspirin and took a sip of water from the glass he'd used earlier. Then she retrieved another ice pack from the bedside table. He never awakened, even when she ripped open the pack and applied it to the swelling. Sighing, she pulled the covers over the both of them and hit the lights off switch. Tomorrow she would work on spending more time with him and showing him how she felt about him.

Chapter 6

Still dreaming, Michael snuggled closer to the fragrant warmth in his arms, a smile on his face. The answering, pleasure-filled sigh rudely jerked him from his pleasant dream. Nikita!

He opened his eyes. Bright sunlight lined the edges of the drapes and partially lit the room. He was lying fully clothed on the bed with Nikita in his arms. The soft globes of her breasts pressed against his chest and the silk of her shampoo-scented hair lay against his cheek, teasing his senses, but his hands rested chastely on one arm and her back. What does a man who hasn't had any in days do with a beautiful woman in his bed? He behaves himself.

Chuckling inwardly he spared another look at Nikita. Apparently, she was still asleep. He pushed the covers back and sat up to examine her leg for swelling. Although both areas were red and bruised, the puffiness was minimal. No running today for this lady.

He found himself looking at her other leg and then the sensual rise of thigh revealed where his T-shirt had ridden up. His fingers itched to trace the curve of that satiny smooth skin and then he caught himself. This isn't a one-night-stand, this isn't flavor of the week, and it sure as hell isn't Chenelle. This is Nikita in your bed and you can't afford to be thinking about her assets. That thought drew his gaze to her shapely rear. Hmmmph! Michael quickly replaced the covers.

Realizing that he wouldn't be able to continue lying there with Nikita and keep his hands to himself, he eased out of the bed, wondering why he was suddenly having this problem. His attraction to Nikita had not dimmed as he'd hoped it would. Instead it was growing stronger. After working with her on different engineering projects for several years, having her as a regular in his Friday night poker game, and occasionally hanging out with her, why did she suddenly seem so irresistible? He'd always liked her and valued their special friendship, but now he was starting to worry that he was going to end up ruining everything. As soon as his feet touched the floor, he stood, silently congratulating himself for not taking any liberties or waking her.

"Michael?"

He turned to find her watching him. "Why don't you go back to sleep?"

"Because I haven't had my morning exercise and I'm hungry." Yawning, she stretched elaborately, her arms reaching high in the air.

Is she crazy? He threw her an incredulous look. "You can't be thinking of jogging or running on that leg."

Lifting a bit of the covers, she gingerly extended the injured leg and thigh. "I guess not."

"I could get you something on deck and bring it down or we could order room service."

"Michael, thanks for the concern, but I'm not an invalid." A tolerant smile transformed her face, her eyes sparkling. "I can make it to the dining room for breakfast. Why don't you take your turn in the bathroom while I get my things together?"

He gave her a critical glance. What is she trying to prove? Noting the determined glint in her eyes, he nodded, gathered clothing from the closet and went into the bathroom. As he stripped and stepped into the warm shower, he decided that this was not the time to stay away from Nikita on the chance that she might make a love connection. Look what had happened when he tried to help Tyson Ward. Nikita wouldn't have been in the taxi with that slug if he hadn't used their bet to force the issue. Now he felt responsible for her getting hurt. The best thing he could do as a friend was to hang tight with her and make sure she was all right and no one took advantage, even if it meant watching her fall on her shapely rear.

Later, as they approached the entrance to the dining room, Nikita turned to Michael and said. "I don't want you to be mad at Tyson about the accident in the taxi yesterday and us almost missing the boat. It's not fair because it's not his fault."

Michael shrugged one shoulder, judgmental anger in his eyes. "Life isn't fair is it?"

Narrowing her eyes, she rolled her bottom lip between her teeth and watched him shrug again in response. There was nothing she could do about his attitude. When Michael was like this, she couldn't reason with him. Straightening her shoulders, she stepped into the dining room.

At the table, Tyson sat eating a pecan waffle and bacon with one arm in a sling. His mother hovered over him, ready to do anything she could to help him.

"What happened to your arm?" Nikita asked as she sat down in the chair Michael had pulled out for her.

"It's just a slight sprain," he mumbled, looking embarrassed.

Nikita saw angry red scratches on his arm and three bandages covering what she assumed were deeper gauges.

"Maybe you guys should consider suing that taxi company or at least writing a letter of complaint,"

Michael said, his gaze boring holes straight through Tyson. "Nikita's leg and thigh are pretty banged up too."

"I'd rather forget about the whole thing," Tyson replied sheepishly.

"Me too," Nikita said, accepting a menu from the waiter. "I've been trying to tell Michael that the accident was nobody's fault."

Tyson's eyes focused on her and then slid away. "I did tell the driver that we were in a hurry and I offered him more money to get us to the ship before it left port."

"Sounds like contributing factors to me!" Michael snapped, leaning forward.

Nikita felt her temperature rising. "Stop trying to push this off on Tyson! He did not tell the driver to go for the spot that opened up in traffic or to go up on the sidewalk when the spot closed suddenly. We were lucky that that policeman saw the whole thing and was sympathetic enough to let the driver continue on in time for us to make the boat."

"Can we all talk about something else?" Alice Ward's eyes were anxious. "I don't know about the rest of you, but I can't digest my food with a lot of arguing and conflict."

Tyson and Nikita agreed readily. Seconds ticked by as everyone waited for Michael's answer.

Tyson cleared his throat and began to speak.

"Michael, I'm sorry about what happened to Nikita and how we almost missed the ship. I've already apologized to her several times. If she gives me another chance, I swear I won't let anything happen to her. Now can we all get past this incident?"

Finally, he nodded in agreement. The rest of the meal was eaten in silence.

As they finished their coffee, the ship's activities director announced the Latin dance class for those who were not going ashore in Manzanillo, Mexico. Tyson and Nikita looked at each other.

"Want to go?" Tyson asked, a hopeful expression on his face. "I figure I can at least go through the steps."

She shook her head negatively. "I couldn't run this morning and it took pure stubbornness for me to walk to the dining room. Maybe you should think about going ashore. The beach and the fishing are pretty good."

"No." Tyson shook his head resolutely. "I've had enough of the ports for now."

"There's only five more after this, if you don't count Miami." Michael stirred his coffee.

Tyson ignored him. "Nikita?"

"I think I'll relax on deck with a book or something."

Tyson struggled to keep from looking too disappointed. "You could borrow my laptop," Tyson said as he pushed his chair back. "I have several games loaded on it."

Nikita smiled. "Thanks. I'd like that."

Michael and Nikita had found a spot on the shady side of the ship when Tyson appeared with the laptop in his good arm. He hovered momentarily until it became obvious that Michael was going to stay. Then he trudged off to the dance class.

Nikita spent an hour and a half playing various games on the laptop and talking to Michael. Then she reclined in her chair with the warm wind caressing her face and the soft rushing sounds of the water lulling her to sleep. When she awakened, Michael was watching her with a solicitous expression on his face.

"Are you worried about me?" she asked, reaching out to touch his hand. At the contact with his warm skin, something like an electric shock flashed through her. "Don't be," she said, removing her hand and trying to cover her reaction. "I'm fine."

"Yeah, right," he quipped, his gaze dipping down to her bare brown legs and thighs, where some of the red bruising had started to purple."

She tugged ineffectively at her shorts. She'd wanted him to look at her legs, but not like this. Instead of admiration or desire, she saw concern in his eyes. "I'll be running again in a day or two."

"We'll see," he said with a half smile. He didn't

even bat an eyelash as an attractive woman in a hot pink bikini strolled by.

"You don't have to babysit me," she said in a rush, "I'll understand if you'd like to prowl the decks, see the sights..."

"Such as Ms. Hot-Pink bikini?" He grinned.

"Yeah." Nervously, she fingered the handle of the laptop, sorry she'd said anything. She didn't want him to take off after some other woman, but she didn't want him sitting with her if that was not where he wanted to be.

This time he took her hand. "Niki, I'm fine, and I'm where I want to be. I can keep my pants up for a few days more."

Her face felt hot. "I didn't mean—,"

"I know exactly what you meant!" he chuckled. "You think I'm one of those A-1 dogs, always looking for the next booty call. Well, believe it or not, this dog has had enough for a while. I'm not looking to replace Chenelle anytime soon."

"I didn't mean that, I just thought—."

A flicker of understanding lit his eyes. "I know, you saw me on deck with that woman the day before yesterday, didn't you?"

She nodded, working to keep her expression neutral as she remembered the hurt and disappointment she had felt as her dreams came crashing down to earth once more.

Michael burst into laughter. "She sat down during you guy's Latin dance class and followed me around for hours. She even sat in your spot at our table at lunch. I told her you were coming any minute and then you didn't show. I didn't have it in me to really be nasty about it."

"Oh." She nodded sympathetically, warmth filling her chest. There was still hope for her.

He chuckled again. "I've been trying to fade into the background to give you a chance to meet someone, make some sort of love connection!"

"You mean Tyson?" she asked in amazement.

"Yeah, until yesterday. I'm sorry I insisted that you go to that restaurant with him. I feel somewhat responsible for your getting hurt."

"Hey, Michael. Hell-o!" she said, emphasizing every word, "Tyson is not my type of guy. And for the last time, the accident was not Tyson's fault. We just had some bad luck!"

"Then I'll drop the whole thing," he said affectionately as he reached out to capture one of her curls and tug gently.

"You'd better," she threatened, playfully punching his arm.

Instead of a formal lunch in the dining room, they opted for pop and a slice of pepperoni and ham pizza on deck. Michael stood in the lunch line and got salad to go with it. A small orchestra played a series of romantic songs while people swam in the pool, lounged in the whirlpool, or socialized on deck. The music put Nikita in such a mellow mood, that she desperately wanted to dance. If it weren't for her leg and thigh, she'd have dragged Michael to the open area on deck and made him dance with her. As it was, she enjoyed his proximity and the sensual charm he unconsciously lavished on her. Occasionally, his arm or hand would brush against her and a liquid thrill ran through her.

"Enjoying the music?" he asked, when she sat with her chin in one hand, a dreamy expression on her face. A man with a pleasant tenor began to sing with the orchestra.

Nikita dipped lower in her chair. "Mmm-hmmm! Recognize that song? It's called 'The Way You Look Tonight'. It's one of my favorites. I wish I could get up and dance to it."

"I know." He patted her arm, oblivious to her resulting shiver of reaction. "You'll get another chance to dance to it. Believe me. We've got more than a week left to cruise and if you want, I'll dance with you."

"I'm looking forward to it," she said softly.

He glanced around at the crowd. Several couples were hugging and kissing. "I think these songs are definitely setting the mood for everyone."

"Mmmh-hmmm," Nikita gave him another

dreamy-eyed look. Her Michael really was a hunk in that white muscle shirt and matching shorts. His muscular legs and thighs were to die for. Her fingers ached to trace the curve of his ribcage down to the flat plane of his stomach. His masculine beauty was all the better because he wasn't one of those guys who was in love with himself.

"Careful Niki," he said in a teasing tone, "Don't look at me like that. You don't want to pull me into this mood and have me forget that we're good buddies."

"And why not?" Nikita raised her eyebrows. That's exactly what I want to do!

" Because you're like a sister to me and I don't have a romantic bone in my body. You know that." He extended a hand to tug at a lock of her hair. "Sex isn't on our menu."

Nikita stared at him, the adrenalin flowing. "Do you think it could go that far?" she asked in a low, daring voice.

"You're a beautiful woman." For several moments his eyes heated—his hot sensual gaze burned hotter than the sun, inciting a lightning flash of desire... Nikita gripped the arms of her chair, certain this was the moment of truth. Then his eyes cooled and he shook his head. "No, it couldn't go that far."

She took a deep breath and blew it out in a huff.

"I think I've just been insulted."

The corners of his mouth turned up, but his eyes were serious and determined. "No, I gave you a compliment. You're only going to get the best from me, Niki."

Staring at him, trying to come up with a snappy comeback, she came up empty. How can you dog a man for ignoring his base urges to treat you with respect? I'm going to have to find another way to get him to think differently about me and love. "It's kind of hard to argue with that."

"You're damned straight!" he replied, inclining his head.

When it got too hot on deck, he dragged her indoors to the horse races in one of the lounges. With the ship's activities director serving as master of ceremony, the betting and the races were lively. Volunteers from the audience rolled the dice to move the six horses along a wooden board. Feeling lucky, and liking the spunky senior rolling the dice, Nikita bet on a horse called True Blue and collected forty dollars.

Walking out just before the crowd, they discovered a wine and cheese tasting just starting in the Lovers Lounge.

"Let's try this," he said, leading her past the heart-shaped doorway to a table on the edge of the room.

They sat down in dainty chairs with delicate legs and heart-shaped backs while the staff finished setting up the wine glasses and the platters filled with fruit, a variety of cheeses, and crackers. Nikita saw that they also had a selection of French, German, and California wines.

"Hey, check this out." Michael leaned forward with a booklet describing the various wines."

"Excuse me, do you mind if we sit here?" A man's voice interrupted them.

They glanced up to see an attractive couple holding hands and hovering near the two extra chairs at the table.

"No, we don't mind. Have a seat," Michael told them. As they sat down, he introduced Nikita and himself.

They introduced themselves as Larry and Carol Powers from Atlanta. "Do you two know anything about wine?" Carol asked opening her brochure.

"Not really," Nikita told her, "We just know what we like."

"We aren't much better," Larry responded, one hand gently caressing his wife's arm and hand, "We've been to a few wine tastings, and we've added some new wines to our lists, but all that stuff about the different regions and the types of grapes in each kind of wine didn't stick."

"Same here." Michael nodded. "I usually drink

the white zinfandel or those German moselle wines. Nikita's more adventuresome."

"What else do you like, Nikita?" Carol asked, her fingers twining with Larry's.

"Oh I like some of the chardonnays."

"I saw some of those up at the sample table. I guess I'll try them." Carol turned and smooched Larry on the lips.

"Are you two newlyweds?" Nikita asked, noting the way they always seemed to be touching each other. The air around them sizzled.

"This is our first year anniversary." Larry lifted his wife's ringed hand to his lips and kissed it. "What about you two?"

"We're good friends," Michael answered, gripping Nikita's hand briefly and releasing it.

She smiled as if in agreement, but she looked at the way Larry and Carol were together and wished she had the same relationship with Michael. She'd been trying to get his attention and it was paying off, but seeing the other couple together made her wonder what she would get if her plans were successful. Michael had been very honest about his views on sex and marriage and the reasons why he would have married Chenelle. Her thoughts were interrupted as the host for the wine tasting lifted a bottle of French wine and began to describe it.

Later Michael and Nikita went to a western

themed dinner in the dining room where he managed to say very little, and afterward they saw a Broadway musical in the ship's theatre. Finally, they stopped by the midnight buffet and sampled some of the fancy desserts, so that by the time they got back to their cabin, they were too tired to worry about the sleeping arrangements. After a quick turn in the bathroom, she donned her sleep shirt and climbed into bed. Michael searched for the blanket he'd been using to no avail. Finally, he climbed into bed with Nikita, careful to keep to his side. Tomorrow he planned to hang out with her again and toss all thoughts of her snagging a new boyfriend to the winds. After all, how much attention was she going to get limping around with that leg and thigh? She was a good-looking woman, but not that good looking!

The sound of sharp rapping on the cabin next door woke Michael. "Room service!" he heard someone call. The clock on the table showed seven-thirty. He sat up yawning, safely ensconced on his side of the bed. He must have awakened at least four times in the night to check his position and make sure he kept his hands to himself, but it had been worth it. He saw that Nikita was still asleep beneath the covers with her back to him.

Sliding out of bed, he walked across the cool carpet to the phone in a burst of inspiration. Why not order room service?

Lifting the receiver, Michael used a low voice to order a poached egg and corned-beef-hash on an English muffin with juice and decaff for Nikita and a Western omelet with wheat toast, juice, and coffee for himself. Then he disappeared into the bathroom to wash and dress.

Half an hour later, Nikita sat in bed, eating breakfast. Michael sat in the chair by the bed, with a tray across his lap.

"This seems decadent", she remarked, cutting a slice out her poached egg and corned-beef-hash on an English muffin and putting it into her mouth. "Mmmmh, and it's so good."

"Mine too," he said, cutting his eggs, "It's worth tipping the waiter."

"So what's up for the day?" She slowly stretched out her legs beneath the covers. "Do you feel like hanging out with me again? My leg is still a little sore, but I've got to start exercising off some of this food I'm eating."

"Since we're in port, we could go into Acapulco. That would give you your exercise."

"I've always wanted to see Acapulco. How long are we here?" she asked between bites.

"We pull out of port at 6pm, so we'll miss the nightlife."

"That just means we'll have to come back and visit when we're not on a cruise." She drank her coffee, blowing across the top to cool it down.

Michael nodded in agreement. "If we like it. So what do you want to do?"

"Let's go on the beach tour. If I recall correctly, they stop in a shopping area on the way back, and if I'm not too tired, I can look for souvenirs."

"That's a good idea", he said scraping the last bit of omelet onto his fork, "I promised to bring my parents something back, too."

"You don't think the beach tour has left already, do you?" she asked, checking her watch. "It's almost eight-thirty."

Michael finished chewing his last mouthful. "I remember two tours, one at ten and one at twelve. Both include a picnic lunch."

"That's good, because I don't want to think about Montezuma's Revenge. You know, that's how we get sick from the parasites in their water." At his nod, Nikita pushed her tray aside. "If you go get the tickets, I'll take my turn in the bathroom first."

"Okay." He gathered the breakfast dishes and set them on the floor in the hallway. Acknowledging him, the cabin steward was already gathering some of the other dishes down the hall. When Michael re-entered the room, he saw her at the closet in one of his shirts, gathering clothing from her still meager selection. "No new information on your suitcase in Puerto Vallarta?"

"No," she answered, turning to face him with a look of disgust on her face, "And apparently not in Mazanillo either! I bet they find my stupid suitcase when the cruise is all over. A lot of good that'll do me then."

Michael tried hard not to stare, but he could just make out the darkness of her nipples beneath the white shirt. As his imagination went wild, he forced himself to look away. On the table by the bed he found his wallet and stuck it into his back pocket. He turned in time to see Nikita walking towards the bathroom.

He found himself staring transfixed at the smooth, fluid movement of her hips beneath the shirt, and the shapely contours of her legs and thighs. His pulse sped up and he swallowed hard as his imagination filled in for the slip of red material covering part of her rounded rear, just visible through the shirt. She was wearing those red thong panties that he'd seen in the ship's boutique. Michael swallowed hard. If it were anyone but Nikita, he knew he'd have taken her to bed long ago and gotten her off his mind. As it was, he was having a hell of a time keeping his hands and his mind off her assets. Man, you really are a dog, in every sense of the word!

Turning abruptly, he forced himself to leave the room. On the way to the ticket booth, he reminded himself of all the reasons why he was keeping his hands to himself. Not the least was his solid friendship with her and her romantic ideas about sex and love. He knew he could never give her what she needed.

At ten to ten, they left the cabin. Dressed in shorts and shirts and carrying Michael's sports bag stuffed with their swimsuits, towels and passports, they exited the ship in the hot, oven-like air, handed their tickets to the tour operator, and climbed aboard the air conditioned bus.

As the bus drove into the Acapulco, the driver got on the microphone and provided a mini-tour of the various sights in heavily accented English. They stopped by La Quebrada to watch people dive from the cliffs, then continued on to the beach where an area was setup with table, chairs, and umbrellas. There was a serving stand in the center with lunches from the ship and a DJ playing music.

Nikita and Michael found a shaded area under one of the umbrellas and spread a blanket across the beige sand. They sat in companionable silence and watched the natives frolicking in the surf. Beautiful, white-capped waves washed into the shore and rushed back out with a comforting rhythm and sound. Fat, fluffy clouds floated on a baby blue sky.

Nikita wished she could change into her bathing suit as she surveyed miles and miles of rippling blue water. Repeated warnings about the water and the undertow from personnel on the ship and the tour operator made her cautious. Michael apparently felt the same way, because he too made no move to go and change at the nearby hotel. So they lazed on the beach, enjoying the view, listening to the music, and people watching.

Close to twelve, they picked up two of the box lunches and ate them beneath the umbrella. When they had finished and disposed of the trash, Michael stood and looked around. Behind his mirrored sunglasses, she couldn't tell what he was looking at, but she assumed he saw a veritable smorgasbord in the number of attractive women dressed in skimpy suits reclining in various spots. "Want to walk on the beach?"

"Until my leg says otherwise." Nikita rose to follow him across the sand and down the beach, suddenly wishing she'd changed into her bathing suit after all. A dark haired woman on the beach was stretched out in a daring white bikini that looked just like the one Chenelle had given her on her birthday. She did a doubletake.

"Something wrong?" Michael turned, apparently noticing her distraction.

"I—I thought I saw a suit just like one I'd packed

for the trip."

He shook his head with a pitying look. "You should know by now that unless you're buying the super expensive stuff, they make a million of them."

"I guess so," she answered with disgust.

They passed natives and tourists alike, enjoying the sun and the view with their families. At first her leg was a little stiff from sitting so long on the beach, but she kept walking until she felt only a slight tenderness with every step. When the tour bus returned with the next set of passengers to continue on to the shopping area, Michael and Nikita walked to it.

The tour bus took them to a shopping area frequented mostly by tourists. Feeling rested, Nikita got off the bus and went into a couple of the stores with Michael. She discovered a black and white onyx chess set for her father and some beautiful beaded necklace and earring sets for her mother. Michael bought a black and a white onyx bull and a copper sundial for his parents. Elated with their purchases, they boarded the bus and headed back to the ship.

As Nikita climbed the gangway, her thoughts centered on soaking her tender leg and her tired body in the big hot tub on deck while one of the bands played soothing music. She couldn't ignore the discreet pitying looks Michael was giving her when he thought she wasn't looking. It was time to give her image and herself a boost. When she got back to the cabin she retrieved the slinky suit she'd purchased in Puerto Vallarta and headed for the bathroom to change. "I think I'm going to go get in the hot tub", she called on her way.

"What?" Michael stirred in the recliner by the bed. He'd been half asleep already. "You sure you want to do that?"

"Why not?" She placed her suit on the little stool by the sink.

"You don't think it's a little too public for you?"

"No." Nikita resisted the urge to come back with a snappy reply. Michael knew her too well. She was betting that he'd follow her up on deck. "There's no music at the one in the spa."

"You've got a point." He sighed and shifted in the recliner.

"So, are you going to take a nap?" she asked, getting ready to close the bathroom door.

Michael yawned. "I'm thinking about it."

"Okay." She shut the door, the nervous energy mounting. If Michael stayed in the room and napped, she was going up on deck and get in that whirlpool if it killed her. *What are you afraid of?* Covering her head, she took a quick shower and slipped into the two- piece suit that was basically a tank top over a bikini bottom. It was made like a tankini, except that everything but the bikini bottom and the bra-like portion covering her breasts was made of a translucent peach material.

Nikita turned in the mirror, feeling naked, and shivering already. She had a nice amount of cleavage, her waist looked small, her stomach didn't sit out too much, and all the essentials were covered. In the suit, she looked just as good as any of the women she'd seen on deck flaunting themselves, and yet... She took a deep breath and opened the bathroom door.

"You going?" Michael mumbled, sitting up. His eyes opened and widened as he stared at her.

Standing in the doorway, it took every bit of nerve to resist the urge to make sure she really did have a suit on. She still felt naked, but the way he stared turned her nervous energy into a hot, thrilling excitement that made her body tingle all over.

"Come here," he said in a low, husky voice that sent waves of heat strumming through her.

The barefoot walk across the carpet seemed like one of the longest she'd ever taken. She stood in front of him, holding her breath and returning his stare. She was close enough to feel the heat of his skin electrifying the air between them.

"Damn", he murmured, dropping his gaze to linger on the curve of her breasts, her flat stomach, and the smooth contours of her thighs. "Double-damn."

He extended a hand as if to touch her, and let it

fall. "You're going to be the death of me", he said, dropping his head, shaking it, and looking away.

She stood there feeling hot and vulnerable, not knowing what to think. "Michael?" Her voice was just above a whisper.

"Are you sure you want to go up on deck in that?" he asked, meeting her stare. His eyes were harsh, his jaw tight.

"Why wouldn't I?" she asked boldly, suppressing the little quiver in her chest.

"Because you're advertising, big time and that has never been your style. I'm going to have to fight them off in droves."

"What makes you think you have to do anything?" she challenged. "I'm a big girl."

"Nikita, I'm just trying to say that I don't think you see guys the way they really are. When they see you in that suit, they're going to have just one thought on their minds."

"I think there was a compliment buried in there somewhere." She moved away from him to go to the closet and retrieve a big shirt to use as a cover-up.

"You look damned good, Niki", he said in a choked voice, "Too damned good."

She whirled around to see him standing behind her, desire burning in the depths of his eyes.

"If we weren't like this," he crossed two of his fingers together, "I'd be on you myself."

Don't let that stop you! Nikita wanted him with a thirst that could never be quenched, but she didn't voice the thought. Instead she put one shaky arm and then the other into the sleeves of the shirt. "Are you coming?"

He nodded slowly and stepped forward, electrifying the air with sensual energy as he reached past her to retrieve his swimming trunks. "Just give me a minute", he said, disappearing into the bathroom.

Out on deck, a jazz band played mellow mood music. In the golden sunlight, Nikita peeled off her shirt. It felt as if she were doing a strip tease for all the attention she was getting, but she saw that several other women were similarly dressed. Maybe it was time for her to stop being so conservative all the time. As she climbed into the whirlpool, she felt as if she was putting on a performance. She saw Michael glare at some of the guys in the crowd. When did he become so protective of me?

Michael took a seat next to her in the hot tub, filling her view with his well-honed body. She shivered when his arm touched hers, and fantasized about touching his smooth, caramel-colored skin. His lips curved into a dazzling smile. Nikita melted, closing her eyes to limit the damage.

"There you are! I've been looking for you all day!" a man exclaimed.

She opened her eyes to see Tyson standing nearby. Greeting him, she went on to explain that she'd gone ashore with Michael.

Tyson acknowledged Michael and dropped into a nearby chair. "I went ashore for a quick city tour and found some things on the way back, but it was nothing like what we saw in Puerto Vallarta. I see you're wearing the suit we picked. You look so good in it that I keep forgetting to breathe when I look at you."

Ignoring Michael's smothered curse, Nikita thanked Tyson.

"Will you be in the dining room for dinner tonight?" Tyson asked. "It's Italian night."

"For sure". Nikita turned her leg against one of the powerful jets in the hot tub. "I love Italian food."

"Me too." Michael added, his voice tickling her ear.

She felt his proximity like an electric charge along the surface of her skin. Nikita suppressed a shiver. The combination of Michael, the hot tub, and their audience was beginning to wear on her.

"What are you doing after dinner?" Tyson asked, excitement sparkling in his eyes. "Why don't you hang out with me?"

"Why don't we discuss it at dinner?" she asked, determined not to hurt his feelings.

"That would be fine." Tyson emphasized the word fine, his gaze caressing Nikita.

She returned his smile and started climbing out,

knowing she couldn't stay in the hot water another moment.

"Let me help you." Tyson recovered her towel from the side of the pool and standing close, draped it around her dripping shoulders. A few of the guys seated nearby threw him envious glances.

As she stood by the tub, clutching the towel to her body, the normally oven-like air actually felt a little cool, but the deck was still hot. She quickly stepped into her sandals. "Do I have time for a nap before dinner?"

Tyson glanced at his watch. "You've got about an hour."

Michael climbed out of the hot tub and stood beside her, drying himself. "If you set the clock, you could probably get twenty minutes to half an hour."

"Then I'm on my way." She started walking towards the cabin. "See you at dinner, Tyson."

"Hey, wait for me," Michael called stuffing his feet into his sandals and then catching up with her within four long strides.

Back in the cabin, she showered and for lack of a robe, slipped into a T-shirt and a pair of shorts. Then she set the clock for half an hour and stretched out on the bed while Michael disappeared into the bathroom.

Chapter 7

An insistent, annoying buzzing sound jarred Nikita from her dream. She slapped at the table by the bed, moving her hand each time in search of the offending device. Finally, she woke up enough to realize that the alarm was ringing and she would have to get up and walk across the room to the chest to turn it off. Grumbling under her breath, she did it.

"Going to dinner?" Michael asked in a sleepy voice. Clad only in a pair of shorts, he was still stretched out on his side of the bed. She was almost too sleepy to enjoy the view of his long, muscular legs and the broad expanse of his chest.

"I think so", she answered, on her way back to the bed. Maybe this isn't such a good idea... Her mind cycled back and forth as she dropped down on the side of the bed. Italian food—sleep, Italian food—sleep, Italian food—sleep. Her pillow was calling to her. Nikita's head dropped.

"We can get a hamburger or some pizza on deck", he suggested in an I-hope-you're-not-really-getting-up-now-tone-of-voice.

That cinches it! Nikita's lids lifted and she forced herself off the bed. She'd had enough burgers and pizza to last her for a couple of days. She needed real food. Glad she'd already showered, she stumbled to the closet and retrieved her red tank dress. "Michael, I'm going down to dinner."

His only response was a deep sigh. He was asleep.

Nikita dressed quickly. As she stuffed her feet into her sandals, the chimes sounded and someone announced their seating for dinner on the PA system. Grabbing her purse, she glanced at Michael. His quiet, even breathing said it all. The man was fast asleep.

"See you after dinner," she called softly, slipping out of the door.

Fifteen minutes later, Nikita sat at the table talking with Tyson and his mother and sipping a glass of red wine when something or someone behind her captured their attention. She turned to look. Michael, casually handsome in a white shirt, light beige sport coat, and matching pants strolled towards them.

"I thought they'd already closed the doors," Tyson remarked as Michael took a seat.

"They had." Michael grinned. "I guess I'm just special."

"I'd have waited if I'd known you were coming," Nikita apologized. "I could swear you were all but snoring when I left."

"I guess I woke up when the door closed." Michael opened his menu and began to read. When the waiter brought Tyson's soup, Michael put in his order.

The food was heavenly. Nikita ate antipasto salad and followed it up with lasagna and stuffed shells filled with ricotta and spinach smothered in a spicy tomato sauce. She was too full to eat dessert.

After dinner, Nikita and Tyson followed Michael out of the dining room and down the main drag into the one of the clubs. Lucky enough to get seats at a table close to the front, they were elated to hear a group of young men imitate the Temptations. Several people, from the very casually dressed to those formally dressed in glittering evening wear, crowded into the club to hear the talented group. The last set ended with a standing ovation that lasted for several minutes.

Nikita stood, yawning. There were too many people crowded in the little club. She felt as if she could barely breathe.

Tyson looked up with concern. "Aren't you going to stay for the next show?"

"I—I've got to get some air." She slung her purse over one shoulder.

Michael stood and pushed back his chair. "I think I'll tag along," he said in a low voice.

Tyson was standing too. His head swiveled from Michael to Nikita and back and he stepped closer. "Are you all right?"

She nodded. Then he startled her by leaning forward to kiss her cheek. "I know you must be tired, so I'll say good night. Are you going to run in the morning?"

"Yes, my leg is a lot better."

"Then I'm looking forward to dance class." He squeezed her hand and then he sat down.

Nikita smiled and nodded. "It's time for me to start exercising again. See you there." Out of the corner of her eye she saw the annoyed expression on Michael's face and wondered if he was jealous.

Michael followed Nikita out of the club and down the corridor to an outside door. Then they climbed the steps to stand at one of the railings. Tiny glowing stars dotted a deep purple sky. The dark glossy surface of the water bounced with a soft, liquid, shishing sound and a cool breeze caressed their skin..

"You okay?" Michael asked, facing her in the semi— darkness. Concern tinged his voice.

Panting a little, she took deep breaths, filling her lungs with air. "I'm okay. I just couldn't breathe with all those people in the club." She eased down into a deck chair.

"It was too crowded," he agreed, taking the seat beside her. "What's next?"

She sighed and drew her feet up into the chair. "I just want to enjoy the peace and quiet out here for awhile, and then I'm going to bed. I'm exhausted."

"So am I," he chuckled. "We've done a lot in the past two days. I think we lost sight of the fact that we've got more than a week left."

"Nah, you were just trying to take my mind off this leg." She tapped his arm playfully. "I appreciate the time and care you've taken with me."

Michael hooked an arm around her shoulders and hugged her gently. "You make it sound like it's been a chore. You know I enjoy your company."

"Thanks. So what's up for tomorrow?" she asked, enjoying the feel of his arm around her.

"I don't know. I'm just going to take it as it comes. Maybe I'll just chill on deck. Feeling better, now?"

"Yes." She stood and stretched. "Let's go to bed." Did she imagine the startled look on his face? It was hard to read his expression in the limited light. As they walked back to the cabin and got ready for bed, the intimacy of their situation wasn't lost on her. Settling beneath the sheets, the distance between them seemed smaller than ever.

Niki awakened slowly with a delicious sense of warmth and well-being. Her cheek nestled against a firm, warm pillow, and her arms surrounded it. Slowly she breathed in the spicy scent of Polo cologne and rubbed her face into the pillow. Realizing that something wasn't quite right, Nikita opened her eyes.

Morning filtered in from the sides of the curtains at the window giving the room a soft natural light. With delight, she saw that her pillow was Michael's muscle-shirted chest. Then she became aware of the warmth of his hand on her waist, and realized that beneath the sheets her T-shirt had ridden up to expose the skin above her silk bikini panties. Would he move his hand? Carefully, she tilted her head to see if he was awake.

"Good morning." The deep rumble of his morning voice went through her like an electric current. His brown eyes sparkled with amusement.

"Good morning," she answered, determined not to blush. This was where she wanted to be. "You make quite a pillow," she said, breaking into a smile.

His slow grin made her heart skip. "And I thought I was standing in for your fantasy man."

You are my fantasy man. Staring, Niki chuckled aloud at the irony of it all. They'd become a lot more relaxed with each other, but Michael had no inkling of the depth of her feelings. Something sizzled between them, whether he acknowledged it or not.

This situation felt so intimate that she wanted him to touch her all over, move his hand from the safety of her waist to the swell of her hips or the aching tips of her breasts. Instead, Niki forced herself to move off him and put a few inches of space between them. She missed the sleepy warmth of his body.

She couldn't just blatantly throw herself at the man, could she? Maybe a little later, when she was more certain she'd get a good reception, she would. "I hope I didn't disturb you."

"No, Niki. We're bound to touch in the night, even with a big bed like this."

"I guess so." Niki turned onto her stomach, propping her face up on her folded arms, and resisting the urge to stare at the prime male flesh only inches from her eyes. "Have you decided what you want to do today?"

Michael yawned. "I thought we could go to breakfast, lie around on deck, try dinner in the Pizzeria, check out the show again this evening, and maybe hit the casino."

"Sounds good to me, except I've got to meet Tyson

in the library at two-thirty."

"I'm sure you can fit that in."

Niki glanced at her watch and saw that it was only six-thirty.

"If you're going to exercise before breakfast, you'd better get going," Michael drawled.

She didn't want to leave him and end the pleasant camaraderie they were sharing. "It's still pretty early. Want to jog with me on deck?"

Smoothly molded muscles rippled as he lifted his arms and leisurely stretched. "I think I'll just lie around a bit more," he said with a half grin.

Niki thought of a big contented cat. "I haven't seen you this happy since we started the cruise. You look as if you're feeling better about everything that's happened."

He gave her an astute glance. "As much as I could at a time like this. I refuse to spend the entire cruise moping about something that's already happened and can't be changed." The bed moved as he turned on his side to face her. "I'm not a big romantic, Niki. You know that. Chenelle was the closest I've come to finding the ideal mate, but I wasn't in love with her."

"Yes, you told me, but you guys seemed as starry-eyed as any of the engaged couples I've seen."

Michael forced a breath out in a huff. "At least until the day of wedding."

"That's true," Niki agreed quickly.

"I've been telling myself over and over that she did me a favor." Michael nestled his head deeper into the pillow. "She never looked at me the way she looked at Lance Coltrane in the chapel. I bet she thought she loved him."

"Yes, she did love Lance. They were engaged."

His expression turned serious. "It really hurt to get dumped like that, Niki. Why didn't you clue me in?"

Niki started at his sudden attack. Why hadn't she told Michael about Chenelle and her ex-fiancé? A guilty voice deep within her spoke. Because although you were praying the whole thing would fall apart, you didn't want to be the cause of it all. No! That wasn't the only reason, she told her guilty conscience. "It—it really wasn't my place to tell you," she stammered defensively. Lord knows, she'd wanted to tell him everything, but sometimes friendship meant keeping silent, even if it hurt. "They had a history, and it didn't work out," she continued, her voice getting stronger with every word. "Chenelle had given up and moved on. Besides, you guys had some sort of agreement."

He nodded then. "We weren't crazy in love, or anything like that, but we were a good match. I may not believe in love, but I do believe in good matches and amiable arrangements. You know, you rub my back and I rub yours."

"Is that a proposition?" Niki demanded in a throaty voice. Take me, Michael, I'm yours.

"No. I wouldn't proposition you, Niki," he chuckled devilishly with a flash of even, white teeth. "I mean that I won't marry someone in love with another man, or someone waiting for me to fall in love with them. That's just asking for trouble."

Shaking his head dismissively, Michael propped himself up on an elbow. "You're just a big romantic. You see love everywhere. I bet you thought I was in love with Chenelle."

"Until you told me differently, yes." Niki studied him, looking for hidden traces of hurt and pain. Despite his comments, there was a hint of sadness and loss in the depths of his eyes. He was in pain, whether he acknowledged it or not.

His forehead wrinkled. "Chenelle was exceptional. I've never meshed so well with any woman. I admit I was hurt and disappointed by what she did."

" And now?"

"And now I'm determined to learn from my mistake. I'm trying to make the best of my vacation, and I refuse to worry about anything."

"That's a good attitude." Niki sat up in bed, noting the considerate way Michael kept his eyes glued to her face as she struggled to keep her panties and the top of her thighs covered with her shirt.

"Go on and run," he urged, changing the subject. "I'll turn over and catch a few Zs."

One more look at her watch, and Niki scooted out of the bed and headed for the dresser. The shirt she wore fell midway down her thighs as she grabbed a top, shorts, underwear, and a pair of socks.

"We'll run together tomorrow," he called, his gaze warming her as she headed for the bathroom.

One backward glance at Michael leisurely reclining on the bed, and Niki laughed. "Promises, promises," she murmured as she closed the bathroom door.

On deck, she started exercising by walking around the track to ease some of the stiffness in her leg and increasing her pace with each lap. With two more laps to go, she saw the dark haired woman standing by the rail on the deck below in a lemon yellow sundress that looked awfully familiar. Nikita stopped abruptly.

Except for the woman on the beach, she wasn't used to seeing other people in her clothes. One of the other runners nearly barreled into her, so she started jogging again. Could this just be coincidence? She wondered, as her attention still focused on the deck below. She had packed an identical sundress in her missing suitcase. Was this woman wearing her clothes? The thought made her blood boil. She was tired of managing with a meager wardrobe.

Nikita started down the steps, determined to get a good look. Realizing that the woman no longer stood at the railing, she covered the entire level searching for her, but the woman had gone. Disappointed, Nikita went back to the sports deck to finish her workout.

Sometime later, a little wet and sweaty from her run on deck, Nikita let herself into the cabin. The bed was empty. In the background, she heard the bathroom shower running. It was just as well, she thought. She could at least run a comb through her sweat-drenched hair. Ruefully, she examined her T-shirt and patted herself with a towel. There was nothing she could do about the sweat stains.

Grateful she'd bought three pairs of shorts with coordinated tops, Nikita rummaged through her meager selection of clothing. She wouldn't look like a fashion plate, but Michael had so much as told her that he didn't care.

She turned at the sound of the bathroom door opening and froze at the sight of Michael in a small pair of black briefs that covered his firm hips like a second skin. Her stomach tightened. Well-formed, muscular legs and thighs danced past her in a series of smooth, athletic motions as he moved towards the closet.

A white towel covered most of his face and head as he vigorously dried his hair and hummed a little song. An expanse of well-toned, caramel skin rippled in the chiseled planes of his chest, arms, and shoulders. Dark, shining hair dusted his chest and trailed down into his briefs. He was beautiful, everything she'd dreamed. Nikita swallowed hard, wishing he belonged to her.

As if sensing her movement to his left, he turned, lowering the towel to his shoulders. "Oops." Quickly grabbing the nearest pair of pants, Michael bent over, pulling them on. With regret, Nikita watched him zip and button them. She could watch Michael all day long.

"Sorry," he murmured apologetically, his expression intent as he tried to gauge her reaction. "I'll try to keep a robe with me from now on."

He was obviously unaware of the sensual power he wielded with that body of his. Nikita wet her lips. "I'm not complaining. I enjoyed the view."

"Did you?" His voice turned husky. The rousing heat in his eyes radiated out to draw her like a magnet.

She nodded, moving closer to him, suddenly unbearably thirsty for his kiss. She stopped only when the heat of his body enveloped her. His hands came up to lightly caress her arms. "I've been checking out the view too, Nikita."

"Did you like what you saw?" she asked breathlessly. A crowbar couldn't have pulled her away from him.

"Mmm-hm." His eyes seared her with their heat. One hand smoothed down the curve of her spine. The other delved into her damp hair as she leaned close to urgently press her mouth to his and kiss him with all the love and passion in her heart. "Nikita," he breathed as he deepened the kiss, sending spirals of ecstasy through her. "I've been fighting it, but you're driving me crazy."

With the quick intensity of a sultry summer storm he delivered a series of devastating kisses as he backed her towards the unmade bed. Michael wants me! Michael wants me! The phrase repeated itself over and over in her mind. Her hands moved restlessly over the warm skin of his naked chest and down to shape his firm buttocks. Moaning softly, she returned his kisses with everything she had.

Nikita felt the edge of the bed at the back of her legs, and then she was falling onto it backwards in slow motion. Michael followed her down, his body covering hers. Her stomach curled at the feel of his hardened length against her. With trembling fingers, she unbuttoned his pants and pulled down the zipper.

Warm fingers burrowed beneath her shirt to unsnap her sports bra and massage the softness of her breasts. Suddenly his hands stilled. Nikita's lids flew open. "Michael?"

Shaking his head slowly, he gently pulled down her shirt and rolled off her.

Tears sprang to her eyes and she blinked quickly, working hard to keep them from falling. "You don't want me?" she asked in an incredulous whisper, then immediately wished she could take it back.

"Of course I want you, Nikita. We could spend the day right here in this bed," Michael said gently as he pointed to his arousal. "But this is lust. I know you, Nikita. For one thing, I'm on the rebound from Chenelle's rejection. That's not fair to you. For another, I bet you don't remember getting drunk last New Year's Eve and telling me all about that guy you loved in college, and how there'd never been anyone else, do you?"

Nikita turned her head from side to side in disbelief. Her entire body burned with shame and embarrassment. Suddenly unable to look at him, she tried to burrow into the pillows with a wrist and hand covering her eyes. Dimly, she recalled having a deep heart-to-heart with Michael on relationships. How could she have told him so much? Where was her pride?

Michael's voice softened as she suffered in waves of humiliation. The fresh scent of soap filled her nostrils as he moved closer. His hand caught hers. "You've been waiting for love, haven't you?"

And I've found it, but I can't tell you this. Nikita

rubbed the back of her wrist across her eyes. "Yes," she whispered, her heart aching.

"I respect you, Nikita, and I know you better than you think. If we'd gone through with this, you'd never have forgiven me."

Clutching fistfuls of sheet in her trembling hands, Nikita forced herself to look at Michael. Massive pain burned in her chest. She felt as if she'd run for miles and then stopped short of the goal. "In case you didn't notice, I wanted you too, Michael."

Michael sighed in frustration. "That's what I can't figure. You damned well aren't in love with me, are you, Nikita?"

She glared at him in stony silence, unable to boldly lie about this, even to save face. "You're an attractive man. I got carried away."

"So did I." He scrutinized her face. "So you were willing to compromise your principles because you were attracted to me?"

"I was willing to sleep with you." Wincing, she sat up, rubbing her arms at the cold harsh words and squeezing out a more honest answer. "I wanted to make love with you." Why did Michael have to push so much? She tried studying the pattern on the bedspread, then closed her eyes instead. She'd never wanted anyone as much as she wanted him and was still reeling from his brutal rejection.

"Nikita?" A hint of vulnerability crept into

Michael's tone. "Were you feeling sorry for me, because of the wedding and everything?"

His question jolted her out of her self-pity. He was a beautiful man, inside and out, and everything a woman could want. Her head snapped up and she forced herself to meet the intensity in his eyes. "I feel a lot of things for you, Michael, but sorry isn't one of them." She could see the stubborn look in his eye. He wasn't going to let it go at that.

"Just tell me..."

Nikita crawled off the bed, determined to end the humiliating conversation. "I can't imagine anyone sleeping with you out of pity, Michael, so get off it," she said sarcastically.

His jaw clenched and he shifted his weight on the bed. "Nikita, I'm sorry, I–"

"I don't want your apology." Nikita's voice skirted the area between a moan and a cry of frustration. The urge to flee, to escape him if only for a little while, rose within her. Choking it down, she stood on shaking legs and retrieved the bundle of clothing with a great show of outward calm.

"This was obviously a mistake. Let's just forget it happened, and try to move on." Nikita strolled into the bathroom. Once she'd shut the door and turned the lock, she collapsed against it in a fit of tears. How would she ever be able to face him again?

Rejected. Nikita's tears mingled with the cold

shower spray. She couldn't seem to stop their flow. Shoulders shaking, she leaned into the spray and cried her heart out. How she loved that man, and he was totally oblivious.

Why was it so easy to successfully implement project plans at work, and so extraordinarily difficult to implement any plan in her relationship? She'd been working on plan one, subtly trying to change the nature of her relationship with Michael when she'd made the mistake of introducing him to Chenelle.

Although she hadn't had the time to fully flesh out plan two, she'd wanted to build on their friendship to show Michael that he could be attracted to her, that he could even fall in love with her. She'd made a mess of things by coming on to him so soon. Then he'd made his newfound desire for her seem like something ugly and dirty. Nikita's heart ached.

I'm a big girl. It's not the end of the world. I can play this off, she told herself once she'd showered and changed. *He can't know how much he's hurt me.*

When she opened the bathroom door, Michael stood blocking her path.

"For a long time, I've considered you a very special friend," he said gently and sighed. His hand extended to touch her face and he pulled it back. "I'm sorry, so sorry if I've hurt you." Sympathy and regret filled his dreamy brown eyes.

"You haven't done anything to apologize for,

Michael." Nikita didn't want his sympathy. She wanted his love more than she'd ever wanted anything before. Friendship, sympathy, and regret. Was this all she could inspire from the only man she'd ever loved? Her feelings for that boy in college paled in comparison. Nikita bit her lip, Michael's careful words wounding her deep in her heart. He'd never felt anything but special friendship for her.

"This cruise wasn't such a good idea after all," he muttered, one hand gently massaging her shoulder.

Nikita stiffened and pulled away. This scenario wasn't even close to the one she'd imagined. Michael should be making love to her instead of treating her like his kid sister and trying to let her down easy. Tears burned the back of her eyelids. "Don't patronize me!"

"All right. I–I, Nikita, I didn't mean..." Michael shuffled his feet uncomfortably.

Unable to look at him, Nikita turned her back. "And please stop apologizing," she bit out miserably as she scraped the back of her wrist across her eyes. It came away wet with unshed tears that he couldn't see. What was she supposed to do? She wanted to go some place where she could be alone with her thoughts, but she couldn't seem to move.

She heard the bedsprings creak as he sat back down on the bed. The huskiness in his deep voice went right through her. Without looking, she could almost see those sensual lips of his forming the words. "I thought we were such good friends that we could talk about anything, Nikita. Why can't we talk about this?"

Why? Nikita turned to look at him then. He seemed genuinely puzzled, his forehead wrinkled, and the fingers of one hand fussing with his towel. How blind could the man be? Before she even thought about it, the words came tumbling out in an emotional jumble. "Because I love you, stupid."

Michael's head snapped up. His mouth opened and closed in surprise, amazement, and disbelief.

Nikita held her breath, the excitement within her at a feverish peak. She'd told him. She'd finally told him.

"Nikita, how—"

Before Michael could say another word, she ripped open the door and raced down the carpeted hall.

"Nikita!" he bellowed. "Come back here."

Pushing open the glass doors, she ran across the sparsely populated deck, into the bright morning sunshine. She was headed up the stairs when Michael came pounding after her.

Her thoughts churned madly. This is stupid and

childish. Stop and face Michael. But Nikita couldn't seem to stop. Bounding up another two flights of stairs, she ran like crazy. Slowing slightly, she rounded a corner where up ahead, she saw a crewman up on a ladder painting one of the inside walls of the ship. Not even winded, she nimbly raced across the deck. It was really silly to be running from Michael like this, but what would she say if she stopped?

He started gaining on her, his footsteps sounding louder and louder. The man was in better condition than she'd thought. Nikita sped up a little more as she scooted around the man on the ladder, almost running smack into a couple of guys running the other way.

She'd gone just a little way up the deck when she turned to see that Michael hadn't been so lucky. Nikita covered her mouth with her hands. He had plowed head on into the runners, and falling, cracked his head on a metal pole. With a loud thwack, the two men fell sideways against the ladder, knocking it and the crewman down onto Michael. White paint streamed across the deck.

The entire sequence seemed straight out of a Three Stooges movie. Nikita wondered whether to laugh or cry, but when reality set in, her steps quickened. What if Michael were seriously hurt? The paint-splattered runners and the poor crewman were getting to their feet as Nikita approached, but Michael remained motionless on the deck. Nikita's breath caught and she struggled to breathe.

"Michael? Michael, say something," Nikita demanded as she dropped down beside him on the deck. He was out cold. With tentative fingers she touched his face, brushing the hair back from his face. It was moist and sticky with something warm. Rubbing her fingers together, she stared down at bright red blood. "Michael!"

Chapter 8

In the ship's infirmary, a doctor quickly examined Michael and determined that although he was unconscious and had some nasty cuts and bruises, there were no broken bones. Then the nurse put him on an IV. Nikita sat by his bed in one of the small rooms that comprised the ship's hospital, holding his hand to her cheek, touching him as she'd never dared before. It hurt to look at the bandages on his head and the bandages covering the gashes on his arms. Whispering a quick prayer that he would be all right, she thanked God there were no broken bones.

She'd told the medical staff she was Michael's wife so that they'd let her stay with him. After all, she and Michael were supposed to be newlyweds. And they were sharing the same cabin. If Michael were himself, he'd thank her for looking out for him, but what should she do now?

Nikita stared at her watch. It was only ten minutes later than the last time she'd checked. He'd been out for twenty-four hours now, and she'd not left his side except to get his medical card and go to the bathroom. Forcing air through her lungs, she realized that she'd never been more frightened in her life. Focusing on his pale lids, she promised herself that if Michael got through this, she was going to love him the way she'd always dreamed of.

"Michael, Michael, wake up." The harsh, hoarse sound of her voice grated on her ears, but it really didn't matter. She'd been talking to him for hours with little result.

Her dry heave split the silence in the room. She bit down on her bottom lip, determined not to start crying again. This was all her fault. All that energy spent trying to get away from him when she dreamed of being with him. What would she do if Michael suffered permanent brain damage?

His hand tightened around hers. She waited, hope building within her once again. He'd moved a number of times in the past hours, but never gained consciousness.

The man in the bed fought a battle deep within himself. Over and over he strained his fractured mind and aching body against the bonds imprisoning him in the pillowy darkness.

"I'm not giving up on you, Michael..."

The voice came to him on thick, dark clouds of

nothingness. He pushed himself towards its welcoming warmth. It was a strong voice, one used to giving orders, yet it drew him with a caressing quality he sensed was for him alone. He couldn't quite make out the words, but he heard worry and despair in its changing pitch and rhythm. It had alternately commanded and cajoled him. Why did he hurt so much?

He clawed his way to the top of the pit. He shook with the agony.

The fresh clean scent of a woman's cologne filled his nostrils.

"Oh, Michael." The cry came out in a choked whisper. Was he Michael? He'd heard the name a lot. He had to be.

A downy soft cheek momentarily rested against his. Something slid along the surface of his skin. His face was...wet? Was she crying over him?

An opaque barrier enclosed him, keeping him prisoner in the nothingness. Gradually the pain leveled, pounding and pulsing within his ears. Was that his heart?

He heard the rustling sounds of the woman's movements. "Michael?"

Very carefully, he peeked beneath the edges of his lids. She'd done something to lessen the light in the room. Blinking, he fully opened his eyes and caught his first look at his dark-haired angel of mercy. Pretty, in a wistful sort of way. The set of her jaw and tilt of her chin hinted at the strength her voice held. Who was she?

The woman's pewter gray eyes lit up, her wide mouth breaking into a smile. "Welcome back." She looked as if she wanted to throw herself at him, her slim, athletic frame fairly vibrating with energy. He stared. At any other time, he would have welcomed the feel of that long, lithe, but surprisingly curvaceous form against his own. But now...he couldn't remember ever enduring such pain. He wasn't dead yet, no. He was simply the loser in what must have been a hell of a fight.

She pulled a device from his bedside table and rang for the nurse. His eyes drifted shut, throbbing head pain threatening to overwhelm him.

"Stay with me, Michael."

He wanted to. He'd followed that velvet-laced-with-steel voice up out of the darkness of a private hell. Once more, he pried his eyes open at the sound of her voice. She rewarded him with another smile that had the impact of a punch to his midsection. Who was she? Girlfriend? Wife? Sister? He hoped not. Down boy, you're not up to this—yet.

Something was not quite right. Her face seemed familiar and yet he'd expected someone different. Now, why was that? He eyed the shiny curls of dark hair and wondered what it would be like to thrust his hands into it.

"Don't just lie there. Say something," she urged, holding his hand and stepping to the side of his bed.

The grating sound from his opened mouth barely resembled speech. He cleared his throat and tried again. This time he couldn't help the low moan that escaped as he held his aching head. "I need a new head," he muttered. "Did someone beat me with an axe? Somebody try to break my skull?"

Eyes widening, she stood like a deer caught in the headlights of an oncoming car. "You—you had an accident on deck," she said nervously, one hand still holding his, and the other creeping up to tentatively touch his shoulder. He liked it. Warmth spread from the tips of her gentle fingers to his battered body.

He peered at her through his fingers, avoiding the bandage on his forehead. "My head is pounding and throbbing so hard I can barely think. What happened?"

She swallowed, her mouth and throat working as she tried to formulate a response. Things were worse than he'd thought. He held his breath while she stammered out an answer. "We're on a ship. You...were running and there was a crewman on a ladder, and some people were running towards you. Then everyone collided and you cracked your head on a post."

Wincing at her description, he still noticed the

excess moisture in those big gray eyes. More tears for him? Gently moving his palm across the bandage on his pounding forehead, he stared, working to keep his eyes open. "I've been out for hours?" At her nod, he continued. "How many?"

"Twenty-four."

"And you've been here all along?"

"Yes." As if remembering her state of dress, she smoothed her gold T-shirt and tugged at her brief navy shorts. With his eyes he followed the line of her long, shapely legs to a pair of running shoes. She caught him looking and flashed him a mischievous smile.

"I heard you talking to me. My mind's been drifting in and out. I could smell your perfume, feel you holding my hand, but I couldn't speak."

"I hoped you could hear me," she murmured.

At that moment, the nurse and the doctor entered the room and in short order were giving him a shot for pain. He winced as the needle slid into his flesh, but was grateful when the pain eased abruptly.

"How do you feel?" the doctor asked, pushing thick wire frame lenses up on his nose.

"Better now, thanks. Of course my head's still one big battered marshmallow, and my body aches all over."

"That's to be expected, given all that's happened

to you. Any nausea? Dizzyness?"

"Just a little, when I got the shot. I'm okay now."

"Good," the doctor said, scrawling a few notes on his clipboard. "What's your name?"

At a loss, the man in the bed tried hard to recall it. He couldn't remember his own name? That was ridiculous! Why his name was...? His name was...? He could almost say his name, but the thought was never clear enough for him to know. Deciding to fall back on the name his angel of mercy had used, he answered, "Michael?"

"Michael what?"

"I don't know," he admitted finally. His angel of mercy gasped softly, drawing his attention. Unconsciously, she clutched his hand against her soft breasts.

"Then what makes you think you're Michael?"

"It's what she called me." He inclined his head towards his angel of mercy.

"And do you recognize her?"

Michael's head dipped. "No."

His angel linked her fingers in his. "I'm Nikita," she said a little breathlessly, her teeth biting into the tender flesh of her bottom lip.

"Nikita?" Her name rolled smoothly off his tongue.

"Your wife," the nurse put in, breaking her silence for the first time.

Michael's thoughts churned. His wife... his wife. She was his wife. He studied her, hard. So he'd taken the plunge. The thought did not disturb him, but his choice intrigued him. He suspected that Nikita was quite a woman, but she was hardly his type. A little too angelic for him perhaps? What was his type? Out of the corner of his eyes, he saw the nurse, an exotic and voluptuous vision in white, and sighed. Trouble lay in that direction.

He felt Nikita tremble slightly through their joined hands and wondered if she could sense what he was thinking. She stiffened and he was somehow certain that she did. He linked his fingers in hers in an effort to comfort her. "Let me guess. We're newlyweds?"

She nodded and then added in a husky voice, "We're on our honeymoon."

He concentrated, trying to remember something, anything. Knife-like pains split the area between his eyes and he broke out into a sweat. "I can't remember anything." Pain and frustration threatened to overwhelm him. Squeezing his eyes shut, he sighed heavily.

"I'll help you," Nikita said, breaking the ringing silence with quiet determination. "And I'm not leaving until I'm sure you're okay."

He sort of liked the idea of this angel as his champion and ally, but the newness of it all gave him pause, and made him slightly uncomfortable. He swiveled his head to look at the doctor. "Doc?"

"In addition to your cuts, bruises and abrasions, you've got a grade III concussion caused by head trauma," the doctor told him. "We've done all the tests we can. There's been some memory loss, but in time, you may get it back."

Michael clenched his fists, repeating to himself that there was some hope of regaining all he'd lost. "How long will it take?"

"Anywhere from a couple of days to a year. Some memories may never be recovered."

Michael closed his eyes, the pulse at his temple jumping. Desperately, he wished himself away, anywhere but here, where no one and nothing was familiar, and a future filled with strangers yawned before him. Nikita stroked that pulse with gentle fingers, watching as his eyes opened in response.

"It'll be okay, Michael," she whispered. "I'll help you through this." He knew then that Nikita would be his anchor. With burning eyes, she turned to the doctor. "Will he be able to work? He's a well established engineer."

The doctor scribbled on Michael's chart. "Most likely, but time will tell." He turned back to Michael. "How's the pain?"

Michael took a long, shaky breath. "Better." He pointed to the rolling table. "Can I get some water?"

The nurse poured iced water into a cup and Nikita held it to his lips while he drank. He watched her the entire time, curiosity burning in his eyes.

"We'll keep you here for a few days, and then let you get on with the honeymoon," the doctor said with a smile. "You're a lucky man, Mr. Matheson, whether you realize it or not. Things could be a lot worse."

"That's what I've been telling myself, Doc," Michael said, his eyes resting on his intriguing wife. The apparent depth of her feelings for him would take getting used to.

When the nurse and doctor had gone, Nikita sat quietly with Michael for several minutes. From the way he stared, she knew he was trying to analyze her, figure her out. He was Michael, and yet he was not. Did she imagine the speculative look she saw in his eyes every now and then?

"You talked a lot more when I was out," he said at one point.

"I wasn't sure you would ever wake up," she confessed. "And now I know that you're tired and in pain. I don't want to keep you awake."

"But I like the sound of your voice."

"Then I'll make sure you hear it a lot—tomorrow."

When she saw that his lids were getting heavy,

Nikita stood up and leaned close to touch her face to his. The short stubble of his beard pricked her skin, but she nestled against him anyway, glad to be close to him, glad that he was alive and reasonably well. She wanted to hold him in her arms and never let him go.

His hand came up to lightly caress her back as she kissed his cheek and slid to the swell of her hips when she kissed his lips. Then, to her surprise and delight, his mouth opened under hers, leading her in a couple of gentle, exploratory kisses. When he finished, she was dazed and trembling.

"That was good. You're a fascinating woman," he whispered huskily, one hand in her hair, and the other cupping her hips. "That's something I don't have to remember."

Nikita smiled at him. "I've been so worried about you." Carefully, she lay her head on his chest, drawing comfort from his touch. Despite the amnesia, splitting headache, and battered body, he'd still managed to kiss her silly. This was the Michael of her dreams. Was it so wrong of her to want it to last forever?

"I'm glad you stuck with me," Michael said, his arms tightening around Nikita. "Everything is so strange. I'm all out of sorts and confused. If I've said or done anything to hurt your feelings—"

"No, Michael, I love you. I'm willing to do whatever it takes. If we have to start over, then so be it," she told him, as she'd never been able to tell him before. More than anything, Nikita wished she really was his wife.

"We have this incredible chemistry between us," he whispered close to her ear, "Can you let that be enough until I can remember how we really are together?"

"It'll be enough," she answered, nuzzling close.

Promising to return in the morning, Nikita trudged back to the cabin alone. In the overwhelming silence, she showered, then lay naked beneath the crisp clean sheets, thinking of Michael. Her lips still tingled from his kiss. She wanted him to finish what he'd started in the cabin yesterday. Visions of him dancing in his briefs, fresh from the shower, filled her mind. He gave her that slow, sexy grin and pulled her close to his warm, sensual body. Nikita closed her eyes as Michael kissed her into oblivion.

Suddenly Nikita sat up in bed, rubbing her eyes in the cool darkness. By the luminous numbers of the clock on the chest of drawers, she knew she'd slept only a couple of hours. She was worried about Michael. Should she tell him that she was not his wife? As long as he was in the ship's hospital, it didn't really matter. Would he remember before he came back to stay in the cabin with her? In the back of her mind, a yearning part of her psyche fervently hoped not.

This was her chance to claim Michael and make him truly hers, to see how good it could get. She'd never loved anyone the way she loved him. Maybe she'd get lucky and he'd fall in love with her. Why not? It could happen, she thought, hoping it would. On that note, Nikita flopped back down on her pillow. She had made the decision to go on pretending and hope for the best.

All night and into the early hours of the morning, Michael tossed and turned through a series of disjointed dreams and flashbacks. He saw himself in bed with a beautiful, green-eyed woman, then in church, watching Nikita come down the aisle. In the final moments of his dream, he saw himself, devastated as he addressed a church full of people. What had happened?

He awakened early, his thoughts a jumbled mess. There was something unpleasant about the wedding. What was it? He tried to make sense of the little he remembered from the dream and failed.

Gritting his teeth, he stared up at the ceiling, determined to remember something. He'd heard Nikita tell the doctor he was an engineer. Examining his hands, Michael wondered what kind. What kind of work did he do? Closing his eyes, he tried to visualize himself working, see his place of employment. For all his concentrated effort, his head began to throb. In frustration, he gave up.

His beautiful nurse came in to check his vital signs and Michael found himself smiling in the face of such beauty. He enjoyed the view, but his thoughts returned to Nikita, his angel. Down boy, you're a married man. Clamping down on the twinge of guilt, he consoled himself with the fact that he'd merely looked at his nurse. What was the harm in that?

When she'd gone, he adjusted his bed to a sitting position and restlessly scanned the room. On the table bridging his bed was a small mirror. Michael picked it up and stared at the stranger reflected there. Did he have a passel of brothers and sisters who looked just like him? And what about his parents? Did he look like them? Brown eyes, dark, curling hair. He grinned at himself: nice teeth. Except for the bandage, the large purple bruise on his forehead, and the angry red scratches, not bad looking at all.

Questions cycled uselessly through his mind. What sort of person was he? He couldn't imagine himself as a sentimental, romantic kind of guy, but he'd gotten married. Most likely, he'd promised to love and honor Nikita. Was Nikita expecting more than steady sex, companionship, and faithfulness?

Was he up to the task? Why had she married him? The questions frustrated him because the answers defined his life and he was clueless.

He thought of Nikita, the kind of woman who'd stand by her man, no matter what. She was beautiful, but not in the classic sense. Beneath those fluffy dark curls, intelligence sparkled in her clear gray eyes. She was an enigma, an open-ended question, but when he'd kissed her, he knew he wanted her.

He heard a tray rattle. Then the door opened and Michael found himself looking for Nikita. The smell of her perfume and the memory of her hand in his as he slept through the night had kept him feeling safe and secure. Had it all been a dream? It couldn't have been anything else because Nikita had left before he went to sleep.

"Good morning. I thought I'd come down and have breakfast with you." Looking more beautiful than he'd imagined, Nikita stood in the opened doorway of his room with a tray of food. Her teal blue sundress emphasized her curves, ending just above the intriguing little mole on her right inner thigh; showing off her long legs and setting his pulse to racing. The dress dipped just a little at her breasts, its halter top leaving the sun-kissed skin on her shoulders and part of her back bare. She'd even taken the time to put on makeup.

"Trying to raise my blood pressure?" he asked as

she stepped into the room on strappy white sandals with glass heels. "Or prove that I've still got the right stuff?"

Carefully setting the tray in front of him, she teased, "Which stuff are you referring to?"

"I'm talking about the stuff I need to finish that honeymoon we started. The fire I'm going to use to send us up in flames."

"The thought of raising your blood pressure had crossed my mind," Nikita said, coloring just a little.

"Then you've succeeded beyond your wildest dreams." Inhaling the scent of her perfume, Michael patted the space beside him on the bed. "Come here."

Nikita stood just out of reach. "Why should I? You don't remember anything about me."

"Ahh, but you're wrong, Nikita. I remember that you've always had the ability to soothe me, to calm me down." He paused, amazed at the thought which had rolled easily from his memory.

"That's true." She took a step forward so that he could just touch the petal soft skin of her hand. "But you don't seem calm now."

Michael threw her a smile of challenge, daring her to come closer. With his fingertips, he traced a provocative pattern that spread across the back of her hand to the sensitive skin of her palm. He watched her take her bottom lip between her teeth, her hand closing over his fingers to halt his sensual assault. "And I remember seeing you in that dress. You bought it aboard this ship."

"Also true." Moving closer till she stood beside him, Nikita hooked an arm around his shoulders and kissed his cheek. "What else do you remember?"

Again he strained, concentrating until his head ached. "Nothing," he muttered in defeat, "Nothing at all. This is frustrating as hell."

"And to be expected, I'm sure." She sat down on the edge of his bed. Studying him, Nikita held his face in her hands, uncertainty flickering in her eyes. If he hadn't known better, he'd have said she was unsure of her reception as she leaned forward and gently kissed his lips. "Welcome to the first day of a wonderful life."

"Tell that to my aching head, my missing memory, and my battered body," he rasped.

"I don't think I need to," Nikita answered. "Everything you've lost can be recovered." Warmth crept into her tone. "You can do this, Michael. I'll help you."

And she would too, Michael thought, staring into her guileless gray eyes, because that's the kind of woman she was. Fear of his vulnerability in the dark, unknown world outside his hospital room had haunted his dreams last night. The thought of Nikita at his side as he rediscovered it was comforting. No matter what he remembered, he felt a sort of link to her.

She was his wife, wasn't she? He couldn't quite bring himself to accept the fact with the confidence and comfort that he should. One thing was certain: Bruised and battered as he was, he wanted to know her in the deepest, most intimate sense. He touched her soft lips with the tips of his fingers and ran them down the downy curve of her cheek.

She leaned toward him, obviously enjoying his attention. Gasping softly, she closed her eyes when he used his hands to trace the length and shape of her legs all the way up past the little black mole on her right inner thigh.

"You've got great legs, Nikita."

"Thanks," she sighed, lying helplessly against him.

She felt good in his arms. He stroked the soft skin at the top of her thighs, inching towards the damp silk between.

"Michael." Nikita moaned and caught hold of his hand, her face flushed and her eyelids fluttering open.

His desire for her was a physical ache, curling deep in his belly. He stared into her pewter eyes, enjoying her obvious sensual daze. The fullness of her parted lips was an open invitation. Her lids drifted closed as he leaned near to kiss her lips. Tentatively, he tasted their sweetness and then dipped his tongue into her mouth again and again in a primitive dance of desire. When Nikita's hand burrowed beneath his pajamas to touch his chest, Michael groaned, urging her into the bed.

Panting, she pulled away. "No, Michael. Someone might come in. I'm not climbing into this hospital bed with you."

"You're already here." He cupped her rounded buttocks, lifting her up until his erection nestled in the vee between her legs.

Nikita squirmed, her warm, soft form dramatically increasing the hot thrill of sensations strumming through his body. Then, breaking away, she sat up to swing her legs over the side of his bed, with the dress exposing most of her legs and thighs.

He caught one of Nikita's soft springy curls and tugged on it playfully. The familiarity of the gesture hit him immediately. His body apparently remembered more than he did.

She got up, smoothing down her dress and moving away to lift the cover on his tray. "Are you hungry?"

"Starving." He gave her a significant look.

"I'm talking about food," she chided.

He shrugged. Between losing his memory and getting hurt, food had been the last thing on his mind. Taking in the soft scrambled eggs, oatmeal, and juice, he wrinkled his nose with distaste. "I can hardly wait to eat all my favorite foods you've got there."

Nikita chuckled. "At least eat some of the oatmeal. Lunch will be better, I promise."

He watched her settle herself into the chair by his bed, enjoying the display of her long, shapely legs. "Do you always keep your promises?"

"Yes. I take them very seriously."

"Good. 'Cause I'm holding you to this one."

"My promise is good only on the condition that you eat some of that oatmeal," Nikita declared flatly.

"I knew that was too good to be true," Michael groaned, as he added butter, milk and then sugar to doctor the oatmeal. "Can I offer you something to eat?"

"Nice try, Michael, but I grabbed something from the breakfast buffet."

"It figures. Well, that's one more thing I've got to look forward to," he muttered. Resolutely, he forced himself to eat half the bowl of oatmeal, and then washed it down with the orange juice.

"Did you call anyone when I had the accident? I was wondering about my family."

"No." Leaning towards him, Nikita answered quickly, looking almost guilty, "I thought about calling your parents, but I didn't want to worry them until we had some concrete information on your condition. If I had, they'd be here now. Do you want me to call them?"

Michael considered it. He was just beginning to reestablish his relationship with his wife. He still remembered little. He wasn't ready to see parents he didn't remember. No, getting to know Nikita again was enough for now. "Not yet," he answered finally. He downed the rest of the orange juice. "Have I got a lot of brothers and sisters?"

"No, you're an only child," she said, throwing him a wide, toothy smile that he couldn't help returning. "But you always wanted brothers and sisters. I did bring pictures from your wallet."

He watched her pull a small stack of pictures from her little clasp purse. "Let me look at them," he murmured, extending a hand and accepting them. For a moment, he held them in his hands, hesitating. Would he recognize them? What if he didn't? Get on with it. The petite woman in the first photo had his almond brown eyes, high cheekbones, and coal black hair. Her gaze held an air of power and command. "My mother?"

"Yes. She's a VP at Ladystyles Inc. Do you recognize her?"

"No." He examined the picture, remembering nothing. The only tie he felt stemmed from his time in the mirror this morning. The physical similarities between himself and this woman were hard to miss. The build of the tall muscular man in the next picture resembled his own. Absently, Michael massaged his scalp with the tip of a finger. "My dad?"

"Yes. He's a VP at the Garron Corporation."

Placing the pictures side by side, Michael examined them. His parents were obviously far from ordinary. "Both heavy hitters, huh?"

"Yes, but look at the next picture. They're human."

In the next picture, his parents posed in a gag photo set in an old saloon. At a table with a bottle of whiskey sat his father dressed as a cowboy, complete with Stetson, guns, and sheriff's badge. His mother sat on his lap in a low cut madam's dress with the ruffles draped up to expose quite a bit of one shapely leg. Something sizzled in the smiles they gave each other.

Glancing up from the pictures, he found Nikita watching him intently. "How did I meet you?"

"We both work for Techno Toys and Gadgets. I'm one of the engineers on some of your project teams. Do you remember RoboChuck?" Michael shook his head negatively and she continued animatedly. "It's a children's robot we've been working on. He responds to voice commands, he's reprogrammable, and the kids can change his configuration with some of the snap-on parts we've designed."

He took in the enthusiasm and excitement in her voice, enjoying this new side of her. She obviously loved her job. He bet she was good at it. "Sounds like an exciting idea."

"Oh, it is." She paused. "You don't remember, do you?"

"No. So far I've only been able to remember the little things."

Nikita covered his hand with hers. "You'll get it all back. If you'd packed your work badge, I'd have brought that too."

"I imagine I'll see that soon enough." He grasped her hand, his fingers massaging the wedding rings. She hadn't been wearing them yesterday. Why not? Michael scrutinized the slightly gaudy rings that must have cost him a mint. Baguettes surrounded a large princess cut diamond, with a matching band. Somehow, it didn't seem like the sort of ring Nikita would pick. But what did he know? "Nice rings," he murmured and felt her tremble just a little. He shot her a quick glance.

She stared at the ring. "A friend helped you pick them."

Michael considered her innocuous words, carefully void of emotion. He'd have bet money that she didn't like them. The truth was, neither did he. "We could get you another set."

Her smile failed to reach her eyes. "Michael, they're fine. I know you paid a lot for them."

He decided to leave it at that. Another mystery

for him to remember, along with the wedding and the feeling that things had not gone as planned. He pushed the table away from him. "What's next?"

Nikita produced a crisp new deck of cards. "I thought we'd play poker," she said with a predatory gleam in her eye.

"Let's play strip poker," he suggested, thinking of how little she wore beneath that sundress.

The naughty smile she gave him made his body tingle. "Let's save that for later," she amended in a seductive tone.

He lifted an eyebrow. "Then we'll play for money."

"Fine, but you can pay me later."

He lifted an eyebrow. "You're awfully certain of your luck. You won't cheat, will you?"

"I don't have to," she replied confidently, her swift fingers expertly shuffling the cards. "Do you remember how to play?" At his nod, she began dealing the cards.

Each started with a five hundred-dollar credit. She was a hell of a poker player, and lucky to boot, but he enjoyed every game. By the time they quit for lunch, he owed Nikita another thousand. Whew! Good thing she was his wife.

"You're damned good," he said admiringly, after she'd beaten him to a pulp.

Nikita stood up and stretched. "Thanks. You'll

get a chance to get your money back."

"Or dig myself deeper into debt."

"It was all for fun. Aren't you glad we didn't play strip poker?"

With a slow, heated perusal, he eyed Nikita from head to toe. Sure, the only garment he wore was that silly hospital gown they made him wear, but the chance to see more of Nikita would have been worth the risk. He threw her a sexy grin. "Anytime you want me to strip, just say the word. Baby, I'm yours."

She blushed. Michael couldn't believe it. Was it possible that he'd had the accident on deck before taking his new wife to bed? Nah, he could never have been into saving it for marriage. He knew that much about himself. So what was the deal with Nikita?

She was quite cute as she stammered out something about getting lunch and shot out of the room. Michael found himself thinking he could hardly wait to get back to his honeymoon. Making love to your wife when you have no memory of being married had to be the ultimate experience. He laughed out loud. Could you cheat on your wife with your wife?

Nikita was true to her word. She rustled up a lunch that easily surpassed the breakfast. Michael found it easy to scarf down the grilled cheese sandwich and chicken noodle soup. For dessert, she promised an ice cream sundae. He found his mouth watering. To keep him company while he ate his meal, she sat in the chair beside him munching on room service pizza.

By the time he had scarfed down the strawberry sundae, Nikita had fallen asleep in the chair. He'd known she was tired because, despite the makeup, there were faint circles beneath her eyes. Amused, he watched her, noting the graceful curve of her neck, and the innocence and beauty of her expression. A dark, shiny curl covered part of one thick-fringed eyelid. He felt a sharp ache deep in his groin and yearned to take her back to the cabin and immediately resume his honeymoon.

A light knock sounded on his door, and then it opened slowly to reveal his nurse and an aide. Quickly and quietly, while the nurse took his vitals, the aide began to gather the used dishes and silverware. The light clatter was enough to awaken Nikita, who nearly fell out of the chair.

"Mmmmph?" she cried, sitting up straight, her eyes dazed with sleep. "I must have fallen asleep."

"You're tired," he told her quietly after the nurse and her aide were gone. "You've been spending too much time in this room."

Nikita caught his hand. "Michael, I want to be with you as much as possible."

"And I'm glad, but I want you to go back to the

cabin and get a good rest, get out on deck for some fresh air, and get dressed up and go to dinner."

She tugged at his hand to emphasize her words. "We can do that when you get out of here. I don't want to do those things without you."

"Promise me," he said obstinately.

"But Michael..."

"Promise me."

"All right, I promise." She lowered her lids over suspiciously shiny eyes. "Are you kicking me out now?"

He pulled on her arm until she moved forward to sit beside him on the bed. Curving an arm around her shoulders, he explained. "I'm not kicking you out. I just feel selfish with you hanging around this place all day."

"Then you don't think I'm smothering you. You're not tired of me?"

"Hell no." With his fingers, he lifted her chin to look into her watery gray eyes. "How could a woman so sensitive be married to a man like me?" he muttered to himself.

She stiffened. When a lone tear trailed down one cheek, he felt like a tyrant. Michael cursed softly under his breath. Pulling her into arms, he nuzzled her face with his, catching the moisture with his tongue. "Nikita, I'm going to talk to the doctor. There's no reason for me to be here. I feel fine. Sure, there's a lot I can't remember, but sticking it out here isn't going to help."

"You don't think it's too soon?"

"No. I'm going crazy and I'm horny as hell. Sweetheart, you keep my motor running in overdrive. You need to rest up because once I get out of here, you probably won't see daylight for at least a week.

Nikita stirred against him. "I wasn't going to say anything, but I talked to the doctor about your release yesterday."

Michael tightened his jaw. "And?"

"And he said that unless you broached the subject, they'd keep you here a couple of days. It's important that you feel ready to face the world."

"Unless my memory suddenly returns, I'm as ready as I'll ever be." With firm but gentle fingers, he lifted her chin. "Don't keep things from me, Nikita. I want everything open and honest between us."

She blinked. "I don't want to lie or keep anything from you, Michael."

"Then don't," he said firmly, reinforcing his earlier words.

Nodding in agreement, she stood up, her expression serious as she prepared to go. Then she kissed him good-bye and left the room, softly closing the door behind her.

Michael lay there, pondering his situation. He couldn't shake the nagging feeling that no matter what Nikita had said, she was keeping something from him. He needed to spend time with her, but he also needed to go through his personal belongings, in order to jar something significant from his memory.

Forcing himself out of bed, he decided to walk the halls of the small ship's hospital. He knew that to get out of this place, he had to be strong enough to make it to his cabin, and he didn't want to be there if he were unable to spend at least a couple of days making love to Nikita. He needed to work on his strength and stamina. At the nurse's station, Michael asked them to page the doctor.

Chapter 9

Nikita hated to leave Michael. She'd always enjoyed his company, but now that he thought they were married, he seemed so loving that she had to tear herself away. His eyes lit up at the sight of her. And wasn't there a tinge of regret in his expression when she left? Suddenly her wildest dreams seemed obtainable. Deep in her heart she prayed he would fall in love with her.

She walked slowly back to the cabin. So far, things had worked to her advantage, but the knowledge brought her little joy. She felt incredibly sad. She loved Michael more than ever, but the moment of truth loomed in her future like a specter of death. At that point, would he hate her? Would he feel betrayed again? More importantly, would he forgive her?

Once inside the cabin, she closed the door and leaned against it, while she studied the fancy rings on her fingers. Twisting them in a circle, she decided that apart from her lie, she hated the rings most.

It had been pure luck that Michael's best man lacked the nerve needed to return the rings at the reception. He'd palmed them off on her, and she'd forgotten about them until they got on the plane where she'd worn them for a short time in order to avoid a lot of questions. She'd found the rings in Michael's things when she went searching for his medical card after the accident. The desire to take them off was strong, but she knew she'd gone too far to turn back. She'd used those rings to legitimize her claim as Michael's wife, and now she burned with guilt and shame. Oh Nikita, just how far will you go in your quest for Michael's love?

Kicking off her sandals in the cool room, she carefully hung the dress in the closet. Her reflection stared back critically as she closed the closet door. Liar! She barely recognized herself these days. Where was the woman who'd worked hard to earn the respect of all her peers at the company? Where was the woman who'd been a true friend to both Michael and Chenelle?

With tears welling in her eyes, Nikita stretched out on the bed. She deserved some happiness, didn't she? Besides, right now Michael needed her in her current role. She promised herself she'd tell Michael the truth when he was less vulnerable. Pulling the sheets up, she dug her head into the pillow and hugged herself.

Hours later, Nikita dressed and went up on deck. Instead of lying out to bake with several others in the sparkling tropical sunshine, she picked the breezy and much cooler shady side of the ship. In the background, a Caribbean band played Reggae music. Selecting a chaise lounge, she settled down with a book.

"Hey stranger, where've you been hiding?" The startling sound of a somewhat familiar voice interrupted her reading.

Over the top of her book, Nikita saw the brown head and questioning green eyes of Tyson Ward. She felt a headache coming on. "Hello, Tyson, what have you been up to?"

"Looking for you." He dropped down onto the chair beside her. "Are you going to answer my question?"

Nikita frowned. No, I'm not, because I don't like the way you're asking. Licking her dry lips, she amended the thought, opting to minimize the information she would give him instead of being nasty. "If you'll give me a minute, I'll try to put together a response."

He patted her hand. "I'm not trying to pry, Nikita. It's just that I was worried that something might have happened to you. We haven't seen you for a couple of days."

"I'm fine, but Michael had an accident on deck. I've been trying to help him as much as I can." Nikita shivered. Just talking about it started a rerun of the entire incident in her mind.

Tyson signaled a passing waiter for a drink. "Really? Where is he? Resting down in the cabin?" At Nikita's negative response, he continued. "What happened?"

"There was a big collision on deck and he was knocked unconscious."

"Is he all right now?"

"Physically, yes, but it's going to take a while for him to recover completely."

He leaned closer, a comforting smile on his face. "If there's anything I can do, will you let me know?"

"Yes, thank you." Nikita took a sip from the water bottle beside her chair.

Tyson massaged her hand. His fingers seemed to stick on the wedding rings. He glanced up quickly, critically scanning her face. "Did you two get married in the last couple of days?"

Blood rushed to her face. She'd forgotten about the rings on her finger. Her stomach rolled. What could she say? They'd told Tyson and his mom that they weren't married. Tyson was bound to give her away to Michael at dinner. "I–I can't talk about this right now," she stammered as the heat rushed to her face. Nikita retrieved her hand and tried to stand.

"I've got to go."

He blocked her path, his voice filled with concern. "No, Nikita. Don't let me chase you away. It sounds like you've been through a lot. Let me help you."

Nikita ran her fingertips across her forehead. She didn't need this added aggravation. The thoug' t of her cool, empty cabin suddenly seemed very attractive. "I'm not good company right now. I don't feel like talking."

"We don't have to talk. Please, Nikita. I just want to sit with you for a while. I'll get my laptop and you can play with it. I'll simply watch, and next time you can give me another lesson, okay?"

She found Tyson's offer hard to resist. She needed something to think about besides Michael. "All right. I'll wait here," she agreed finally, seeing his use of the laptop as an excuse to remain in her presence. At this point, she didn't care. Surfing the Internet for a while through the hook up in the ship's library or even playing a few games of computer solitaire would definitely relax her. If he started asking questions again, she'd simply go back to the cabin.

True to his word, Tyson sat quietly and observed. When the sun started going down, she slipped back to the cabin to shower and dress for dinner.

Dinner was pleasant with Tyson and his mother working hard to keep her entertained, but her thoughts centered on Michael. Afterward, Nikita made a beeline for the ship's hospital. To her dismay, Tyson tagged along, sticking like glue.

Wrinkling her nose at the antiseptic smell of the hospital air, Nikita did her best to discourage Tyson. Nothing seemed to work. Checking her watch, she reminded him about the show starting in the lounge. That didn't work either.

Through the open doorway of his room, Michael looked incredibly handsome as he sat in bed watching a football game. He'd combed back his dark hair, shaved, and dressed in the short pajamas she'd brought.

"Nikita." His expression brightened with obvious welcome when he saw her standing in the doorway. He ignored Tyson. "Come here."

Nikita went to him, her heart soaring when he pulled her into his arms and kissed her like a dehydrated man getting his first taste of water. The sexy citrus smell of his cologne, the wild, mint-flavored taste of him, and the sensual swirl of his tongue combined to scramble her senses and give her everything she needed. Afterward, he pulled her down to sit on the side of his bed, turning her gently within the circle of his arms. "Missed you," he whispered huskily in a voice only she could hear. "I wanted to go looking for you. Can't wait to finish that honeymoon." His hands massaged the bare skin of her arms, then settled at her waist.

Nikita shivered.

Then Michael seemed to notice Tyson. "Hello. Do I know you?" he asked, eyeing Tyson critically.

Tyson grinned. "We've met, and eaten dinner together."

"Then we're friends?"

"Acquaintances." Tyson sat in the chair by the bed, keenly mindful of Nikita.

Michael's eyes narrowed and met hers for just a moment. "You've been keeping Nikita company," he said in a flat tone that made her feel as if she'd been accused of something.

"As much as she would allow. Today I had to bribe her with my laptop and promise not to talk."

"Well, I hope you enjoyed it, because I'm getting out of here in the morning and Nikita's going to be real busy. We've got unfinished business."

"Yes, we've got the whole day planned," she told Tyson. Michael's just putting on a show for Tyson, she told herself, but something within her melted and flowed beneath his heated stare. She was unquestionably his and he knew it.

Tyson's glance fell on the gaudy wedding rings. "I'm glad to see you're feeling well. Nikita says you've got amnesia."

Her stomach tightened. Had Tyson figured everything out already? Why hadn't she made up a plausible cover story? Because you hate lying to anyone, a voice deep within her replied.

She watched Michael scrutinize his expression. Her pulse sped up. "Is there something in particular that you want to remind me of?" Michael asked.

The knowledge shining in Tyson's eyes was hard to ignore. She covered the fisted hand in her lap as she bit into her bottom lip. This was it. He was going to give her away. Helplessly, she waited for the words that would end it all. Maybe she deserved it.

"I—I just wanted you to know that we're all rooting for you." Tyson's smile was all goodwill and innocence, but Nikita suspected that he'd merely postponed the moment of truth.

"Thanks." Michael relaxed visibly and Nikita released the breath she'd been holding. He lifted the deck of cards from the table and waved them in the air. "Do you want to play cards or something?"

"I think I'll leave you and Nikita to spend some time alone."

"Well, I appreciate your stopping by," Michael said. "The four walls of this room have been driving me nuts. Tomorrow I'm going to resume my life, whether my memory cooperates or not."

Soon after that, Tyson left for the lounge show. Once the door closed behind him, Michael tugged gently on one of her curls and said, "Stay away from him, Nikita."

On her knees, she shifted to face him. "That

won't be hard, but why?"

"Because he wants you. The man couldn't take his eyes off you. He'd like to come between us."

She linked her hands behind his neck and laid her cheek against his. "Then we won't let him, will we?"

"No, we won't. He seemed to be pretty persistent. For a minute there, I thought he had something really unpleasant to tell me."

Nikita buried her face in the warmth of his neck. "So did I."

Michael froze. "Is there something I should know?"

With her chest burning, Nikita chewed her bottom lip. This was her chance to set things straight, yet she couldn't quite bring herself to do it. "There's a lot you should know, Michael," she managed, pushing back to look into his eyes. "You've got amnesia."

He sighed with frustration. "I keep remembering bits and pieces of my life, but nothing seems to make sense. I see jumbled pictures of you, me, and a woman with green eyes, but nothing much about the church and the wedding. Something bad happened at the wedding, didn't it?"

She nodded. An awful burning sensation rose in Nikita's throat, making her gag. "Nothing turned out the way we planned," she said carefully. "Nothing." The rings flashed with rainbow fire and

Nikita looked away. No, she couldn't talk about the wedding.

He scanned her face. "Who was the green-eyed lady?"

With difficulty, she swallowed. "Chenelle, my best friend."

Michael's eyes widened with shock.

Clasping her shaking hands in her lap, Nikita was silent, certain this was the moment of truth.

"Chenelle and I... We were— pretty close," he said hoarsely, searching Nikita's expression. Watching him squirm, Nikita guessed he remembered sleeping with Chenelle.

"Yes." She croaked, afraid he'd remember it all. He and Chenelle had enjoyed each other. She couldn't forget that she'd almost lost Michael forever, and now, because of her own lies and actions, she might lose him again. Despite her best efforts, a single tear rolled down her cheek.

He smoothed the tear away with a fingertip and pulled her into his arms. "I'm sorry, Nikita. From what I can gather, I wasn't much of a fiancé. I hope to be a much better husband."

Nikita felt miserable. Michael had nothing to be sorry for. Did he think Chenelle had came between them? She couldn't let him feel guilt because of her lies and manipulations. Swallowing, she found her voice. "Maybe we should talk about it, Michael. It's not what you think."

"No, it's probably worse."

"Michael, I've done some things I'm ashamed of, things I thought I'd never do."

"I don't care," he insisted stubbornly. "We're a couple, aren't we? Stay with me, Nikita, and I'll dedicate everything within me to making you happy."

Nikita rapped his shoulder. "You're not listening. If you knew everything, you might not want to be with me."

"Don't worry about that part of my memory. It'll come back soon enough," he said roughly. "Of all the things I've forgotten, I don't want to remember hurting you."

"You've done nothing to hurt me."

"Haven't I?" He fluffed her hair. "Sometimes when you think I'm not looking, you look sad. It's almost as if you're waiting for me to lower the boom. Nikita, trust me, you can relax. Everything is going to work out fine. If we can get through this, we can survive anything." With his fingers curving around her face, he leaned close and kissed her lips.

Almost faint with relief, Nikita traced his lips with a finger. "Are you sure?"

"I'm sure." He hooked an arm around her shoulders and pulled her close. "There is something I need to know."

Nikita swiveled her head to look at him. "What's

that?"

"Have you been carrying on with that guy?"

"Tyson? No!" She brushed her fingers along his jaw, surprised that he'd fallen for Tyson's game, surprised that he cared. "How can you ask me that? He likes me, but believe me, you have nothing to worry about. You are the only man I've ever really loved."

"That's good," he said, his eyes darkening to a royal blue. "Because I don't believe in sharing, and what's mine, I keep." His mouth swooped down and captured Nikita's in a wild kiss that left her tingling clear down to her toes and wishing for more. Weakly, she leaned against him on the bed while his hands reverently traced the soft curves and valleys of her body.

She burrowed her hands beneath his pajama top to caress the warm satiny skin on his chest and tangle her fingers in the fine sprinkling of hair there.

"I want you, Nikita," he whispered, close to her ear. "I'm burning for you." Lifting her completely into the bed, and easing her back against the pillows, Michael covered her body with his. He drew down the top of her dress, freeing the soft globes of her breasts. Nikita gasped as he dragged his open mouth across the sensitive skin, pausing to suck gently on the tender brown berry nipples. Through her thin tank dress and the material of his pajama bottoms, the hardness of his erection burned against her inner thighs.

A brisk knock sounded and the door swung open. Nikita and Michael froze. "Excuse me. Sorry to interrupt," the nurse said pleasantly. "I know you're going back to your cabin tomorrow, Mr. Matheson, but I need to take your vital signs for the charts."

He shielded Nikita with his back while she fixed her clothing. Then with a look of apology, Michael rolled off Nikita and covered himself with the sheet. Too embarrassed to look at the nurse, Nikita took the hand he offered and got down from the bed on shaky legs. She'd never done anything this bold and daring. Her heart thumped madly, her body still throbbing from Michael's caresses.

Nikita trembled at the hot smoldering looks Michael threw her while the nurse took his vital signs and carefully wrote them down. She felt almost naked. The tension in the air was so thick she could have touched it. She was in for the loving of her life with Michael.

"Another fifteen minutes, and you'll have to leave," the nurse told Nikita on her way out. "Visiting hours are over."

The minute the door closed behind her, Nikita nestled back into Michael's arms. Sighing heavily, he caressed the length of her back, his hands drifting down to knead the fullness of her hips. "Wish I could go with you."

Nikita locked her arms around his neck. "Me too."

Gently, he bit her lip, then his tongue darted into her mouth to dance with hers. "Mrs. Matheson, we have a date for tomorrow that's going to last all day long."

"And maybe into the day after that?" She sighed.

"I can if you can," he said boldly.

Nikita let her gaze drift over the length of him. "You're on."

He caressed her face. "So get here bright and early tomorrow, 'cause they'll probably let me go after breakfast."

Filled with happiness and anticipation, she smiled. "I will." She'd almost begun to believe in this fantasy they were playing out. No matter what happened, she would always remember this time she'd had to be Michael's wife.

After Nikita left, Michael got up and prowled the halls of the ship's hospital. He'd taken another look at the pictures and remembered nothing. He kept telling himself that it had only been a couple of days, but it did nothing to calm his restless spirit. The feeling that he had things to do, things that couldn't wait for him to regain his memory at a leisurely pace, overwhelmed him.

After leaving Michael, Nikita restlessly prowled the decks from one end to another, knowing that she wouldn't be able to sleep. She didn't see Tyson again and she was glad. For a while, she sat in the piano bar that Michael had discovered and drank juice while a little old man played melancholy songs. Later, in the casino, she ran into Carol Powers at one of the quarter machines. Larry was at the blackjack table.

"You look kind of worried," Carol said with a sympathetic look. "Everything okay?"

"Michael's in the hospital." Nikita fitted a five-dollar bill into the machine and watched the counter go up.

"No!" Carol whipped around to face her. "What happened? Is he going to be okay?"

Nikita explained and found Carol staring at her hand. Those damned rings again!

"I hope he gets back to himself soon," Carol said in a sympathetic tone. "It's a shame that this had to happen in the middle of a cruise. Try not to worry so much." She focused on Nikita's rings once more. "Hey, nice rings! Did you guys get married? I thought I detected a little bit of something between the two of you." Carol smiled.

Biting her bottom lip, Nikita pressed the spin

button on her machine. She couldn't bring herself to repeat the lie. "No, we didn't get married, but I told the doctor we were on our honeymoon so that they would let me stay with Michael when he was unconscious. And now—now... "

"Michael thinks you guys really are married," Carol said shrewdly.

Nikita nodded uncomfortably. "He's going to be furious when he finds out."

"If it were me, I think I'd just tell him before he remembers," Carol said gently.

Nikita blinked hard and stabbed the button repeatedly. "I can't. I've let this go on too long and he's really vulnerable right now."

"I see." Carol patted her shoulder. "You don't have to worry about me or Larry saying a word. And if there's anything we can do to help, let us know."

Chapter 10

Warm sunlight filtering into the cabin's window awakened Nikita early. Michael would be released from the hospital today. Smiling, she yawned and stretched in the king-sized bed. Closing her eyes and rubbing her cheek against the crisp cotton sheets, she imagined that Michael was with her. Yes. Yes. Today she would realize her dream of loving him in every sense of the word. It couldn't get much better than this.

Having him with her would be like being out in the sparkling sunshine all the time. Just thinking about it made her toes curl. Now she wouldn't need to spend so much time imagining herself with Michael, she reminded herself as she rolled out of bed and landed on the thick carpet.

Padding to the small bathroom, she turned on the shower and looked in the mirror. "He liked what he saw," she told her reflection with a grin. Despite his fascination with curvaceous and exciting women like

Chenelle, he'd had his hands in her short, dark hair and he'd had his hands all over her slim form. And what about those hot simmering looks he'd thrown her, and the provocative whispers of all the ways he planned to make love to her. Oh yes! With that thought, she stripped off the T-shirt and stepped into the warm shower spray.

She was going to enjoy her "husband," she decided as she soaped herself with a perfumed gel, and she would do all she could to help him regain his memory. But what happens when he remembers that he's not your husband? It's only a matter of time, a little voice whispered at the back of her mind.

Taking her bottom lip between her teeth, Nikita scrubbed her knees harder. If Michael remembered enough to know she wasn't really his wife, she'd just deal with it then. Having made her decision, she pushed the negative thought to the back of her mind. Today they would be a couple of newlyweds.

Waltzing out of the bathroom, Nikita donned the short white jumpsuit she'd worn on the plane. Then she took a comb and played with her ebony curls until satisfied with the effect. She applied a little makeup, and had just stuffed a fresh change of clothes into a duffel bag for Michael when a knock sounded on her door.

Nikita checked her watch. It was only seven-thirty in the morning. Who would be coming by at a time like this? When the knock sounded again, she walked to the door and peered through the peephole.

She should have known, she thought as she opened the door. "Hello, Tyson. What's up this morning?" she asked, taking in the blue muscle shirt that seemed to reveal more than it hid of the rippling golden skin of his chest and arms and his trim waist. His matching blue shorts virtually showcased his athletic legs and thighs. Yes, she acknowledged, he looked as if he'd stepped out of a magazine ad. If she weren't so much in love with Michael, she'd have been drooling about now.

"I was hoping you'd be up," he said, placing a hand on the doorframe. "Can I come in for a minute? I don't want to talk in the hall."

Nodding, Nikita stepped aside to let him pass, then closed the door. She should have known when he followed her to the hospital yesterday that he'd have something more to say to her. His glance darted quickly around the room, his eyes resting momentarily on the king-sized bed and then on to catch her staring at him.

"Like what you see?" he asked in a teasing tone.

"Is that why you came by?" she quipped smartly. "I'm sure the girls out there are drooling, but I've only got eyes for Michael these days."

Obviously, he didn't believe her, she thought as he grinned, one green eye winking at her. "Want to pound the deck with me this morning? I know you like to run everyday."

Nikita thought of telling him to go pound sand. "No. Michael's getting out the hospital today."

"No wonder you look good enough to eat. I tell you, Nikita, you're too good for him."

"Then I'm lucky he doesn't agree with you."

Tyson shifted his weight. "Doesn't he?" He grabbed her left hand and lifted it so that the gaudy wedding rings sparkled in the light. "I bet he figures it's a moot point because he thinks you guys are married."

A wave of apprehension coursed through her, eroding her self-confidence. Stiffening and tugging her hand loose, Nikita held her ground. "What's your point?"

Tyson lowered his voice and leaned forward. "How do you think he's going to feel when he finds out?"

Her stomach clenched. "This is not a conversation I want to have with you. Why don't you mind your own business?" Nikita hated the sound of the pleading note that had crept into her voice.

Ignoring her, Tyson pressed further. "Don't you understand? You are my business, Nikita. I don't want to see you hurt. Can't you see that you and I would be better suited?"

Nikita shook her head from side to side. "No. No.

I love Michael. I have for a long time."

"And I bet he's been totally oblivious of that fact," Tyson said, quickly sizing up her situation. "Why else would he tell everyone at dinner that the two of you were just friends?"

Hot blood rushed to her face and she wanted to sink through the floor. Briefly, she wondered, Are you desperate enough to keep this going? But what choice did she have? She loved Michael and there was no way she was going to abandon him now, even if it meant continuing with her lie. Licking her dry lips, Nikita answered, "I don't know. Why don't you ask him?"

"Maybe I will." Tyson stroked the tip of her chin with a finger. "I'll make sure you're around to hear the answer."

He was threatening her, she was certain. Her hands clenched into fists as she thought of telling him where to go. Then reason cleared her mind. There was a method in his madness. If Tyson couldn't have her love, then he'd see to it that he had her hate.

"Can we continue this later?" Turning away, Nikita stuffed the rest of the clothing she'd selected for Michael into the bag. "I've really got a lot to do."

"Sure, I don't want to hold you up. If you want, I could help you get Michael from the hospital down below."

The thought froze Nikita's blood. Lowering her lashes, she lifted them slowly to find him watching her intently. "No, I think I can manage."

"I wish you would give me a chance," he said softly.

"And I wish you would leave me alone," she tossed back.

"I'm going, I'm going," he said, deliberately misunderstanding her. He opened the door. "See you later, Nikita."

What will he do next? she wondered as the door slammed shut. Deciding not to waste precious time worrying about it, she pulled the short-sleeved shirt from the bag and held it up. Somehow, she thought Michael would look better in one of those muscle shirts. Striking her first choice, she pulled a muscle shirt from his drawer and stuffed it into the bag. It wouldn't hurt to see more of Michael's manly chest, she decided. Now she was ready to go.

When Nikita reached Michael's room, she found him sitting up in bed, hunching forward to watch "Looney Tunes." A wave of familiarity washed over her. How many times in the past had they stopped working a problem to do the exact same thing?

Closing the door, she strode across the room to place the bag on the floor and take a seat beside him on the bed. Without turning to look at Nikita, he hooked an arm around her shoulders and they watched the cartoon in companionable silence for several minutes. When Bugs Bunny delivered his signature line once more, she turned and greeted Michael.

"Hello sunshine." He pulled her close, opening his mouth to slide his tongue along hers in a kiss that sent shivers of desire coursing through her. She closed her eyes, savoring the moment. How she loved this man.

A thrill of excitement ran through her at the sight of his bare muscular chest and arms rising above the sheet. Despite a few healing bruises, he was still a visual treat for the eyes. She couldn't help wanting to see what lay below the casually draped material covering his lower body.

He grinned, enjoying her rapt attention. "I hope you brought some clothes because I'm ready to go."

"I've got your clothes." Placing a gentle kiss on his lips, Nikita picked up the bag and set it on his bed. Afterwards, she lay her cheek against his, enjoying the warmth and texture of his skin.

"They promised to have the discharge papers ready by the time I showered and dressed," he said.

"Good." She smoothed her fingers through the thick softness of his hair. "What do you want to do first?"

"Don't you know?" He threw her a hot glance, his finger tracing a heated path along the neckline of her jumpsuit. "I think we should do it on the bed first, then in the shower, and then on the floor. What do you say?" Nikita blushed, her mind filling with several vivid erotic pictures of the two of them. He chuckled. "A few days in bed with me and blushing will be a thing of the past."

She found herself trembling. "Is that a promise?"

"Oh yeah." His voice deepened. "I can hardly wait to resume the honeymoon." His mouth caught hers in another dizzying kiss. Then he cupped her chin gently, his chocolate brown eyes simmering. "Guess I should go on and take the shower."

"I guess you should."

Flinging back the sheets, he leapt from the bed in a sudden flurry of activity. "I like the view," Nikita called at the sight of his well-shaped buns clad in black briefs, not to mention his strong, beautifully proportioned legs and thighs. "Mmmmm."

Turning his head, he grinned and winked at her, then disappeared into the bathroom. Smiling, Nikita stood and began collecting his belongings. She paused to glance at the pictures of his parents, wondering how they'd feel if she actually married Michael. They hadn't cared for Chenelle, but they had always seemed to like her. Would they feel differently if he loved her? Slipping the photos into a side pocket, she hoped she got the chance to find out.

She had everything in the bag when the bathroom door opened and he walked out looking fresh and handsome in his muscle shirt and khaki trousers. His freshly washed hair was still damp. "You look good."

"Thanks. And thanks for packing my stuff." He walked over to Nikita, kissed her cheek, took the bag, and slipped an arm around her waist. "Let's just stop by the desk and get the papers. I'm anxious to get out of here."

"Sure." Nikita walked out of the room with him.

At the front desk, they collected Michael's discharge papers then went out the double doors and up two flights of stairs to the Lido Deck.

The sight of endless blue sky, bright sunlight, and rippling waves of ocean held Michael enthralled on the way to their cabin. Breathing in the smell of the ocean, he paused to stand at the railing and stare. "It's all so beautiful."

"And peaceful," Nikita added, a dreamy look in her big gray eyes.

"How many days do we have left?" he asked, watching her black curls dance in the warm breeze.

"Five."

He smoothed her soft cheek. "Don't look sad. We can always take another cruise."

"You're right," she murmured, dropping down into a chair.

"No, Nikita. Don't sit down. Let's go to the cabin

first."

"Won't you feel a little claustrophobic after being cooped up in sick bay for days?"

"No, not if I'm with you." Taking her hand, he pulled her up from the deck chair and into his arms. "Besides, I thought we had some unfinished business," he whispered close to her ear.

She leaned into him for a moment so that he felt the full length of her slight but soft frame. Her gray eyes sparkled wickedly. "I didn't forget," she murmured, wetting her lips.

Michael took her hand and turned her around. "Okay, that's it. We'll go right now." Together they climbed two sets of stairs and walked a long corridor. Nikita stopped at a door near the end and Michael opened the door to their cabin. Briefly, he took in the image of the king-sized bed covered with a floral spread, the table cluttered with both their things, and the single suitcase visible from the open closet. Bright sunlight from the large window filled the room, spilling over the small sitting area and the bed.

He heard the soft catch of her breath when he bent to lift her slight form and then carry her over the threshold into the sunlit room. "Mrs. Matheson." As the door closed, he feathered a kiss across the soft fullness of her lips and let her body trail along the length of his till her feet reached the floor.

"I—I love you, Michael." Emotion gripped her voice.

Her words filled him with a warm, aching feeling. Despite the loss of his memory, he knew that being loved by Nikita was a rare and precious thing. The tears shimmering in her eyes tugged at his heart. He wanted to answer with loving words of his own, but something held him back. He didn't know if he loved her, wasn't even sure such a thing really existed. He did know that he did not want to hurt her, because he cared a lot.

"Nikita, you mean so much to me," he groaned, knowing his words were inadequate. "I can't imagine a future without you." He bent and kissed each dewy eyelid, whispering nonsense. He didn't consciously know what he said, but she trembled and lifted her hands to delve deep into his hair and pull his head down to fuse their lips in a passionate kiss. He ached to take her, right then and there. His hands found her perfect breasts, kneading the soft globes until Nikita's head fell back and his mouth followed the warm scented path down the side of her neck to the valley between her breasts. He slid down the zipper on her jumpsuit, easing it over the silky skin of her shoulders until it dropped at her feet. His breath caught. Oh yeah. Nikita stood there, his fantasy in a tiny black lace bra and a miniscule pair of black lace panties. This was his wife. The ache in his gut deepened.

Swallowing hard, he unsnapped the clasp on her bra and looked his fill. He massaged the warm mounds, enjoying the sound of Nikita's soft sighs and the electrifying contact with her skin. "Oh lady, you are perfect. I've got everything I want, right here." Bending down, he sucked hard on each swollen, brown nipple. Blood raced through his veins. When Nikita swayed on her feet, he lifted her again and carried her to the sunlit bed. She pulled back the sheets and he followed her down, rolling with her on the cool crisp sheets.

"I want to feel you." Nikita lifted the bottom of his shirt and pulled it over his head. He lay back and let her flick her tongue across his nipples while her hands worked at his fly. She slipped her hands in the opening and then smoothed the pants over his hips and down his legs. His heart hammered his chest like an engine running full bore. Oh yeah. I've died and gone to heaven.

"I always thought you had a nice butt," she whispered, grabbing his rear to pull him closer to the sumptuous heat of her body. He grinned at the compliment and covered her sassy mouth with his, hungrily devouring its softness. Sliding his hands along the tanned silk of her thighs and the swell of her hips, he hooked his fingers in the black lace and slid her panties down her legs and over her dainty feet. He wanted her so badly his hands shook.

"Michael!" she urged hoarsely when he cupped her heat, dipping his fingers into the warm, slick moisture. The heady aroma went to his head. Oooh yeah. He gently spread Nikita's legs and bent down to give her an intimate kiss, savoring the taste of her on his tongue. Mmmm. Her fingers caught in his hair while she writhed against him, alternately pushing and pulling until her body tensed and she cried out in release.

"Michael..." Her eyes were glazed with passion. He fell into the open welcome of her arms, touching, feeling, kissing... Her hands gripped him, massaging and stroking until he threatened to burst. Oh yeah.

"Now Michael. I can't take much more...," Nikita cried. She lifted her legs and he settled in the warm cradle of her thighs, pushing into her tight, moist heat. With a sharp cry, she gripped him as he thrust himself home with long, deep strokes that left them both gasping. Holding the firm pillow of her bottom he rocked, increasing his speed. Hot, unadulterated pleasure rushed to his senses.

Yeah! Yeah! Yeah! Nikita's sexy little moans and the wild, uninhibited way she thrust back urged him on, until they both exploded in a gripping avalanche of fiery sensation. Light-headed, he floated down to the bed. Still shaking from the sheer intensity of their lovemaking, he held his wife close, his fingers stroking the damp curve of her back.

Nikita awakened in the dark feeling more relaxed and content than she could ever remember. Michael lay draped over her like a blanket, his naked chest against her back, and one arm hooked about her waist. She heard the slight, even sounds of his breathing as he slept.

She nestled back against him, enjoying the heat of his body and the way it contrasted with the coolness of their room. She was living her dream. He'd hadn't said he loved her, but he'd done everything else. For Michael, that amounted to a lot. It amazed her that despite getting nowhere with years of planning, she'd fallen into this honeymoon trip and made her wildest dreams come true.

In the darkness she turned to face him, the tips of her breasts burning against his chest. With a finger she traced his features, glorying in her counterfeit right to touch him at will. Whispering her name, he stirred a little, his hand lowering to caress the curve of her hips and then moving up to gently knead her breast. When she pressed her lips to his, she realized that he'd fallen back asleep.

Nikita sighed. Poor Michael was apparently

worn out. They'd made love three times and each time had gotten pretty intense. Her stomach rumbled and she checked the clock across the room. Nine o'clock. Too late for dinner. Slipping from the warm bed, she decided to shower and then search for something to eat.

Closing the bathroom door as quietly as she could, Nikita ran the shower while assembling her toiletries. She'd just stepped into the shower and closed the curtain when it opened again.

Michael stood in the opening in all his glory. She swallowed hard at the sight, need burgeoning up within her again.

"I missed you." The sexy rasp of his voice and the memory of all the things they'd done in bed made her tremble. He climbed into the small stall with her, closing the curtain again. "Now I know why I couldn't sleep in the hospital down below. I'm used to sleeping with you in my arms."

His words filled her heart, but an attack of conscience stole her pleasure, especially since she knew that he'd never intimately slept with her before. She stepped into his embrace and the warm velvet of his kiss. Her head fell back as he explored the recesses of her mouth with his tongue.

Then she soaped her bath mitten with jasmine-scented gel and proceeded to wash his magnificent body. If it all ends badly, I have enough memories to last a lifetime, she found herself thinking as she soaped the padded curves of his chest, his muscular arms and strong legs.

Eyes closed, he groaned as she washed the firm curve of his buttocks and at last the hardened length of his arousal. Lovingly, she rinsed him off with the warm shower spray. Opening his eyes, Michael took the gel and mitten from her. "Your turn."

Nikita trembled all over at his gentle massage of her breasts with the bath mitt. He stared at them the whole time as though he'd never seen them before. Then he soaped her thighs and buttocks, lingering sensuously between her legs until she clung to him, gasping. Quickly rinsing the lather from her body, he switched off the shower and ripped open the curtain. "Enough of this teasing," he growled.

She reached for one of the thick white bath towels and he stopped her. "No, let me." Then he surprised her by sensuously licking and kissing the water droplets from virtually every inch of her body. Waves of pleasure raced through her. Nikita writhed beneath his passionate assault until she fell against him, no longer able to stand.

Chuckling, Michael lifted her and carried her back into the bedroom to deposit her on the bed.

"Michael," she cried weakly.

He stood between her legs, his hands gripping her thighs. "Yes," he answered, plunging deeply into her. Nikita gasped at the hot, hard thickness of him filling her so she thought she would burst. This time his rhythm was slow, steady, and relentless. Hot currents of sensations rippled through her. Pressing his open mouth to the sensitive skin on her neck and shoulder, he moved down to suckle her aching breasts. Crying out, Nikita strained with him in a growing storm of fevered passion. Together they hung on at the peak, shivering, shaking, and clutching one another until they sank back on the bed dazed and spent.

"Wow," Michael whispered, holding Nikita tightly to him. "You are incredible."

She buried her face in the warmth of his neck. "I didn't know it could be like this."

"Believe it." His fingers tangled in her hair. "It's only going to get better because you're just right for me."

Pressing her lips to the pulse at the side of his neck, she said, "Write that down, 'cause I want you to remember those words forever."

"I won't forget." He framed her face with his fingers and gently bussed her lips. "I may have lost my memories, but I haven't lost my feelings for you."

Wishing she could believe that, Nikita looked into his eyes, her lips forming an appropriate smile. She knew what was coming and her heart quivered at the thought. She'd probably lose Michael forever.

The sudden loud growling of his stomach startled them both. "I think we'd better get something to eat," Nikita said quickly. "There is a pizza parlor a few decks up."

"I've got a better idea." He got out of the bed to rummage in the middle drawer of the dresser. Finally he produced a black plastic folder that he brought back to bed with him. "Let's call room service."

Sitting up against the pillows, they pored over the menu. Tentatively, he selected an appetizer and a steak, checking with Nikita to make sure it was something he usually liked. For herself, she selected a seafood pita and ordered wine for both of them.

While they waited for their food, he stretched out crosswise on the bed. Nikita sat beside him, on her knees, rubbing the smooth expanse of his back and kneading the rope-like muscles of his shoulders. Closing his eyes, he spoke in a lazy tone. "Mmmm. I wasn't tense after all that time we spent making love, but this feels great. Can you cook too?"

Nikita found it hard not to laugh. Her cooking talents were so pitiful that they bordered on the negative. She'd always intended to learn how, but somehow she'd never found the time. She shifted her weight to her hips. "Not that well, but I make a mean salad, and I can't be beat when it comes to getting a carry out."

Michael's shoulders shook with laughter. "That's all right, because I can cook." His blue eyes widened in amazement. "That just slipped out! I hope its true. I can cook, can't I?"

Was he starting to remember already? The thought set her stomach to fluttering. She really hated lying about anything. Deep within she prayed, Dear God, please let me have him just a little longer. Michael repeated his question. Inclining her head, she raised her eyebrows. "You've never cooked anything I didn't like."

"Sounds like you're tiptoeing around the tulips." He rolled over onto his back and pinned her with a glance. "So I'm not a gourmet cook, huh?"

Nikita's head swiveled from side to side.

"But I'm at least okay at it." At her nod, he grinned and stretched leisurely. "I can live with that. Maybe we can take gourmet cooking lessons."

"If we can find the time." Bending at the waist, she eased her form down next to his.

"So besides making love, what do we do all the time?" There was a weird sort of challenge in his rough tone.

A heaviness rose in her chest. She should have anticipated this, but Michael's questions made her uneasy. She wanted this dream to continue, but even she wasn't sure how far she would go to maintain it. Shifting to her right side, Nikita faced him.

"We work, play cards, you bowl, play handball and basketball and sometimes you build computers for your friends. I run almost everyday, surf the Internet, help you with the computers..."

"Sounds like a nice life, but I don't recognize any of it." A tinge of worry colored his voice.

"You will." Taking in his expression, Nikita scooted closer. He was obviously worried sick.

"Sometimes I wonder, what will we do if my memory never comes back?"

"Continue living our lives and make the best of it." She brushed a thick lock of black hair away from his face, admiring the unique shape of his features. "I thought you said you weren't worried because it would come back soon enough."

"I did," he rasped. "But I was just putting up a good front and hoping for the best. You didn't really believe me, did you?"

She'd wanted to believe that he didn't care if his memory returned because he was happy with her. Nikita swallowed and rubbed her cheek against smooth skin above his razor stubble. "I wondered, but I had 'high hopes'..."

"The truth is that I'm scared as hell that I'll be like this for the rest of my life. Except for you, I'm alone in a world full of strangers and I bet you could write a book about the things I've forgotten about you.."

"You could always establish a new relationship with everyone. You're very good with people. You always were." She climbed on top of him, legs and arms on both sides of his body. His fingers traced the sloping curve of her back and hips. Cupping his head in her hands she whispered, "As for me, I will never leave you unless you decide you don't want me anymore, or you tell me to go."

He eyed her steadily for several moments, then pulled her close to brush her lips with his. "I can't even imagine that."

The knock at the door startled both of them. "I'll get it." Michael gently covered her up to her neck with the sheet and stepped into his khakis.

The pungent smell of sex permeated the room. More than a little embarrassed, Nikita turned her head, determined not to look at the waiter. She heard the clattering sounds of plates and silverware, and of Michael accepting the tray and placing it on the dresser. Her stomach growled as the pleasant aroma of food floated on the air. She was happy!

Chapter 11

Immersed in a warm pool of lapping water, she floated on her back, watching fat, fluffy white clouds drift across a dreamy blue sky... Sighing with pleasure, Nikita awakened to incredible silence and the sensual thrill of Michael, naked in her bed, one arm casually draping her waist, the hand extended to rest, palm down, on her breast. Could he have been the warm, lapping water in her dream?

She heard nothing but the soft sounds of his even breathing. They'd stayed in the cabin talking, playing, and making love for two days straight with only the occasional visit from room service. She'd lived one of her most passionate dreams. For the hundredth time in the past two days she wished the fantasy she was acting out could be real.

Her lips curved into a satisfied smile as she turned on her side. "Ooh!" The throbbing ache at her very core and the brush of the sheets against the tender tips of her breasts evidenced the fact that her body needed a break. Who would have believed it? She lifted her head to find Michael watching her indulgently.

"You're sore too?"

She nodded.

Michael chuckled. "I didn't count how many times, but we must have set some sort of record. We'll have to do something else, at least for a while."

Nikita touched his cheek. "I'm not complaining. We more than made up for any time lost by the accident."

"So what do you want to do today?"

She noticed the odd silence of the ship. There was no vibration, no movement, and no sound from the engines. "The ship's engines have stopped." She got out of bed and lifted a corner of the drapes to bright sunlight and a partial view of a busy dock. "We're in port. Let's go ashore."

"Where are we?" Michael sat up, pushing back the covers.

"I'm not sure. Let me check the daily newsletter." She found it on the floor by the door. Scanning it quickly, she sighed. "We missed getting off in Costa Rica, and we missed seeing the ship go through the Panama Canal, but we can go into Aruba today." She crossed the room to sit beside him on the bed.

"What's there to do in Aruba?" He snuggled closer to read over her shoulder.

Nikita read on. "There are some city tours, restaurant tours, watersports, and gambling." Then she continued with the details for all the tours.

"I vote for the watersports. Let's go snorkeling." His warm lips nuzzled her neck.

"I want to see some of the city too," Nikita said.

"Is there any reason why we can't do both?"

"If we leave soon, no. And I've heard you can get through a tour faster if you hire a Taxi and let the driver conduct your private tour."

Michael shrugged. "Let's just pick one of the ship's short tours and go snorkeling when we get back."

"Fine," Nikita scooted off the bed. "We should dress and get going."

Michael took her by the hand and led her to shower. "Let's save time and water," he said as he turned it on. "You're spoiling me. It's going to be hard to take a shower alone again." Pulling her into the stall, his mouth covered hers and his tongue danced wildly. Then he lathered the bath mitten and gently washed every inch of her tender skin.

I'm going to miss this, Nikita thought as she returned the favor, then rinsed him off. She'd always thought he was a very sensual guy, but she'd never imagined the full extent. They dried each other with the large, white bath sheets and dressed.

Sitting by the bed, he watched her pack for the

beach. "Nice suit." Michael fingered the net material of her tankini.

"I got it in Puerto Vallarta." She placed a couple of towels in the bag and went to the closet to scrounge around for Michael's beach shoes.

"There's not much in there that belongs to you," Michael said from his spot on the bed. "Nikita, we need to get you some clothes."

Retrieving the shoes, then standing to stuff a pair of sunglasses into her pocket, she murmured, "You know that my suitcase got lost somewhere between the airline and the ship. It'll turn up."

Michael shook his head. "I don't think so. This cruise is almost over. There are only four days left."

Not wanting him to buy her clothes, she shrugged and sighed, "All the more reason to just let it be."

"No," he insisted stubbornly as he extended a hand to her. "Let's compromise. We'll get you a few new things in Aruba or Ocho Rios."

Taking his hand, she dropped down beside him on the bed. "All right," she agreed reluctantly.

Outside the ship, they stood in a long line of passengers with their tickets and ran into Larry and Carol, who'd had the same idea. The couple sat in seats across from them on the air-conditioned bus.

"I heard you had an accident on deck," Larry said, "It looks like you've recovered."

Michael nodded and clasped Nikita's hand.

"Everything but my memory and a few healing scrapes and bruises."

"I can't even imagine forgetting Larry and all my family and friends," Carole's voice rang with sympathy. "I hope it's not too lonely."

"I haven't really been lonely. Nikita's been my rock," Michael replied, lifting her hand to his lips for a kiss. "I'm looking forward to remembering our past. I can't imagine a better wife. She's damned near perfect." He planted a kiss on her lips, oblivious to the fact that she was blushing beneath her natural coloring.

A heavy weight of guilt pressed in on Nikita, almost choking her. She knew she should tell Michael the truth right now, but she couldn't seem to find her voice. After a moment of stunned silence, she saw Larry's gaze dart to the gaudy rings on her finger in surprise, while Carol simply looked a little uncomfortable. A trickle of sweat ran down the side of Nikita's face.

"Hey, I'm glad you guys tied the knot!" Larry said enthusiastically, leaning across the aisle, "We thought you might get around to it."

"You did?" Michael threw Larry a puzzled look.

"Of course we did," Carol said carefully, "Whenever we're around you guys we can feel the attraction between the two of you."

Michael turned to Nikita, a question in his eyes.

"Is there something bothering you?" Nikita asked in a voice that only wavered slightly. *If he asks me, I'm going to tell him the truth.*

He stared at her. "I—I 'm not sure. I was thinking that something wasn't quite right and while I was trying to define it, I lost the thought. Isn't that crazy?"

"No, it isn't." Nikita placed her free hand on top of his and spoke from her heart. "If there's anything you want to know, anything—just ask me."

Michael shook his head, a frustrated expression on his face. "It's gone."

Nikita sagged in relief, but guilt made her add, "If you just…"

"Let's not worry about it now," Michael said with a wave of his hand. "Let's enjoy the tour."

Nikita nodded and they both started listening to the tour guide's running dialogue describing the various historical sights they passed. The bus took them to the historical museum of Aruba, which was inside an old Dutch fortress, and on to the Chapel of Alta Vista, the first chapel of Aruba. Then they went on to Mt. Arikok, which was near the center of the island and a natural preserve with some of the oldest Arawak Indian drawings and trails featuring some of Aruba's divi-divi and kwihi trees, rare and exotic cacti, aloe, and tropical birds, flowers, and iguanas.

By the time they got back to the ship, they were

too tired to go snorkeling. They watched a movie and relaxed in their cabin instead. In an effort to avoid Tyson as long as possible, Nikita ordered room service for dinner. Later that evening they went out and visited nearly every nightclub on the ship. It was very late when they crawled into bed together.

Nikita's head ached from the previous night's tequila binge. She barely remembered dancing till the nightclubs closed, returning to the cabin, and making love with Michael until the wee hours of the morning. Lord, that man had stamina and technique. He'd begun to exhibit a definite tenderness towards her that she hadn't noticed with his previous relationships.

Last night at the last club, he'd held her close while they did a slow dance and whispered, "Nikita, you're my star, you really are. Through all the problems I've had with the accident and my loss of memory, you have been the bright spot, my shining star. I feel so lucky. I just want you to know that I'm yours, for as long as you want me."

She sighed, knowing she'd treasure those words forever. Could he be falling in love with her? Her pulse sped up at the thought. Not likely. This from the man who did not believe in love? He'd still neglected to mention love. She discarded the thought.

Focusing on the window, she saw the first rays of morning light poking around the edges of the drapes. Massaging the sudden cramp in her leg, Nikita sat up on the side of the bed. She hadn't run in days. She couldn't put it off any longer. Slipping out of bed as quietly as possible, she got underwear, shorts, socks and a T-shirt from the chest of drawers and slipped into the bathroom to dress.

Minutes later, Nikita eased back into the room. Bending down by the bed, she searched for her running shoes.

"Nikita? Where are you going?" Michael sat up rubbing his eyes, his voice rough with sleep.

"I need to run. I thought I'd get it out of the way while you slept."

He yawned, stretching his arms to each side. "Want some company?"

She stared at him in surprise. "Sure. But you never ran with me before."

Getting out of the bed, he pulled on underwear and a pair of shorts. "I probably do a lot of things I never did before."

Nikita stepped into her running shoes. "That's true." The truth was that the thought of Michael running with her made her stomach quiver. What if he had another accident? And what if he remembered everything? She'd been expecting it, but did she have to help it along?

Michael pulled on a T-shirt. "I thought you said we were out running on deck when I had the accident?"

Nikita's heart fluttered. Holding the laces of her shoe she tied a double bow. Memories flooded her mind, and she felt the prick of tears behind her eyelids. She couldn't lie about this. "A-actually, we had a little spat and I left in a hurry. You chased me."

He came over to gently tilt her chin up. "What were we fighting about?"

"Our relationship." Her pulse sped up.

Nikita saw him set his jaw and close his eyes.

She covered his hand with her own. "I didn't mean for you to get hurt."

"It wasn't your fault, it was an accident."

"Do you want to talk about it now?" she offered, determined to tell all. Nervously, she rubbed her cold and clammy hands together. The moment seemed to stretch forever.

Michael shook his head. "No, because I really don't remember. I don't know what I was thinking and feeling at the time, and your telling me just wouldn't be the same."

Nikita released the breath she'd been holding. Her shoulders sagged with relief. "Should I go run alone?"

"No. I really do want to go with you, if you want

me, that is."

Standing, she leaned up to kiss his cheek. "I'll always want you, Michael. I love you." She ignored the uncomfortable expression on his face because she also knew why he'd never say those words to her. Michael didn't believe in love.

When Nikita reached the door, he was right behind her. Within minutes they were up on deck warming and stretching their muscles in the brisk morning air. The sun floated on the ocean like a great golden orange ball.

Jogging in place, she turned to Michael. "Ready?"

"Sure." He matched her pace as they started down the deck with a number of other runners and joggers.

As they finished the second lap, she felt her head clearing. Her muscles were warm now. So far, so good with Michael. Maybe she'd been worrying for nothing. Nikita increased her speed.

They were on the fifth lap when a familiar looking group of men approached. It took all she had not to stop in her tracks. The sweat she'd worked up turned cold against her skin. It was the group of guys Michael had collided with several days ago. Would he recognize them? Stomach fluttering, she halted and watched in dismay. Nikita bit her lip. How had she gotten herself into this mess?

The group stopped to surround Michael, patting him on the shoulder, and shaking his hand. "Hey man, you all right?" the short, thin one asked. "We are sorry for our part in your accident." The others spoke in a language Nikita couldn't recognize.

"I'm fine." Michael shook all their hands. "I just wish I could remember everything."

"You lose your memory, eh?" the man asked with concern. At Michael's nod, he said, "We will pray for you." Then they all nodded and continued their exercise.

That was just too easy, Nikita thought, her body chock full of adrenaline. Oh God, I can't live like this. Despite the warming air, she shivered. "They were coming the other way that day," she mumbled inanely, fighting a wave of acute guilt.

Michael didn't answer. He had a strange, wondering expression on his face. He took a step. Holding her breath, she saw him extend an arm as if to balance himself. Michael stumbled suddenly, fear flickering in his brown eyes as he blinked rapidly.

Her eyes widening, Nikita's voice was close to a sob. "Michael?" He looked as if he were going to be sick. "Are you feeling all right?"

"No," he gasped, swaying almost drunkenly. "I–I don't know what's going on, but I feel pretty weird.

Nikita stared in concern, her world narrowing down to Michael's struggle. Tendrils of fear crept down her spine. Running to his side and slipping an arm around his waist, she helped him balance himself. He looked a little green. She touched the cool moisture covering his forehead and her pulse sped up.

"This buzzing in my head is so strong I can barely see."

Nearly panicking, her gaze darted around the area frantically. About twenty feet to their left she saw a couple of empty deck chairs. "Come on, let's go sit down," she urged, nudging him towards the chairs. Again he stumbled, and they both nearly fell.

"Senora, do you need assistance?" A burly crewman stood nearby.

"Yes," Nikita said gratefully. "Please help me get him to the hospital."

"No. No, I don't want to," Michael protested. "It's a prison down there. I can lie down in the cabin."

Torn, she hesitated, not sure what to do, while the crewman slung Michael's arm over his shoulder, taking on most of his weight.

"Which way to your cabin?" he asked, "The doctor can see him there."

By the time they got Michael back to the cabin and in the bed, Nikita was a nervous wreck. When she made an anxious call to the hospital, his doctor came almost immediately.

After a thorough examination he told Nikita that

Michael was having an 'incident' resulting from the accident, his concussion, and the loss of memory. Advising that he rest, he told Nikita to call the hospital if things got worse.

Here I go again. Michael, please be okay. For hours, Nikita sat by the bed, holding his hand while he slept. He looked like an innocent, lying there with his ebony hair rumpled and his face alternately troubled, then relaxed with sleep. From time to time he awakened, calling her name. With all her heart, she lovingly reassured him.

Her stomach burned. Nikita realized that she hadn't eaten, but how could she with Michael in such bad shape? The thought of food made her nauseous. Skipping a few meals wouldn't kill her.

As the day wore on, weariness overtook her. The bed looked inviting. She was thinking of climbing onto it with him when he stirred and mumbled.

"Michael?"

When his eyes opened, she saw that they were clear.

Smiling, Nikita leaned closer. "You're feeling better."

"Yes." His voice seemed hoarse, his eyes narrowed. He turned onto his side, so that his hand shifted from hers. Nikita saw anger burning in his eyes.

Her stomach roiled with uneasiness. She stared, her heart in her mouth. "Are you angry with me?"

"Yes." This time Nikita recoiled from the harshness in his tone. "You lied."

"I—I'm not sure what you mean," she stammered, afraid that she did. Her dream was crumbling before her eyes.

"I think you do." His eyes speared her with a look. "Nikita, I remember everything now, the accident, the hospital, and this charade you've been playing for the past few days." Anger and disgust filled his voice.

She stood, her heart threatening to burst from her chest. The moment of truth had come at last. Guilt and shame filled her as one cold-fisted hand went to her chest. "I—I didn't plan it. It j—just happened. I always meant to tell you, but it never seemed to be the right time."

"I never thought you'd do something like this." He scrambled to sit up on the bed. "You didn't even call my parents."

"You didn't want me to. Besides, I didn't want to worry them. Until you woke up, the doctor really couldn't say what your condition was. Then you seemed okay except for the memory loss. I did look out for you."

"I thought we were friends. Best friends. I trusted you. Now I don't know what to do."

Despite the choked anger in his voice, she also heard his hurt and pain. Nikita's hands flew to her mouth, hot tears slipping down her cheeks. The wedding rings flashed in the late afternoon sun. She hurriedly slipped them off, offering them to him.

Michael shook his head, his expression filled with disgust. "If they hadn't cost so much, I'd throw them in the trash," he muttered, his fury a palpable thing.

As if they were hot, Nikita dropped the rings on the chest of drawers. The urge to flee ate at her will, but she held her ground. In the past, she'd always run away from conflict. This time she would not because if she couldn't work this out with Michael now, she'd never get another chance.

Straightening her shoulders, Nikita swallowed against the tears clogging her throat. "I–I love you, Michael. I have for a long time," she said breathlessly. "Before I introduced you to Chenelle I thought…"

"Do you know what I see when I look at you now?" he snapped. "I see you and me and all the things we did in bed and in the shower. I can't forget that."

Those images played in her mind. Nikita's knees shook. Her voice quivered a little when she stood up to him. "Is that such a bad thing? You like sex."

Michael exploded with fury. "You've got that right. The difference between us is that I don't pretend it's love."

She flinched, blood pounding her temples. So he thought she'd pretended to love him.

"Yeah, I liked sex with you, Nikita, but I've never lacked a sexual partner when I wanted one. What I really needed was a friend and you just royally flunked the test!"

Humiliation consumed her. Michael's cruel words ate at her pride. He'd taken something they shared, something that still resonated deep within her heart, and made it seem cheap and ugly. The pain of his rejection rocked her. She understood his anger, but knowing she'd been wrong did nothing to lesson the pain. Nikita felt her heart breaking. He was the love of her life. She wanted to crawl under the bed and die.

Dropping her head, Nikita backed a step towards the door. A voice whispered deep in her mind about love and forgiveness. She lifted her chin to meet his furious glare. "I'm sorry. I didn't mean to hurt you."

"Nikita, I can't talk to you right now. If you think you're hurting, that's nothing compared to what I'm feeling. I really bought into your little charade." He shoved his hair back from his face. "Just go. Maybe we can talk later."

The buzzing in Nikita's ears nearly deafened her.

She felt physically and emotionally beaten and battered. This morning his behavior could only have been described as loving. Her relationship with Michael had changed so fast. What would she do now? Love wasn't something she could turn on and off at will. She knew she would love him forever.

Slowly, she turned and wearily made her way to the door. Opening it, she turned to face Michael once more.

"Just go," he said, turning away to stare out the window.

So she did.

Nikita spent the next couple of hours aimlessly wandering the various levels of the ship like one of the lost. When she could no longer put one foot in front of the other, she dropped into a lounge chair far back from the rail on one of the topmost decks. Sheltered by an outcropping, she stared at the rippling blue water, wishing she could just float away.

She simply ran out of tears, but Michael's words still burned her ears and made her heart ache. Yes, he'd liked the sex, but he had never lacked sexual partners. He'd really needed a friend, something she obviously wasn't. She'd given him the special gift of herself, and her precious love, and he'd simply used them and then tossed them back.

"What are you doing up here?"

Nikita lifted her head to find Tyson strolling towards her. She shook her head, hoping he would get the hint and go away.

He reached her side and stood assessing her with concern. "Hey, isn't it a bit cool to be sitting out here in your shorts and T-shirt?"

When she simply shrugged her shoulders, he peeled off his sweater and put it around her. She felt a little better. She hadn't noticed the change in temperature.

Dragging a chair near, he sat next to her. "You look like you've been through hell."

Nothing like a compliment to lift a girl's spirits. When she stared down at her fingers in her lap, he continued, "He found out, didn't he?"

"I don't want to talk about it," she croaked, her throat clogged with tears.

"So what are you going to do? Spend the night out here?"

"I don't know." Shivering, Nikita pulled the sweater closer to her body. Her thoughts had centered on Michael's anger and his apparent inability to talk to her rationally. Could she go back to the cabin? Did she want to? She'd had enough pain and humiliation to last for quite a while.

"You're welcome to my cabin if you like." When

she rolled her eyes at him, he added sheepishly, "Let's go down to Hotel Services Center and see if they've got a room for the rest of the cruise."

Recognizing the wisdom in his words, she followed him back inside and down to Hotel Services Center. To Nikita's amazement, the staff found her a very small single room on the same floor as the engine room and supplied her with toiletries. The solitary privacy of her room was worth hearing the constant hum of the engines.

Numb, but weary from the day's trials and tribulations, she stretched out alone on the narrow bed. It took some getting used to.

Despite the blanket on his bed, Michael felt cold. Restlessly turning over in his sleep, he extended an arm to touch the soft, warm body of his wife, and encountered nothing. That awakened him. He was in bed alone. "Nikita?"

Michael sat up in the early morning light. The couch in the little sitting area was also empty. Then he remembered that he didn't have a wife. Where was Nikita? As his anger and the evening temperature cooled yesterday, he'd gone out to look for her. He'd been worried because she'd just been wearing a T-shirt, shorts, and a pair of tennis shoes.

After several frustrating hours of wandering the various decks, restaurants, and clubs, he'd checked at the desk and been assured that she was safe and had made other arrangements. He cursed softly and punched his pillow. Nikita really wasn't his wife, so why did he still feel like the deserted husband?

He checked the clock on the table by the bed. The glowing dial showed seven-thirty. Grumbling, he lay back on the pillows, adjusted the sheets, and closed his eyes. It didn't take long to realize that despite the hour, he couldn't sleep. Disgusted with himself, he got out of bed and went into the bathroom.

Moving past Nikita's lipstick, toothbrush, and comb on the sink, he turned on the shower. In the caddy inside, he spotted the scented shower gel they'd been using. Before he really thought about it, he flipped the cap and let the provocative aroma fill his nostrils. Erotic images played in his head and clouded his mind. This fragrance on Nikita's silken skin had driven him wild.

Shaking his head, Michael closed the tube and tossed it on the counter. "She really did a number on you. You're hopeless," he told his reflection in the mirror. Grabbing the deodorant soap from the sink, he got back into the shower.

Later, as he climbed the steps to the deck where people jogged and ran in the morning, he wondered, Am I really looking for her? It didn't matter because she wasn't among the crowd of health enthusiasts. He walked the track four times and decided to try breakfast in the dining room.

The combined aromas of bacon, sausage, and corned beef hash assailed Michael as he strode into the restaurant, but left him strangely unaffected. When he arrived at their table in the sumptuous blue room, it was empty. The waiter took his order and quickly bustled off. Shortly thereafter, Tyson Ward and his mother arrived and put in their food orders.

Mrs. Ward set down her juice glass and turned to Michael. "Mr. Matheson, I heard about your accident. How are you feeling?"

"All right, I guess." Michael fiddled with his silverware. "Thanks for asking."

"I hear you've got your memory back," Tyson said.

Something in Tyson's tone rubbed Michael the wrong way. He quickly glanced up at the other man. "Oh?"

"Well, I saw Nikita on deck yesterday and it sort of came up." Tyson grinned challengingly.

A tide of jealousy knocked Michael for a loop. He felt his blood pressure rising. Had Nikita spent the night in Ward's cabin? Just thinking about it made him want to explode. Then reason won out and he decided that she would hardly need to go through Hotel Services to sleep in Ward's room. Taking a deep breath, he counted to ten and forced himself to speak calmly. "Where is Nikita?"

Ward fixed his gaze on a point somewhere behind Michael. "She's coming this way."

Michael swiveled his head till he saw her approaching in a new pearl gray dress that matched her eyes. You're still angry, he reminded himself. She lied to you. She betrayed your trust when she pretended to be your loving wife and made you like it. That stung most of all.

"Good morning." Her voice was soft and hesitant. Hope lit her eyes, animating her face as she paused near his chair for a fraction of a second.

"Morning." It didn't matter that she looked fresh and beautiful despite the puffy eyes and the faint circles her makeup failed to conceal, or that he really wanted to kiss her. He got a whiff of a new provocative scent on her skin when she sat down, and his jaw clenched.

She watched him, her hands folded almost primly on top of the menu. She was nervous. He narrowed his eyes and saw the hope in her eyes die like a candle in the wind. Her head dipped.

Nikita's hand shook a little as she picked up her glass and took a sip of water. Michael fought a battle within himself. He felt tense and agitated with the need to touch her, comfort her. He'd always liked her, but this was ridiculous. When she turned to give her order to the waiter, he stared down at his bowl, concentrating on his grapefruit.

Michael couldn't taste his food. He simply shoveled it in and chewed. In the background, he heard Ward and his mother laughing and talking with Nikita. The forced sound of her laughter spoke volumes. Studying her unobtrusively, he saw that instead of eating, she was nervously rearranging the food on her plate.

Suddenly she was pushing her chair back and standing up. "I—I guess I wasn't hungry after all." Nikita's lips curved into a smile that failed to reach her eyes. "See you all later." Briefly, darting a glance at Michael, she headed for the entrance at a brisk clip.

It took everything he had to remain in his seat.

Chapter 12

She'd run away again. After showing up in the dining room to face Michael, she'd withered in the face of his obvious anger and reverted to her old habit of running away. The realization hit her when she stopped to catch her breath at the rail on the Atlantic Deck. The pleasant breeze did nothing to ease her thoughts or alleviate the tingling of the sun against her skin. Panting, she lifted the damp hair off her neck and groaned. Would she ever learn?

She should have stayed and had it out with him instead of cowering in the face of his anger and outrage. Her love was a force to be reckoned with and infinitely worth fighting for. Why didn't she make him admit that his time with her had been special? He couldn't have faked the way he reacted to her, the way he made her feel. Deep inside she'd even begun to think that he might be a little in love with her. That dream would die hardest.

For most of the night she had tossed and turned,

unable to sleep with the nagging anguish dragging her into the depths of despair. When sleep finally came, persistent loneliness and the heavy ache in her heart awakened her again and again. Oh how she'd missed Michael's warmth beside her in the bed and his arms holding her in the night. And then she'd worried about him and the lingering effects of his accident. It hurt too much to think he simply didn't care for her.

Rhythmic, Caribbean music floated up from the deck below. Grabbing the rail with both hands, Nikita gazed down into the deep blue water, swaying slightly with the sensual rhythm of the steel drum band. It seemed that she'd been in love with Michael forever. Surely they could work through their relationship... Somehow, the lilting music filled her with hope. When the song ended, she was walking down the metal stairs, on her way back to Michael's cabin.

Before she could lose her nerve, Nikita rapped sharply on the door. When she heard the muffled sound of Michael's voice, she quickly opened the door and stood in the opening. Exuding a masculine appeal she couldn't ignore, he sat on the loveseat going through a bag of books. Waves of apprehension coursed through her.

"Nikita!" His brows lifted in surprise, a question glimmering in the depths of his eyes. He didn't seem angry, but he wasn't exactly welcoming either.

Her stomach churned with nervous energy and frustration. Nikita pushed herself past the crippling tenseness in her legs to step into the sunlit cabin. Closing the door, she leaned against it. "I—I think we need to talk."

"I agree." Michael scooted sideways, highlighting the space beside him on the loveseat.

She hesitated, not certain she could talk at all while sitting so close to him.

"Afraid I'll bite?" His lips twisted in annoyance.

"Just stop it," Nikita retorted, steeling herself inside. She knew that backing down right now would be the worst thing she could do. When he simply continued to look at her, she braced herself and dragged a chair from the desk to sit across from him. Despite the negativity emanating from him, the citrus scent of his aftershave teased her senses.

Swallowing, she blurted out, "This anger of yours is more than I can stand. I've never seen you so furious. I'm sorry I lied, and let you live the lie for the past few days. I regret it more than I can say, but I need to know why you're still so angry with me."

Michael's features hardened. He spoke vehemently. "You want to know why I'm so angry? You took advantage of me when I was vulnerable. When I realized it, I felt betrayed. I still do."

The validity of his claim hit her like a fist to her

stomach. Nikita slumped in her chair. She had taken advantage of him to cash in on her own dreams and there was no way to undo the deed. She burned with shame and regret. Deep in her heart, she'd never imagined that her seemingly harmless lie would affect him this way. She'd never really thought past being with Michael, loving him.

He pinned her with a glance full of hurt and anger. "You were so special to me. My special friend. I'd never been this close to anyone. I told you things I never told another living soul."

Guilt suffused her, battering her heart and mind until her body fairly vibrated with it. With her heart in her eyes, she reached out to take his hand in hers. "I–I guess I did take advantage, and I regret it more than anything. I'm sorry. I never meant to betray you or our friendship. What I did, I did because I wanted to experience everything with you."

Michael's eyes darkened as he retrieved his hand. She could almost see him hardening his heart against her. "Are you really sorry? Or just sorry you got caught?"

Nikita gasped, raw hurt and pain clawing at her insides. Tears burned the back of her eyelids, threatening to overflow. She knew she deserved that. "I'm sorry I lied and that it has hurt you and caused this rift between us."

"When were you going to tell me the truth?"

With the crook of her arm, she blotted the moisture from her eyes and let out a shaky sigh. "After my morning run. I was trying to get up the nerve."

His lips twisted with exasperation. "Give it up, Nikita."

"I can't." Nikita bit her lip, almost shivering despite the heat of his anger. "Michael, I truly value your friendship. It means more than you can imagine. I've always been there for you, respected your confidences, and kept your secrets."

"Well, I can't get past what you did," he snapped, one hand gripping the arm of the loveseat. "You made me into someone I'm not."

Pausing to gauge his expression, she noted the straight line of his mouth, and the inherent disgust in his expression. The futility of her dream threatened to overwhelm her. What could she do? "I'm sorry. I didn't mean to betray your trust. I think I just got tired of being on the outside looking in." Her voice broke a little, but she continued anyway. "Michael, I can apologize until the cows come home, but I can't take back something that's already happened. Isn't there something I could do to make it up to you?"

Several moments of tense silence met her request. "No. There's nothing you can do," he replied tersely, without a hint of compassion.

He doesn't love me. He never cared at all, Nikita

realized with hopeless clarity. She took in the obstinate expression on his face, the knowledge twisting and tearing at her heart. His lips tightened, his nostrils flared. Active anger sparked in his eyes.

Nikita choked back a sob and blinked rapidly to keep tears from falling. In the space of a few short days, she'd blown all her dreams. Her breath froze in her throat. This is the end. This is the end, a voice chanted in the back of her mind. In her heart she'd been afraid this day would come from the time she took her first step aboard the ship. On its own accord, her hand touched his for what was sure to be the last time as she spoke in a voice that sounded harsh and strained. "So, this is it? We can't make-up because you'll never forgive me?"

"I don't know. I can't say that."

Nikita rose slowly, her heart breaking. She tasted blood where she'd bitten through the skin of her lip. She's known that the moment of truth would be hard, but hadn't imagined this hard. The clog in her throat made her voice hoarse. "Then I'll just get my things and go."

As her hopes spiraled downward, her thoughts were a jumbled mess. She was leaving the cabin and Michael for good. It hurt to think that he probably relished the idea. He watched silently as she walked to the closet and withdrew the dresses he'd selected in the ship's boutique, only days ago. Carefully folding them, she placed them in a neat stack on the bed. Then she removed the shorts and T-shirts from the chest of drawers. "I actually thought you might...love me," she mumbled under her breath.

"I don't believe in love," he said in a voice that lacked conviction.

She paused in the act of adding her load to the stack on the bed to look at him. "I know that you've been saying that, but I don't know why."

"My mother killed herself for love." His voice broke and he continued, "I realized long ago that love is a fairy tale, and decided that I would not follow in her footsteps."

"Michael, your mother is alive and well. She was at the wedding. Don't you remember?"

He scowled. "I remember seeing my aunt at the wedding, not my mother." The harshness in his voice eased. "I've told you a lot about myself, but I —I've never told you I was adopted by my aunt," he said in a strangled tone she'd never heard before.

Nikita's mouth dropped open in surprise. She saw threads of loneliness and vulnerability in his determined expression and realized that his mother's choice had profoundly affected his life. The tangled emotions he spewed were coming from the very heart of the man. "No, you never told me."

"My mother killed herself when my father abandoned her. She was desperately in love with him, a married man. You see, her romantic love for him was stronger and more passionate than her love for her only child."

"Oh." Nikita's breath came out in a sympathetic sigh. She experienced a wave of compassion for the small child who had been abandoned by his mother and then grown into a man who did not know how to love. She was beginning to understand some of the reasons behind his tough stand against it. Crossing the room, Nikita went to him, her fingers kneading the knotted muscles of his shoulders. "I'm so sorry, Michael. I wish she'd been there for you."

Michael shook his head matter of factly, but his voice was still harsh. "Don't be. Mom was her sister and a lot more practical. She married the man her father chose and has lived happily ever after. I've had a good life."

Caressing his cheek, she saw through his bold declaration. Deep inside him lived a little boy who was afraid of being abandoned. She tried to phrase her words carefully. "Michael, it's obvious that you were emotionally scarred by the entire situation. Maybe that's why you don't believe you could love someone romantically, or that someone could feel that way about you..."

"Oh, I gave it a shot," he interrupted her defiantly. "A few times several years ago, in fact. Somehow, no matter how much I thought I loved each woman, or she seemed to love me, we could never make it work. Eventually, I reached the only conclusion I could. Love is a condition we talk ourselves into. We use love to justify and glamorize the things we do for companionship and sex."

Though Nikita mentally recoiled in reaction to his words, she restrained herself in consideration of all he'd just revealed. "No, Michael." Her fingers slipped from his shoulders and down to his arms in a caressing gesture. She spoke close to his ear. "You couldn't be further from the truth. Maybe those women didn't really love you. Maybe you didn't really love them. For what it's worth, I love you. I have for years, and until this cruise, we never made love."

"The thought never really crossed my mind. Maybe you should have left it that way," he put in nastily.

Wounded, Nikita snapped back. "Too late now." Striding back to the chest of drawers, she pulled open the underwear drawer. Just looking at the contents made her flush with embarrassment as her mind flooded with memories of the pleasurable and exciting ways they'd used to take them off. He was a sensual man, the best lover she'd ever had. *Of course there's only been one other,* a voice whispered in the background of her thoughts. *And the two of you thought you were in love.*

With quick, agitated movements she began sorting through the pile of sexy underwear mixed with men's briefs. She slapped the jewel-toned satiny lace bras over her shoulder, aware that he was watching every movement. "I didn't exactly tie you down and force you to make love to me."

"The operative expression is 'have sex.'"

That hurt. He might as well have kicked her. A single tear rolled down one cheek and she quickly wiped it away. Suddenly Nikita's temper flared and burned hot and reckless. Grabbing one last handful of the matching silky, sexy briefs, she stalked back to the bed and tossed them on the pile. Glaring at Michael, she hissed, "I made a mistake. That doesn't give you the right to talk to me like this. I've admitted my mistake and apologized."

"Do you think that makes everything okay?"

Nikita stared at her love. He'd become someone she barely recognized. "I guess you're going to have to make do, because once I've packed all my things, I'm out of here." She pulled an empty sport bag from underneath the bed and began stuffing the clothes into it.

"Go ahead, run away again."

"I'm not running, you're forcing me out," Nikita cried in frustration. "You refuse to see reason. You won't let us get past this one mistake. You don't really want me." You don't really love me, she added in her thoughts.

"You pretended to be something you're not, something you had no claim to. And you took advantage of me. Do you know I actually felt guilty when I thought I'd hurt you by sleeping with Chenelle?"

"You did. It hurt like crazy. How do you think I felt? I was devastated. I never dreamed that the two of you would hit it off like that, or that I would have to see it up close." Another tear slipped down her cheek and she wiped it away angrily with the back of one hand.

"You made me think I had this virtuous wife, who was much more than I deserved, when I'm not even married."

Jerking the bag off the bed, Nikita huffed, "Well, now you can go back to that hard reality." Hopelessly, she took one last look around the cabin where she'd experienced the closest thing she'd ever have to a honeymoon. She'd gambled and lost. Her chest was so tight she could barely breathe. She forced the words past her aching throat, "Good-bye, Michael." A haze of pain and anger blinded her as she headed for the door as fast as she could. When the door slammed shut behind her, she waited outside for several moments, hoping he would call her back. He didn't.

She took her things back to her new room and cried until she had no tears left. Then she went to the ship's Cyber Café and surfed the Internet. Hours later, Tyson found her there.

"Niki, I'm worried about you," he said, taking a seat beside her.

"I'm fine," she assured him in a hoarse voice. She cleared her throat.

"This is me, Nikita. I was there with you last night and I was with you this morning in the dining room. I know that you love him more than anything and he's going out of his way to hurt you. Maybe it's time to move on."

"That's what I've been telling myself," she admitted, clicking the mouse on an icon. "Because I've done everything I can think of to make things right."

"If you loved me like that, I'd never let you go," he said earnestly.

"Can we talk about something else?" She put her face in her hands. "I've got a terrible headache."

Leaning close, he put an arm around her shoulders. "Not eating can do that to you. You didn't eat a thing this morning. Have you had anything since?"

When she shook her head, Tyson urged her up off the chair. "Let's get something out on deck."

On deck near the pool, a band played rumba music. Nikita sat and listened while Tyson stood in the buffet line. It was hard to be sad with the lively music playing. By the time he came back with a burger, fries, and salad, she was feeling a little better. With his urging, she managed to eat half.

Afterward, Tyson followed her to the sports deck to watch the sunset. For most of the time, they sat in companionable silence, but when it began to get dark, he turned to her and said, "I know that you probably think I'm a poor substitute, but I'd like to spend the rest of this cruise making you happy."

Nikita shook her head negatively. "It wouldn't be fair to you."

"Then let me stay close and be your friend, because I really do care about you." With an arm around her shoulder her pulled her close. "I know you're hurting right now, but it's going to get better."

"It has to," she agreed, briefly returning his hug, and then moving out of his embrace to stand. "I don't feel like talking right now. I think I'll go lie down."

"What about the show tonight?" Tyson asked as she turned to go, "We're supposed to be dancing with Maria Rosa and the class. That would cheer you up."

"I can't because I don't have a costume."

"I already spoke to her about it and she said she had something that would fit you."

A glimmer of excitement lit her eyes as she stopped and faced him. "Doesn't she care that I haven't been to class in about three days?"

"No, because you know the dance. You and I were some of her best students. Come on Niki, say you will. It'll be fun."

"All right, I will," she said, allowing Tyson to pull

her into the excitement.

That night, the Latin dance portion of the two shows was a big hit with the audiences. Maria Rosa and her class performed two dances for each show and for two hours that evening Nikita forgot about her problems while she lost herself in the dance. Later, as she lay in bed, she wondered if Michael had been at the performance and if he had seen her. Was he missing her the way she missed him? Still hurting, she doubted it. After all he'd said when she'd tried to apologize, she wouldn't try again.

Michael spent the evening walking the ship, hoping for a glimpse of Nikita, and not knowing what he'd do or say if he saw her. In anger he'd said things that she would never forget or forgive. No matter how many times he told himself he didn't care, he did. It didn't feel right to be angry with Niki and not be able to talk to her.

In the Big Show Lounge he spotted Nikita and Tyson laughing, twirling, and stepping among the crowd of Maria Rosa's Dancers. Jealousy slammed into him so strong, that he didn't realize he was standing until several people asked him to sit down. His chest burned and his stomach gurgled. Gripping the armrests, he stared at Nikita, certain that she hadn't meant anything she'd said.

He waited in the lounge after the show, for a chance to ease the anguish growing in the back of his mind. When she didn't appear, he searched the public rooms on the ship once more. After, he sat among the crowd in the piano bar with a glass of cognac, listening to the music. Although he talked with some of the other people, and women still flirted with him, he couldn't rid himself of the feeling of being alone. When he realized that the song being played was "The Way You Look Tonight", one of Nikita's favorites, he returned to the cabin.

It was a long night. Michael watched movie after movie on the television in his room. The movie staff was obviously on Nikita's side, because the movies were all romances or romantic comedies where the couples were apart because the men were obviously wrong, or they needed to realize their love for the woman. He wasn't wrong for being angry with Niki and he wasn't in love with her. Michael switched the set off in disgust at about 3 am. Then he read a technical journal until he fell asleep.

The next morning, Nikita forced herself to eat breakfast in the dining room. It was all she could do to swallow oatmeal with apples and cinnamon and a side of fresh fruit. When Michael arrived, her radar went off the scale, but she pretended to ignore him. Her heart was pounding as she excused herself and got up to leave. Releasing her chair with a cold, clammy hand, she made the mistake of looking at Michael. He looked about as miserable as she felt in his rumpled tan shirt. The whites of his eyes were a dingy gray, and the laugh lines in his face looked more like grooves. Ignoring the expectancy in his eyes, she turned and walked out.

Sitting in the sun, two decks up, she congratulated herself. Maybe I can make this work. Maybe I won't have to quit my job. She closed her eyes and let the sun warm her skin. It's going to be all right. Then she opened her eyes and saw him standing there.

"Niki?" he said in a husky voice, "Can we talk in private?"

She shrugged. "Why bother? You said it all yesterday and I'm trying to move on."

"Please? I was mad, and that's what you heard more than anything. There are some things I need to say."

Inclining her head in reluctant agreement, she followed him down to the cabin on shaky legs. Once the door closed, he gathered her into his arms and held her tightly. "I'm sorry," he whispered. Within seconds, she abandoned her stiff posture and melted against him, returning his embrace.

Releasing her abruptly, he moved away, and then turned back towards her, shifting his feet. "I'm still mad at you, but I can't let you go like this. I missed you too much."

She scanned his face, trying to gauge his expression. Her pulse hammered like a carpenter's gone crazy. She saw a mixture of fear, regret and surprise that he'd actually risked rejection by blurting out his feelings, and a bone deep sincerity that couldn't be faked. "I missed you too," she admitted softly, dredging the words up from the depths of her soul and putting herself on the line. "I couldn't sleep and I worried all night long."

His eyes intense, his hands rested on her shoulders. "Don't go, Nikita."

"I don't want to." More than anything she wanted to stay here with him, but fresh hurt and fear held her back.

Moving closer, he stared into her eyes. "I didn't want to admit it, but I need you. I want you with me."

"I want to be with you," Nikita whispered, "But you were so busy pushing me away that I thought you didn't care."

"I care." Michael opened his arms. "I don't want to, I didn't plan to, but I do. Come here, Nikita. Stay with me, please?"

With a small cry, she went into the warm, welcome comfort of his arms to lay her face against his chest and lock her arms about his waist. For precious moments, he held her tightly, their hearts beating as one. Then his hands eased apart to stroke up and down her back. Nikita inhaled his unique scent and thought of burrowing beneath his clothes to stay forever. She felt loved and treasured, as if she'd finally arrived home from a long, difficult journey. They gently rocked from side to side.

"That was too close," he rasped, his voice rough with emotion. "I almost let you walk away for good." Michael framed her face in his hands. With exquisite care, he smoothed the moisture from her cheeks with his fingertips, his brown eyes looking deep into the depths of hers. "I'm sorry, baby," he whispered, as he covered her face with soft, breezy kisses. "You just sort of sneaked up on me and I didn't know how to act."

"I'm glad you didn't let me stay away." Nikita nuzzled her cheek against the smooth skin on the side of his face. "Are you still angry with me?"

"Yes. I'm furious." He held her so tightly that it almost hurt. Then he was touching her, as if he needed to feel that she was real. "But I'll get over it. Eventually."

Fascinated, she gazed up at him, trying to reassure herself that they'd actually weathered the storm. He smiled, and Nikita shivered at the strong emotion and need she saw shimmering in his eyes. Love filled her heart and mind, spilling out into her answering smile.

"Trust me." Michael's lips brushed Nikita's, and then his mouth covered hers in a gentle kiss. Carefully lifting her into his arms, he lay her back on the bed and followed her down. She felt his fingers on the buttons of her dress, and soon he was widening the opening and kissing every sensitive inch of flesh uncovered as he slid it from her body.

"I want you Nikita," he whispered as he kissed his way back up her body to feast on her breasts. "It seems like it's been years."

Her hands slipped beneath his shirt to caress his warm, smooth flesh and help him pull the garment over his head. "I want you too."

He came back to her, his mouth meeting hers in a hot, sensual exploration that left them both trembling. Then they made slow, passionate love to each other.

Much later Nikita gazed out the cabin window and saw the orange globe of the sun slowly sink into the rippling, blue ocean. Against her back, Michael's body covered her like a second skin, his hands extending over her breasts and stomach. Defying all odds, she was where she wanted to be, in Michael's bed, in his arms. Already he'd admitted to wanting her and needing her. Would she ever have his love? she wondered, her heart filling with hope.

As the warmth of his breath fanned her ear, she found herself wondering if he would marry her. Would he even think of it? After coming so close to losing him forever, she was too happy to push, plot, or plan for anything, but she wanted so much from Michael. Most of all she wanted his love.

He stirred, and his lips brushed her temple. "Nikita? You awake?" he whispered close to her ear.

"Yes." She turned to face him and their lips met in a passionate kiss. Then they simply lay on their sides and held each other. She was so content she could have purred as his hands gently massaged her back.

He tilted his head back to look at her, a shadowed expression in his eyes. "I've been thinking about the wedding and remembering everything that happened."

Nikita shifted on the bed, uncomfortable with her own memories of the wedding fiasco. "I know you had strong feelings for Chenelle. Does it still hurt?" she blurted out and then caught herself. "Sorry, of course it still hurts. It's only been ten or eleven days since it happened."

"Actually, it seems like it's been longer than that." He eyed her thoughtfully, one finger tracing the shape of her nose, then dropping to outline the curve of her lips. "It was like being drop-kicked in the middle of a slow dance, but now that I've had time to think about it, I see that everything happened for the best."

"You do?" she squeaked, then cleared her throat. She could barely believe his words.

"Sure. Chenelle's relationship with me was based in reality, but she obviously thought she was in love with Lance."

Nikita watched his hand smooth up and down her arm, her uneasiness growing. "Do you think I'm being unrealistic because I love you?"

Startled, he shook his head. "No. No. You're an incurable romantic." He kissed her lips, her chin, and her forehead.

The anxious butterflies in her stomach refused to go away.

Michael gave her a charming grin. "I'm no good at this. I've been trying to work up to saying that I think we should get married."

"You do?" Her eyes widened as she stared in surprise. "Pardon my limited vocabulary, but you never cease to amaze me."

He chuckled, but she saw a hint of vulnerability in his eyes. "Do you want me to get down on my knees and ask properly?"

It was something she wanted and needed. The

mere thought made her pulse race. "Would you?" she asked as the butterflies threatened to rush her throat.

"If that's what you want." Pulling back the covers, he treated her to a delicious view of firm, rounded buns that stood at attention, well-shaped masculine thighs, and his semi-erection.

She propped herself up on an elbow, smiling in anticipation, as he got out of bed and dropped to the floor.

Michael took her hand in his. "Nikita, will you marry me?"

Nikita's smile faded. She wanted pretty words, hearts, and flowers. What had she expected? She knew him very well, and thanks to their conversation earlier, she knew why she'd probably never hear a declaration of love. Trembling with excitement and the tiniest bit of disappointment, Nikita stared at him. So he wasn't proposing with flowery phrases or declarations of love. Why does he want to marry you? He's certainly not in love with you, a voice whispered in the back of her thoughts. Unable to dismiss the thought, she asked carefully, "Why do you want to marry me?"

"Because I want you and need you. You're more than I deserve." He pressed a warm kiss into her palm. "You're beautiful, intelligent, fascinating, and loving. I've never clicked better with anyone. All the time you pretended to be my wife, I knew I was the luckiest man imaginable. When I got my memory back and you left, I felt like the abandoned husband."

"You asked me to leave," Nikita protested, trying to jerk back her hand. Against her will, painful memories of the past couple of days replayed in her thoughts.

Michael held on persistently, refusing to let her pull away. "I was angry. And I seriously regret it. If you weren't with me now, I'd be miserable." He cupped her cheek with his free hand and whispered huskily, "You're not going to hold it against me are you?"

Nikita simply melted. Michael had that effect on her. To satisfy her ego, she pretended to consider his words for a few precious moments, then shook her head negatively. She loved this man. He was a good man, so handsome, so perfect, and hers for the taking. Bending forward, she combed her fingers through his hair, kissed his lips, and then deepened the kiss. "If you can forgive and forget, so can I."

They shared a smile. "Where's my ring?" she quipped mischievously.

"I thought of it, but I'm not stupid enough to propose to you with the rings I bought for Chenelle. Besides, you hate them. They're definitely not your style." He chuckled at her surprised expression. "Didn't think I knew, did you?"

"No." Nikita linked her fingers in his. "You get two gold stars for being observant. Now here's the kicker. What is my style?"

Lowering his sooty black lashes, he seemed to turn his thoughts inward. "A single stone. A solitaire. No, that's too plain." He glanced back at Nikita and smiled. "I see you with a marquise or princess cut diamond."

"How'd you guess?"

"They're beautiful and graceful, like you. I know you well. Remember? I still can't believe that I didn't know how you felt."

"Neither can I," she mumbled under her breath.

Michael's tone grew slightly more insistent. "We would be very happy together, Nikita. Say yes."

He's finally gotten around to proposing to you. A voice urged in the back of her mind, Hurry! Accept his offer before he changes his mind. Nikita wanted to, but something deep in her heart kept her from committing. "I–I can't imagine saying anything else. Just let me think about it for a while, enjoy the fact that you've finally asked." Extending her arms into a slow, languorous stretch, she eased down on her side.

Standing, he climbed back into bed to face her incredulously. "You're turning me down? After all we've been through?"

"No, no." Pulling him close, she hugged him

tightly. "I love you. I just need a little time."

He pushed back to look at her, the concern in his eyes growing. "I don't want to pressure you, but if it's something I've said or didn't say..."

"It isn't," she lied. They tumbled on the bed until she lay on top of him, breast to chest, hip to hip.

His fingers kneaded her neck, causing her to close her eyes with pleasure. "And if you think I'm on the rebound from getting dumped by Chenelle..."

This had occurred to her so she needed an extra bit of reassurance. Flexing her knees, she sat up on him and peered down at him. "Are you?"

"No. No way." His hands slid down to cup her hips.

Scanning his face, and seeing only sincere emotion, Nikita was satisfied.

"As a matter of fact next time I see her I'll thank her," Michael added as his hands smoothed up and down her thighs. His eyes sparked with desire.

Bending forward till the tips of her breasts met the warmth of his chest, she sighed, "So will I." Her lips met Michael's in a caressingly sensual kiss that expressed her love more eloquently than any words could.

He groaned, his hands sliding up to massage her breasts and roll the hardened tips between his fingers. "I can't get enough of you."

Waves of desire peaked within her to flow down

in a hot pool of moisture. She breathed his name, propping herself up with the shaky palms of her hands and undulating against his hot hard length.

His tongue swirled within her mouth, delving deep inside to incite and thrill. Nimble fingers glided across her naked back, over her hips and down her thighs to slide between and move in and out of the slick moisture there. "Nikita," he whispered.

Lifting her hips she impaled herself on the pulsing thickness of his erection. Michael thrust hard and deep and Nikita undulated and rolled with each counter thrust. Together they rocked frantically, settling into the deep, pounding rhythm ingrained deep within their hearts and souls.

Later, they showered, dressed, and then went to celebrate with a sumptuous dinner in the formal dining room. Afterward, they danced till the early morning hours in one of the ship's romantic clubs.

Chapter 13

Slipping out of bed in the predawn light, Nikita quietly gathered the clothing needed to run. As she tiptoed into the bathroom, she glanced back at Michael's sleeping form. Yes, she acknowledged, between the breaking-up and making-up, and all the loving in between, she could understand his exhaustion. She was simply too keyed up to stay in bed.

Although she'd made her decision, it weighed heavily on her, making her uneasy. After her run, she was going to accept his marriage proposal because when all was said and done, she loved him with all her heart. She couldn't stand the thought of not being with him, loving him.

In the bathroom, she dressed quietly. She caught sight of herself in the mirror and stared. Her eyes looked large and soulful, with a few red lines marring the whites. And her lips were only millimeters away from forming a pout. She looked as if she would break into tears any minute now. With a shock, she realized that she did feel like having a good cry.

"What's wrong with you?" she whispered to her reflection. "The man you love wants to marry you. You should be ecstatic."

And a little more than ten days ago he wanted to marry Chenelle, a dissonant voice echoed in the back of her mind. Does it really mean anything? Maybe you're little more than a convenience.

The thought burned her heart like acid because no matter what, her love for Michael was powerful, deep, and consuming.

On a shaky sigh, she switched off the light and left the bathroom. As she passed the bed on her way to the door, she saw Michael sleeping with his arms wrapped around her pillow. It tugged at her heart. You're going to say yes, she told herself. You're going to marry the man of your dreams.

Up on deck she warmed her muscles quickly, then ran six laps as if the hounds of hell were chasing her. Sweat trailed freely down her chest, arms, and legs, and tingled the sensitive skin on her face. Her heart thundered like a drummer gone mad. The muggy air made it hard to catch her breath.

For the next two laps she slowed her pace to get her heart rate down. That's when she realized that much of the moisture running down her cheeks was due to tears. This is reality, she told herself. Why can't you be happy with the way things are?

A voice from deep within her answered. Because Michael was right about you. You're waiting for true love. You still want pretty words, flowers, and romance.

And love. Most of all love, Nikita added mentally as she fell into a lounger to rest for a minute. She was too tired to run back to the cabin. Waiting for her body to return to normal, she sipped from her water bottle and closed her eyes.

Footsteps sounded as someone approached. When she opened her eyes she saw Tyson perched on the lounger next to her. "Did you have a good run?"

"Oh yeah." Feeling grungy, she ran a hand through her damp hair and shifted uncomfortably.

"I haven't seen you in the last day or so."

She threw him a frank expression. "Michael and I made up."

A tinge of regret flickered in his eyes. "I hope you know what you're doing."

She knew Tyson was interested in her, but she'd never encouraged him. Throwing him a sympathetic look she said, "I love Michael."

"I realize that." Tyson's eyes narrowed. "But does he love you?"

She recoiled a little in shock. He'd zeroed right in on her thoughts and fears. "It's really none of your business," Nikita snapped as she felt the heat rushing to her face.

"You have serious doubts, don't you?" he asked astutely.

Was it that obvious? she wondered. Unwilling to lie, Nikita shook her head and tried to formulate a response.

"Love, marriage, children, romance—you deserve it all, Nikita. Don't shortchange yourself."

"And how would she do that?" a new masculine voice interrupted. Obviously startled, Tyson fell silent.

Turning her head, Nikita caught sight of the newcomer. "Michael!" He'd dressed quickly, it seemed, in a slightly wrinkled white T-shirt, shorts and tennis shoes. "I wasn't expecting to see you any-time soon."

Carefully stepping between their deck chairs, he deliberately ignored Tyson and looked down at her intensely. "I missed you," he said, his stare covering her in a silent caress. "If you'd just awakened me, I'd have been glad to work out with you."

Out of the corner of her eye she saw Tyson bris-tling behind Michael's back. "You were exhausted. I didn't want to wake you," she mumbled, not sure she liked his newfound willingness to exercise with her.

"Did you have a good run?" His fingers touched the moisture on her cheeks and somehow she knew that he knew she'd been crying.

"Yeah." She wet her lips. "I was just trying to catch my breath before going back to the cabin for a shower." Standing, she wrapped her towel about her shoulders and patted her face with one end. "I should get out of these wet clothes."

Michael turned as if he would go with her quietly, then suddenly turned back to face Tyson. "I heard some of what you said to Nikita. Just what were you trying to imply?"

"I wasn't 'trying to imply' anything." Narrowing his eyes, Tyson rose from his lounger, ready to argue. "Nikita is a beautiful, intelligent, and caring person. She's a treasure and a romantic at heart. If she wants true love and romance, why should she settle for less?"

"And I suppose marrying me would be settling for less?" Michael took a threatening step towards Tyson.

"You said it, not me," Tyson smirked.

Michael glared at him, the pulse at his temple jumping. "I've had it with you interfering in my relationship with Nikita," he growled. "I'm going to knock that stupid smirk off your face!"

"Not up to the verbal battle, huh?" Tyson flexed his fingers and moved away from his chair. "Some people can win in either arena. If you think you're man enough to take me, give it your best shot."

Nikita stared at them in amazement. Had they

lost their minds? When both men raised their fists and Michael charged forward, Nikita stepped between them. "Michael, Tyson, please stop it."

She might as well have been speaking a foreign language. Both men ignored her.

"Maybe you should rethink this," Tyson snickered as they easily maneuvered around her. "When my fist connects with your face, you might lose your memory again and then where would that leave Nikita? She'd probably have to go through another bout of pretending to be your wife, you ungrateful bastard."

Nikita's temper reached a boiling point. She'd never been the sort of woman men fought over and she didn't want to start now. Besides, the thought of Michael getting another head injury bothered her, no matter who initiated it. There was always the chance that his luck would fail and he'd suffer permanent damage.

So angry that her body shook, Nikita put a hand on each man's chest and pushed those immobile walls of beefcake with all her might. They barely moved.

In an uncharacteristically loud and cutting voice she blasted them. "I've had about all I can take from the both of you. If you think I'm flattered by the threat of the two of you fighting over me, you're sadly mistaken. So you want to fight, do you? Why don't you go down to the gym and put on gloves? All I can say is that I'm not going to stand here and watch you two brawl on deck with me as the excuse. You'd better think again. I've got nothing further to say to either of you."

Giving each of them a look of disgust, she thrust past the gathering crowd of onlookers and headed for the cabin at a brisk pace. From the silence that followed her, she was certain that she'd effectively stopped the fight.

Nikita let herself into the newly cleaned cabin and made a beeline for the bathroom. Stripping off the wet clothes, she turned on the shower. For several moments she stared at the door in a quandary. Should she lock it? She wanted to. Finally she did.

As she opened the door to the shower she heard the knob on the bathroom door rattle and then the muffled sound of Michael's voice. "Nikita? Can I come in?"

"Not now. I'll be out in a minute," she answered. Stepping into the shower, she turned beneath the warm, needle-like spray. Steam filled the air. Wistful thoughts of Michael washing her body, then covering it with hot open mouthed kisses, made her want to rethink the decision to shower alone. Building lather with the perfumed gel, she reined in her thoughts. Yes, it was a lot more fun to shower with Michael, but right now she needed to clear her mind.

What was she going to do about Michael? Was she settling for less as Tyson suggested? Did it really matter? Of course it did. The idea of going ahead with her earlier decision and accepting his marriage proposal made her uneasy.

Stepping out of the shower, she dried herself and started her daily routine of applying moisturizer, lotion, deodorant, and brushing her teeth. To her dismay, she'd forgotten to bring her clothing into the bathroom. Annoyed with herself, she fastened a dry towel around her body. It wasn't as if he hadn't seen it all before. Besides, she told herself as she unlocked the door, she wasn't so hot for Michael that he could diffuse the current situation with sex.

He was lying on the bed, watching the bathroom door when she walked out. His eyes darkened in appreciation as she stepped across the room in her towel. "Hey," he called out in his raspy voice.

"Hey." Nikita sifted through the neat stack of clothing for underwear. You are not going to scurry back to the bathroom with your clothes like a scared little rabbit, she told herself.

"Still angry?" Michael asked. She heard him shifting on the bed as she found a delicate pair of red panties.

"Just annoyed," Nikita said. Defiantly, she dropped the towel and felt his heated stare caressing her naked flesh. As she stepped into the panties, their glances held and unwelcome excitement fluttered in the pit of her stomach. Michael will always excite you, the voice whispered in the back of her thoughts. Accept it. That does not mean you've got to jump into bed with him now.

She might as well have been doing a reverse strip tease. Unabashed desire smoldered in his eyes as he watched her pull the scrap of material up over her legs to settle on her hips. Her nipples hardened and her resolve along with them.

"I guess we were a little ridiculous." His voice warmed.

Nikita found the matching bra and put her arms into it. "You said it."

Michael sighed. "I'm sorry, okay?"

She nodded, clasping her bra and unfolding a bright red dress.

He continued in a rough voice, "That guy has been drooling all over you and waiting for me to mess up for most of this cruise. We've finally settled things between us and now he's trying to make you unhappy with your decision. It just makes me want to smash his face in." His voice softened in appeal. "Can you understand that?"

She nodded and pulled the dress over her head. "But you should understand that I don't care what he thinks. Neither should you. You and I are the only people who matter here." Thrusting her arms through the straps, she pulled the garment into place at her waist. As the hem fell to a couple of inches above her knees, she saw a flicker of disappointment in Michael's eyes. She knew he wanted to make love to her. Despite her need to feel that there was more than sex and friendship in their relationship, she wanted him too.

"Kiss and make-up?" he offered, extending his hand to her. "I'll try to ignore him."

She went to him then, climbing up on the bed and let him sweep her into a warm embrace. Desire and love bubbled within her. She saw a question in his eyes, before his mouth drifted down to hers in a deeply passionate kiss. Nikita melted. As she held on, her hands shaping the strong muscles of his arms and shoulders, she felt his fingers delve beneath the hem of her dress to firmly caress the length of her thighs.

Slipping her hands between them, she pushed against his chest. Gasping, Michael broke the kiss. "Not-not now," she managed in a low tone. "Let's do something else."

"All right." They both trembled as he simply held her, stroking her back. "You really get me going," he whispered close to her ear. "I want you, Nikita, all of you. If I don't watch it, I'll be spending all my time in you, on you, or trying to get to you. I know there's more to life than making love with me."

"Yes, there is." Nikita tilted her head up to kiss his jaw. "Let's enjoy this last day of the cruise."

Grinning sheepishly, Michael said, "There's a mechanical horse race starting up in about an hour. Do you want to go? Are you feeling lucky?"

"Yes, very." She smiled up at him. "We could get something quick to eat on deck first."

He cupped her cheek. "Now that you mention it, I am hungry."

"You might want to change clothes," she said, eyeing his wrinkled shirt and shorts.

He tried to smooth his wrinkled shirt with little success. "You've got a point." Scooting off the bed and heading for the closet he added, "Just give me a few minutes."

"Sounds like I've got time for a nap." Nikita sank back against the pillows.

"Yeah? You wish." Michael increased his speed, sorting through a stack of clothing and selecting a blue print shirt and pants. "Five minutes, tops." He called as he pulled his shirt over his head.

Shortly thereafter they left the cabin.

A late afternoon breeze caressed Nikita's skin as she sat in the shade on deck. Shifting in her chair, she realized that she would be glad to get back home to her computer and her job. It was hard to believe that she actually missed her demanding job.

Lifting her arms, she stretched lazily and then turned towards the sound of approaching footsteps. Michael strode towards her, looking handsome and well rested. He'd changed into a tan shirt and slacks. She wanted to run her hands through his freshly washed hair and smooth her hand across his clean-shaven jaw. "Looks like you had a good nap," she called as he neared.

"Yes, I did." He flopped down into the chair beside her. "I can't believe you weren't tired. Two straight hours of Reggae dancing is enough to do anyone in."

Nikita grinned. "I'm in a little better shape than you are."

"You think so, huh?" His expression turned skeptical. "I think you'll have to prove that one."

"I think I just did," she smirked.

"Maybe, maybe not." His facial expression turned deep and assessing. "I've got something for you."

"Really?" She sat up, excitement rising within her. "I like presents."

"And I like you. Very much." He took her hand in his. "I know it hasn't been that long since I've been myself and we've really been together, but I've known you for years. I've always had special feelings for you. They've just never affected me this way." To her surprise, he lifted her hand to his lips and kissed it.

Nikita shivered at the contact and looked straight into Michael's eyes, trembling all over. She knew where he was going with his declaration and she didn't know what she would say, because her love was deep enough to drown them both.

He spoke in a husky, halting tone. "I want you to know that I've never felt this way about anyone. You're the only one for me. I know it, and I was a fool to ever think otherwise. I look at you in the morning and it's like the sun's come up. I can't seem to sleep at night without seeing your face, holding you in my arms, and making love to you. I can give you forever, Nikita. I can get as close to what you need as an honest man can get. Will you please marry me?"

Michael's words warmed her through and through. Her eyes filled with tears of joy and sorrow. This was the closest to a declaration of love that she would ever get from him. With all her heart she wanted it to be enough, but it wasn't. She opened her mouth, but no words came out.

Michael pulled a small, black velvet box from his pocket and opened it. "I saw this in the ship's jewelry store and it had your name all over it." Resting on the velvet was a large, flashing marquise diamond mounted on a curving gold band. He gently slipped it on her finger.

The ring fit perfectly. Nikita stared down at its blinding beauty. It was exactly what she'd wanted.

Michael watched her intently. "Nikita? Say something."

A tear slipped down her cheek. "I can't," she croaked.

In exasperation he framed her face with his fingers. "Can't what? Can't say anything? Can't marry me?"

She bent and wrenched the ring from her finger, reluctantly placing it back in the box. "Can't marry you."

"Why not?" He stared at her as if he were trying to see into her brain, and somehow read her thoughts. "You love me."

"Yes." Nikita sniffed.

"And I'm yours. I've never felt this way before." He brushed the hair back from her face. "You've become an essential part of my life."

"It's not enough." Nikita covered his hands with hers. "I wish it were. You've been very honest with me about your feelings and your past and I-I appreciate it, but until now, I haven't really been honest with myself. Love is very important to me. I love you, Michael, but I need to be loved in return." She studied her love and hope and fear seized her heart; hope that he would declare his love, and a fearful certainty that he never would. She pressed the velvet box into his hands.

Michael glanced down at the box, up at Nikita, and back down at the box. His jaw tightened, hurt and pain creeping into his expression. "I've never lied to you, Nikita, and I'm not going to start. You've got all I have to give. "

"I know." Biting her lip, she looked out over the churning water, where the horizon met the dreamy sky. Was there any hope?

He touched her arm. "We've come a long way."

"Yes, we have." She swallowed against the awful dryness in her mouth. "And it wasn't easy."

His hand clasped hers and tightened. "Don't give up on me, Nikita. I don't want to lose you."

Bending towards him, Nikita caught her breath. "You can't lose me. We're friends, aren't we? I'll always love you."

Michael scanned her face, raw emotion roughening his voice. "Then what's the problem? Why can't you marry me?"

She stared at him, her body aching with sympathy. Despite her need to reach out to him, support him, she had to stand up for herself, she simply had to. "I don't want to settle for less. No matter how much I love you, I need to marry a man who loves me."

"So Tyson managed to get between us after all."

"This has nothing to do with Tyson. Long ago I

promised myself that I wouldn't marry until I found a man I loved, who loved me in return. I fit in nicely with your sex, compatibility, and companionship theory, but I can't see you adding love to the equation. From what you've told me about your past, I understand where you're coming from, but it's not enough. You don't love me."

Michael's brows furrowed. "How can you be so sure when I don't know myself?"

Something deep within her responded to his words, but Nikita hardened her heart against it. "You don't believe in it."

"But you've made me question that conviction. I've never felt this way about anyone else. Maybe I do love you."

"And maybe I've just won the lottery," Nikita put in.

A trace of sadness flickered in his blue eyes. He made a clicking sound with his teeth and said gently, "No sarcasm, not from you. I believe in us, Nikita. Don't walk away from me."

"You know how I feel. What do you want me to do?"

"Keep the ring." He smiled a little nervously as he lifted the top of the box. "You like it, don't you?"

The diamond flashed in the sunlight and reflected a rainbow of colors on her arm. Nikita stared at it lovingly. Michael had given her this ring in her dream, only then he'd also declared his love. "I simply love it," she said. With effort, she closed her eyes and turned away from it. "It's gorgeous, but I can't accept it."

Michael gently pressed the box into her hand, his expression serious. "Keep it for me. Keep it until you feel you can wear it, until you're certain you can marry me."

Nikita realized that he wasn't going to give up. Her stomach churned. She felt torn between what she wanted and what she needed. Swallowing, she asked, "And if that day never comes?"

Nuzzling her cheek and caressing her fingers, he answered. "Then you can give it back, and I'll deal with it, but I'm asking you to try. Will you?"

Michael stared at her with such longing that she trembled. How could she deny him a chance when her own heart cried out for him? Reaching past the negative voice at the back of her mind, she smiled, her heart full of hope and love. Then she gave the only answer she could. "Yes."

He chuckled in relief. Nikita's eyes misted over at the newfound promise of the future. It was as if a heavy load had been lifted from her shoulders. When she looked at Michael she had stars in her eyes.

Gently gathering Nikita in his arms, Michael tenderly kissed her lips. "You won't be sorry."

Later they went to the cabin to dress for the formal dinner party and concert in honor of the last night of the cruise. As Nikita combed the closet, trying to decide what to wear, Michael pulled a bundle of packages out of the life vest compartment.

"For me?" she exclaimed in excitement as he placed the white boxes in her arms.

"Yes." Michael's smile was warm and intimate. "I knew tonight would be special because it's the last night. I wanted you to have something to remember this time."

Her smile widened. She loved surprises. "What is it?"

"Open it," he said, taking a seat on the bed.

Nikita opened the largest box, peeled back the tissue, and gasped. Black satin spaghetti straps edged and tapered into silvery panels that crisscrossed at the chest. The dress nipped in at the waist to flow into a long black and silver patterned skirt that was cut a lot shorter in the front. "Oh Michael," she said, carefully lifting the black and silver creation from the box. "It's beautiful!"

"I thought it would look good on you," he murmured. "That silvery color will bring out your gray eyes."

Prancing over to the mirror, she held it to herself, turning from side to side. "I saw this dress in that little shop on Lido Deck two days ago. When I went back to get it, it was gone. How did you know I wanted it?"

"I've got ESP," Michael said smugly. "Now open the other packages."

Placing the dress on the loveseat, she sat down with the other packages. In one she found stockings and a sexy silver pair of panties. "Thank you. No bra?" she asked, throwing him a suggestive look.

Michael grinned. "You don't need one with that dress."

"Don't I?"

"Quit fishing for compliments and open the last box."

She placed the box top on the arm of the loveseat and dove into the mound of tissue paper. "Ooh!" she cried, pulling out a delicate pair of black and silver evening shoes and examining them in the light. In a flurry of activity she tried them on. "They fit." She whirled around.

He rolled his eyes. "Of course they do. I know your size."

She didn't miss the silent implication that he knew everything about her. Nikita went to him and gave him a special hug. Framing his handsome face in her hands, she kissed his mouth. "Thanks for being so thoughtful."

"You're welcome." He smoothed her hair and caressed her cheek. "Are you happy?"

"Oh yes." She leaned against him. "I'm glad we're together."

"Me too," he replied, holding her close for several minutes, his hands idly massaging up and down her arms. Nikita felt so relaxed and content that she nearly fell asleep.

Michael seemed more aware of the time. He pushed back and studied her intently. "Don't you think we should get ready?"

"Oh. I didn't know I was so tired." Nikita scooted off the bed and ran for the bathroom. She was already in the shower when he joined her.

"I'm going to miss this when we get back home," he said as he took the shower mitt and began scrubbing her back.

"Me too." She sighed, bracing herself against the wall for support and waiting for Michael's next comment. Was he going to ask her to move into his condo? She couldn't do that. Staying in his room on a cruise was one thing, but openly living with a man without being married to him was quite another. She hadn't been raised that way. And what would she tell her family? And his?

Under his silent urging, she turned so he could wash the front of her body.

"I guess we'll have to find a way to make things work," he said in a husky whisper as he swirled the mitt over her breasts and stomach. "Because there's no way we could just stay together. I wouldn't even ask."

"I'm glad." Nikita leaned forward and smacked him on the lips. "We'll work something out."

Once dressed for the evening, they went to the Captain's Farewell Party to dance, enjoy cocktails and appetizers, and have pictures taken. Later they went to dinner in the formal dining room.

Entering the room, they saw that champagne graced every table, courtesy of the cruise line. When they arrived at the table holding hands, Tyson and his mother were already ordering food. Tyson looked up from his menu to stare at Nikita and Michael for several moments. His glance darted from one to the other a number of times before his eyes dimmed with disappointment. Then he gave his food order to the waiter.

Nikita and Michael ordered lobster dinners with seafood chowder. As the waiter left with their orders, Tyson turned to Nikita. "I want to apologize for this morning," he began. "I guess I got a little carried away."

Nikita relaxed, glad that dinner would not be as tense as she'd imagined. "It's all right, Tyson. I'm glad it didn't go any further."

Tyson sipped his wine. "So I guess you guys have settled things between you?"

"Yes," Michael answered quickly, as his hand covered Nikita's. "Wouldn't you say so, Nikita?"

"Yes." She met Michael's gaze. "We're going to take each day as it comes. If things work out, we should be married before the year is out."

"We will be." Michael's hand tightened on hers.

Watching him, Nikita's heart filled with hope and love. Maybe this relationship could become everything she'd dreamed after all.

As Nikita and Michael exited customs the next day, they were both a little subdued. Thoughts of home and work intruded as their idyllic interlude ended.

The mystery passenger loomed up ahead of them in an outfit that didn't match any that Nikita had packed, for once. Still, Nikita wanted to say something to her. How much coincidence could there be? She walked faster, determined to catch her.

"Hey," Michael said, suddenly lifting his finger to point. "Can you believe that?"

Nikita turned her head to follow the direction of his finger. She chuckled at the sight of her missing suitcase awaiting her in a lonely corner of the luggage area. She hadn't needed it after all. As she watched the other woman disappear in the distance, she decided that you never could tell how much of life was a coincidence.

Michael reached it first and checked the tag, verifying that it was her bag. "So what's in here? What did I miss?"

Throwing him a provocative look, she answered, "I'll have to show you sometime."

Exiting the port, they boarded a bus for the airport. On the plane they sat in first class again, but they didn't talk much. Nikita's thoughts kept returning to her home life and reconciling Michael's possible role in it. Finally she fell asleep with her head on his shoulder. When she awakened, he was smiling at her and was holding her close.

At baggage claim in the airport, Michael took her bag pulled it alongside his. "I'm still getting used to the fact that I'm going home to my place and you're going home to yours.

Nikita couldn't ignore the unhappiness in his expression. "We can see each other. We will see each other," she said carefully. Then waited for him to ask again, why don't we just get married now?

Michael touched her hand. "We'll talk tonight after we get home and then we'll have dinner tomorrow, okay?"

"Okay." Her hand slid up his arm to pull him close for a quick hug. It was going to be all right.

"Michael, Nikita! How was the cruise?" Nikita's mother approached them. She was smiling but there was a tentative expression in her eyes.

"Mom, it was great!" Nikita hugged her mother

hard, glad to be home.

"I'm glad." Mrs. Daniels returned the hug and searched her daughter's face. "I missed you."

"It's good to be missed," Nikita said, then added, "And to tell you the truth, I was starting to get a little bit tired of being on a boat."

"We'll have to take a shorter cruise next time," Michael said.

"I guess so," Nikita answered, not sure if they would ever go on a cruise together again, but not about to voice her thoughts.

"How are you, Michael?" Mrs. Daniels asked sympathetically.

"I'm fine Mrs. Daniels." He kissed her cheek. "Nikita and the cruise did wonders for my disposition."

"Do you have a ride home?" Mrs. Daniels asked as they headed out of the baggage claim area.

He thanked her for asking. "I was planning to take the limousine."

"Don't be silly. You're riding with us," she ordered.

"Yes ma'am!" Michael moved closer to Nikita and followed them out of the automatic doors and across the street to the parking area.

Mrs. Daniels located the car and opened the trunk. "Honey, your dad asked me to tell you that he'll call you this evening. He wants to take you to dinner."

"That would be nice." Nikita helped Michael put her heavy suitcase and his Pullman in the trunk. "When did you see him?"

"Last night." Nikita's mother closed the truck and colored a little. "We ran into each other and decided to have dinner." She shot Nikita a warning glance, signaling that she did not want her daughter to make anything out of her dinner with her ex-husband.

"Is daddy still in town?" Nikita asked innocently.

"Yes, he is," her mother answered in an animated tone. "He took a promotion in the city and he's here to set up the office." She used her remote to open all the car doors at once.

"Where's he going to stay?" Nikita got in closed the door, and clipped on a seatbelt.

Mrs. Daniels shrugged. "I don't know, but you know he's always loved certain parts of the city."

"That's true," Nikita said happily.

At the red light, Mrs. Daniels turned to Michael and Nikita and said, "All right you two, I'm getting some strange vibes. Tell me you didn't do anything stupid like get married."

Michael's laugh seemed hollow. "We didn't get married, Mrs. Daniels, but I did ask Nikita to marry me. She turned me down."

Mrs. Daniels' head whipped around and she studied her daughter's face. Then she drove to Michael's place in silence.

Chapter 14

Bone tired from a long day at work, Nikita closed her front door and put her briefcase in a corner. In the weeks following the cruise, she and Michael had found it difficult to resume their career and home lives. Each was thrown into engrossing and time-consuming new projects at work that made long hours unavoidable. This made it hard to be together. If that wasn't enough, co-workers, friends and family members seemed to sense the change in her friendship with Michael and therefore put the relationship under a microscope.

Checking her watch, Nikita sighed. She was too old for this. It was nine o'clock, and still no Michael. Yes, she wanted and needed to see him, but she was exhausted. Helplessly, she stared longingly at the couch and finally sank down on the cushions. Just a few minutes' rest, that's all she needed. What could it hurt? Her eyes closed.

The people upstairs were working on that deck

again. The furious pounding rocked the room so hard that Nikita was certain that the front door would fall off its hinges. At the sound of Michael's voice, she turned towards the door. He was yelling, and he sounded angry and frustrated...

"Michael?" Disoriented, Nikita sat up on the couch. The pounding continued. She'd fallen asleep. Yawning, she stood and made her way to the door. "Just a minute."

When she opened the door, he stood leaning against the frame with a large white bag in his arms, looking tired and more than a little angry. Her heart beat faster just from looking at him.

His hair stood out from where he'd thrust his fingers through it in frustration, and his normally crisp white shirt looked rumpled. He'd taken off his tie. "I've been pounding on your door and shouting for at least ten minutes."

"I'm sorry, I guess I fell asleep. Come on in." Nikita grabbed his free hand and pulled him into the front hall. "You don't look too lively yourself," she muttered softly as she shut the door.

"I know. Working those two new projects is taking all my free time." Placing the bag on the hall table, he took Nikita in his arms. Then his mouth came down on hers in a deeply sensuous kiss that had her clinging to his shoulders.

Afterwards, she faced the passion in his eyes

with a slow smile. "Apparently, working two projects gets you all worked up."

"You get me all worked up." He said, cupping her face with one hand. "I've been thinking about you all day." When Nikita blushed with pleasure, he fingered a curl and murmured, "You're beautiful, you know that?"

Leaning forward, she kissed his lips and said honestly, "Never so much as when I hear you say it."

His hands smoothed down her back to cup her hips. "Then I'm going to have to say it every day."

Extending her arms, she locked them around his neck, pressing her breasts against his chest and immersing herself in the sensual excitement of holding Michael in her arms. "Mmmm, you feel good. It's been too long."

He traced her lips with a finger. "Three days and two hours to be exact."

Nikita grabbed the front of his shirt and started pulling him towards the bedroom. "I was thinking that we'd eat first, but it sounds like you need some sexual healing right away."

Michael stopped short, throwing her a penetrating glance. "You know I didn't just run over here to get laid. I really missed seeing you, hearing your voice, having you tease me, touch me..."

Nikita took in his words, and examined them in her thoughts. Sex was really important to Michael, so they spent a lot of their time making love. She enjoyed being with him, no matter what they did, but she also wanted him to be happy and satisfied. With the tips of her fingers, she massaged a bare patch of his skin through the opening of his shirt. "Are you turning me down?"

"Me? Never." He sighed. "I'm just trying to tell you that I'm hungry for everything, starving in fact. If you want to eat food first, I'll still ravish just as enthusiastically."

She appreciated the thought. Her gaze softened. "What did you bring?"

"Charlie's chowder and some of that bread they serve with it."

She grinned. It was her favorite seafood chowder. He had to have driven way out to the restaurant and stood in line to get it. "Wow. Thanks for the thought." Her stomach whined and she rubbed it gently. "I guess that settles it. Let's eat now," she said leading him towards the kitchen.

Michael set the food on the counter in the great room while Nikita went and found some white wine and a couple of glasses. Then she poured the wine and he opened the cartons and set out the silverware.

Delving into her chowder, Nikita closed her eyes, savoring the blended flavors of shrimp, crab, lobster, and fish. When she opened them again, she found

Michael watching her with a smile on his face. "What? What did I do?"

"Nothing," he chuckled. "Enjoy your food. I just like to watch you, see you do the things you like."

"Then see me get fat from eating this rich stuff and going to bed on it," she finished for him.

"Oh, I'll help you work it off before you go to sleep," he promised, throwing her a hot look. Their mouths fused together in a moist kiss over the counter. Both moaned, broke apart and then ate faster.

When they'd finished, he pushed the cartons and glasses out the way and reached for Nikita. "Want to get creative?" He shaped the curve of her breasts with both hands.

She stared down at the counter and back at Michael. "I want you here and now, but I'm so tired I'd probably fall asleep on the counter afterwards."

"Let's compromise." His hands moved lower. "How about me, in your bed, in two minutes?"

"You're on." Nikita turned and they both raced for her bedroom.

Sated in the warmth of Michael's arms much later, the sound of the alarm jerked her from the depths of sleep. Quickly leaning over to shut it off, she fell back against him. "Time to get up and go home."

Michael's arms tightened about her. His eyes remained closed. "No. I'm not leaving."

"Michael, it's two-thirty in the morning," she said, shaking him gently.

"Exactly," he grumbled. "I'm not going anywhere." His eyes opened and she saw frustration, determination, and a hint of vulnerability glinting their brown depths. "I can't take being separated anymore. I think about you all the time, and I barely get to see you."

She too was tired of sneaking around and getting little bits of time together when she needed a lot. She ran her fingers across the short, dark razor stubble that gave him a slightly disreputable but sexy look. "When our project work advances a little..."

"Then there'll be other projects," he finished for her, a question in his eyes. "I'm talking about us. Don't you miss me?"

"You know I do." She nuzzled his nose with her own in a sensual version of an Eskimo kiss. Her thoughts reflected back to the cruise, when he'd been all hers, and she moved closer.

"Then why should I go home?" he asked, rubbing a hand up and down her arm.

Nikita stared back at him, her thoughts racing. *Because I wasn't brought up this way. It would hurt my family. Because I'm just not up to the raunchy comments we'll draw or the necessary explanations.* "Michael, you know how it is in this town. The cruise caused enough gossip and innuendo. If they knew we were carrying on like this..."

"Do you think they don't? And does it really matter?" He scanned her face and she instinctively knew that the moment of truth had arrived. Her gut clenched as he continued. "On the cruise, I asked you to marry me. Maybe it was a little premature then, but now you've had several weeks to consider it."

She swallowed hard, trying to think of something to say. Her heart pounded in her chest, the noise filling her ears.

Crawling from beneath the covers, he got down on his knees beside the bed and took her hand. "Did you know that you're the first thing on my mind when I wake up each morning? I go to sleep each night with thoughts of you. Nikita, you are my dream." He bent to press a warm, moist kiss to her fingers. "My heart, my body, my mind and my soul belong to you. Won't you please marry me?"

Bending over their joined hands, Nikita's eyes filled with tears. She'd gotten her pretty words and there was no way she could doubt the sincerity in Michael's voice and his expression. Should she hold out for the one word he hadn't used? Could she, now that she loved him more than ever? "Oh, Michael," she sobbed and began crying in earnest.

"Don't cry, sweetheart." Michael nuzzled her cheek and got back into bed to pull her close. "I do love you. I guess I saved the best for last." He pulled a tissue from the nightstand and patted her face with it. "It's not an easy thing for me to say, but I mean it with all my heart."

"When? When did you realize it?" She sniffed, anxious to hear each precious word.

"When we got back from the cruise and had to be apart. When the load at work made things worse. It wasn't a single point in time. You spoiled me. I've been starving for your love and affection. I've got this void inside me that only you can fill and the little time we spend together seems like a few drops in the bucket." Tilting her chin up, he kissed her moist eyelids and asked in a voice rough with emotion. "So, are you going to marry me?"

"Yes, Michael." Nikita's lips met his in a sizzling kiss. "I'll marry you."

Laughing in relief he gathered her close, his hands caressing her arms and back. "Yes! It's about time! When?"

"Whenever you want." Still a little dazed, she lay against him, her head on his naked chest.

"How about right now?" His gaze turned daring.

Nikita shook her head. "My mom will want a big fuss and so does yours. Besides, I've always wanted a formal wedding."

"What do think? Can we do it in a month?"

"We'll have to, because I'm not waiting any

longer. I don't like being apart." Nikita's arms locked around his neck, as happy as if she'd gotten Christmas in July. Love made all the difference in the world.

Michael's arms tightened about her, his hands touching her with wonder. "We'll be happy, Nikita, I swear it."

"This is my dream," Nikita said, fresh tears sparkling on her lashes. "I love you Michael..."

One month later Nikita and Chenelle stood together in church.

"This feels so unreal. I can't believe I finally made it." Nikita sighed at her beautiful reflection in the full-length mirror. The pearl-rimmed neckline of the dress dipped over her breasts to reveal a becoming bit of cleavage and the sides nipped in to flatter her small waist. To complement the headpiece, her stylist had applied a fall of hair that brushed her shoulders. Right now, she felt more beautiful than she had her entire life. Laughing, she whirled in a white cloud of silk and chiffon.

"I'm just glad that everything worked out for all of us." Chenelle hugged her tightly.

"Me too," Nikita agreed, returning the embrace.

Chenelle sighed. "When I think that all the time Michael and I were planning our stupid arrangement you were such a good friend, even though you were in love with him..."

"It's a good thing Lance found the guts to take you away from it all," Nikita said.

"That's for sure." Chenelle smiled.

"And I think Michael's happy with the way things turned out," Nikita added.

Chenelle raised her eyebrows. "Are you kidding? He personally thanked Lance for preventing him from making what would have been the biggest mistake of his life!"

Both women chuckled. As they separated, Chenelle patted her burgeoning belly and sat down in a nearby chair.

"Baby bothering you?" Nikita asked sympathetically as she threw her pregnant, but still beautiful friend a look of concern.

"Always." Chenelle smiled. "He's a busy little beaver."

At the knock on the door, they both turned to look at each other.

"Well, it's not Aunt Doris, bless her heart," Chenelle whispered.

"I'll get it," Nikita said, lifting the hem of her dress from the floor.

"No, let me." With amazing speed and agility, Chenelle jumped up and went to answer the door. She held the door open just a bit, covering the opening with her bulky body. Nikita heard her talking in a low tone and an answering masculine whisper. Abruptly, Chenelle turned to face her. "Michael wants to talk to you."

"No!" Nikita started nervously. "He shouldn't come in here. It's bad luck for the groom to see the bride before the wedding."

Chenelle spoke with Michael and then back to Nikita. "He says he'll talk through the door."

As Nikita approached the door, Chenelle said, "I've got something to do. I'll be right back."

The next thing Nikita knew, Chenelle was slipping out the door. "Chenelle?" she called out in surprise.

"Are you all right, sweetheart?" Michael spoke from the other side.

Nikita leaned against the back of the door. "Just a little nervous." Although she wasn't particularly superstitious, she didn't want to tempt fate.

Then Michael eased around the door and shut it, looking as handsome as ever in his black tux. Nikita's heart fluttered. Just looking at him made it hard to breathe. "Michael, you should have stayed on the other side of the door."

He gave her a mischievous grin. "I had to see how you were holding up. Mmmm, you smell good." Pulling her into his arms, he kissed her with a wild, passionate hunger that set her body to tingling.

Nikita felt a little dizzy. It was going to be some

honeymoon. "I'm fine," she murmured in answer to his question. "You know it's bad luck to see the bride right before the wedding."

"Don't worry, it'll be all right. Besides, I've done a hell of a lot more than look at you today." He chuckled, his eyes darkening.

"True," she acknowledged, blushing at the memory of their early morning rendezvous. He traced the pearl neckline of her dress with the tip of a finger. "Did you bring cognac?" she managed to ask.

Raising his eyebrows and opening his mouth, he parodied a scandalized expression. "In the church? What would the reverend say?"

Nikita rolled her eyes. She would never forget Michael drinking cognac with her just before his wedding fiasco with Chenelle. "Come off it, Michael. Remember last time?"

"Don't remind me." He sighed. "I needed every bit of the alcohol to get me through that disaster." Gazing at her wonderingly, he lifted her arm and whirled her around. "You're beautiful, Nikita. I don't need a drink to watch you join with me forever. Just looking at you intoxicates me."

Hugging him close, her fingers brushing the soft, ebony hair curling just above his collar, Nikita's eyes sparkled with tears. "I love you, Michael."

"I love you too." He touched the moisture on her cheeks. "This is what I want and I have no doubts,

no regrets. How about you? You still want me forever?"

"Forever and ever," she breathed, her heart
swelling with emotion. "You'll always have my
heart, and my love."

"And I'll treasure them and you forever," Michael
whispered with a husky sincerity that made her
want to cry with happiness. He dropped down into
Chenelle's chair and pulled Nikita onto his lap, wedding finery and all. "You're not nervous now, are
you?"

"No," she answered quickly and then realized
that her teeth were actually chattering. How could
she be nervous when she was about to fulfill all her
dreams? she wondered. Her hand resting on his
shoulder actually trembled. "I—I guess I am. I don't
know what's wrong with me."

"It's all right, baby." Carefully pressing her head
to his chest, he slowly rocked her back and forth, his
soothing voice caressing her ears like music. His
scent mixed with aftershave filled her nostrils and
her mind with pleasant memories. "You know this
whole show today is just about you and me. Don't
worry about all those people out there, because they
don't matter when it comes down to it."

"Yes, I know," she whispered, imprinting this
moment in her memory forever. "Everything is fine,
Michael. Just give me a few minutes. I'll be okay."

For several moments, he continued to talk while holding her close. Gradually, Nikita stopped trembling. A loud knock on the door startled both of them. They'd forgotten themselves.

The knob turned and someone cracked the door open. "Coming in," a familiar voice called.

Nikita scrambled off Michael's lap. "Daddy!" She met his gray gaze and stared for a moment. It sometimes startled her to look at her father and see so many of her own features reflected in his face. He'd moved back to town, but with their busy schedules, she didn't see him as much as she wanted. They used the phone a lot.

"Hi-ya, princess. You look beautiful. Your mother wanted to come, but she'd already been here with you for more than an hour. I persuaded her to give me this final chance to be with you before you walk down the aisle and become an old married lady." Crossing the room, he hugged her hard and kissed her cheek. Nodding at Michael he added, "Did you two forget that you have a whole church full of people waiting to see you take the final step?"

Michael stood, straightening his tux and shuffling his feet. "I just needed to talk with Nikita for a moment."

Cupping her chin, he gently kissed her lips. "Meet me in the chapel?"

"Oh yes. There's no place I'd rather be."

Tangling her fingers in the thick hair above his collar, she drew him close for another warm, velvet kiss. When her father cleared his throat for the second time, they broke apart, laughing.

"I'm leaving." Michael chuckled as he blew her a kiss.

"What was that really about?" her father asked when Michael had gone.

"I was nervous," Nikita admitted as she lifted the fancy hatbox from the floor and opened it.

"Why?" Her father wrinkled his forehead and shot her a skeptical look. "A blind man could see that you're crazy about him."

"It's just that I'm finally getting what I've wanted for so long. Everything has a dreamlike quality. Even your presence adds a bit of unreality to the whole situation. Before we started the wedding preparations, when was the last time I saw you?" She lifted the pearl and lace-covered circlet from the box.

"I'm too ashamed to say." he mumbled.

"It's been too long Daddy."

"That's for sure. You've grown a lot since I last saw you, and your mother..." He watched her peel back the cloud of chiffon and place the circlet on her head. "Do you want me to find Chenelle or your mother so that they can help you with that?"

Nikita smiled and began to strategically place

the hanging loops of pearls and arrange her hair. "I'll manage. "Now, what about mother?" she asked quickly.

"When I look at her I find it hard to remember how I ever found the strength to leave. She's a wonderful woman."

Nikita turned to him, hardly daring to hope. "Oh Daddy, do you think you might..."

"Stick around for a while? Try and stop me. I don't particularly care for the company she's keeping right now anyway."

"I must have been good this year, because I'm getting all my wishes," she exclaimed, giving her father another quick hug.

"Are you ready?" he asked as she slipped the veil back in place.

"One more thing." Sighing, Nikita retrieved the bouquet of blue and white flowers from the other florist box. Satiny white ribbons trailed as she lifted it to her nose and sniffed the exotic fragrance. Her hands trembled.

Her father gently hugged her shoulders. "Okay princess, time for the royal walk?" When she nodded he took her arm. "Let's go."

In a flurry of activity, they made it to the chapel door. On cue, the wedding march began. Once again, the wedding began, but this time, Nikita was the bride and at the altar, Michael watched her with eyes of love. Chenelle's little sister, Nina, went down the aisle throwing rose petals. Michael's nephew, Andy followed her with the ring.

This is it, Nikita thought as the bridesmaids began to pair with the groomsmen. Michael and I will be married in the next few minutes. She floated on a buoyant cloud of happiness. Her knees trembled with nervous excitement.

She peered into the church and saw all her friends and family members chuckling at the antics of the children going down the aisle. As the bridesmaids followed, Nikita peeked towards the front of the church where her beautiful mother sat alone in a blue and white evening suit. A jaunty little pillbox hat sat atop her head with its sassy net veil hanging down as she stared anxiously towards the door.

The last of the bridesmaids walked the baby blue and white-ribboned aisle with the groomsmen. She caught sight of Michael's parents as Chenelle started down the aisle with the best man. Lila Matheson's dark head turned and she smiled encouragingly at Nikita. Michael Sr. nodded in approval.

Michael drew her eyes like a special treasure. His expression shone with a heady mixture of pride, hope and love. She trembled, her heart full, and said a quick prayer of thanks.

As he had in her dream, Nikita's father took her arm, and they followed the same narrow path through the silent crowd, virtually floating down the satin expanse. She could barely hear the music. Instead, she heard the excited beating of her heart.

At the altar, Michael waited, his expression intent, an air of breathless impatience swirling around him. His lips formed her name and he extended one hand, palm up. As she reached his side, he clasped her hand and the glow of his smile warmed her all over.

Reverend Adler began his part of the ceremony, and they shared another smile, lost in each other. Neither wavered as they repeated their vows. Then Reverend Adler asked if anyone knew a reason why Nikita and Michael should not be joined. Unafraid, Nikita and Michael held hands and gazed into each other's eyes.

There was an almost audible sigh amongst the crowd in the church as the ceremony proceeded. At the last, when the reverend pronounced them husband and wife, Nikita lifted her face for Michael's kiss. His moist mobile lips covered hers in a gentle kiss that flamed into a hungry, passion-filled joining of their lips and tongues. Michael held her tightly, his fingers caressing the lace covering her back and shoulders. Nikita sighed happily, secure in the knowledge that she had finally come home.

Have you read a book Today?

If not

Why don't you try our line of books meant to satisfy your literary taste.

Genesis Press Inc. is the home of the nation's leading line of African-American romance novels, Indigo Romance. We want everyone to read and enjoy novels with characters they can relate to and identify. We want to bring quality novels to the market that build positive self image and reflection. Genesis plans to continue to build and grow its' Indigo Romance line, offering love stories to fill all hearts.

Thank You
for reading a Genesis
Book.

PATH OF FIRE
by
T. T. Henderson

Fighting depression over the failure of her marriage and her inability to have children, Tia Algod flees to Africa as an aid worker for Feed the World. When the raging war between the Tutsi rebels and the Hutus encroaches on the refugee camp in Zaire where Tia is working, she suddenly finds herself a refugee with her life in danger. To escape, Tia must reach Kigali, Rwanda, and the Feed the World headquarters.

If not Call us and order today
at

INDIGO

Winter & Spring 2002

❧ June

Still Waters Run Deep	Leslie Esdaile	$9.95
Indigo After Dark Vol. V		$14.95
Ebony Butterfly	Delilah Dawson	

OTHER INDIGO TITLES

A Dangerous Deception	J.M. Jeffries	$8.95
A Dangerous Love	J.M. Jeffries	$8.95
After The Vows (Summer Anthology)	Leslie Esdaile	$10.95
	T.T. Henderson	
	Jacquelin Thomas	
Again My Love	Kayla Perrin	$10.95
A Lighter Shade of Brown	Vicki Andrews	$8.95
All I Ask	Barbara Keaton	$8.95
A Love to Cherish	Beverly Clark	$8.95
Ambrosia	T.T. Henderson	$8.95
And Then Came You	Dorothy Love	$8.95
Best of Friends	Natalie Dunbar	$8.95
Bound by Love	Beverly Clark	$8.95
Breeze	Robin Hampton	$10.95

Cajun Heat	Charlene Berry	$8.95
Careless Whispers	Rochelle Alers	$8.95
Caught in a Trap	Andree Michele	$8.95
Chances	Pamela Leigh Starr	$8.95
Dark Embrace	Crystal Wilson Harris	$8.95
Dark Storm Rising	Chinelu Moore	$10.95
Eve's Prescription	Edwinna Martin Arnold	$8.95
Everlastin' Love	Gay G. Gunn	$8.95
Gentle Yearning	Rochelle Alers	$10.95
Glory of Love	Sinclair LeBeau	$10.95
Illusions	Pamela Leigh Starr	$8.95
Indiscretions	Donna Hill	$8.95
Interlude	Donna Hill	$8.95
Intimate Intentions	Angie Daniels	$8.95
Kiss or Keep	Debra Phillips	$8.95
Love Always	Mildred E. Riley	$10.95
Love Unveiled	Gloria Green	$10.95
Love's Deception	Charlene Berry	$10.95
Mae's Promise	Melody Walcott	$8.95
Midnight Clear (Anthology)	Leslie Esdaile	$10.95
	Gwynne Forster	
	Carmen Green	
	Monica Jackson	
Midnight Magic	Gwynne Forster	$8.95
Midnight Peril	Vicki Andrews	$10.95
Naked Soul	Gwynne Forster	$8.95
No Regrets	Mildred E. Riley	$8.95
Nowhere to Run	Gay G. Gunn	$10.95
Passion	T.T. Henderson	$10.95

Past Promises	*Jahmel West*	*$8.95*
Path of Fire	*T.T. Henderson*	*$8.95*
Picture Perfect	*Reon Carter*	*$8.95*
Pride & Joi	*Gay G. Gunn*	*$8.95*
Quiet Storm	*Donna Hill*	*$10.95*
Reckless Surrender	*Rochelle Alers*	*$8.95*
Rendezvous with Fate	*Jeanne Sumerix*	*$8.95*
Rooms of the Heart	*Donna Hill*	*$8.95*
Shades of Desire	*Monica White*	*$8.95*
Sin	*Crystal Rhodes*	*$8.95*
So Amazing	*Sinclair LeBeau*	*$8.95*
Somebody's Someone	*Sinclair LeBeau*	*$8.95*
Soul to Soul	*Donna Hill*	*$8.95*
Subtle Secrets	*Wanda Y. Thomas*	*$8.95*
Sweet Tomorrows	*Kimberley White*	*$8.95*
The Price of Love	*Sinclair LeBeau*	*$8.95*
The Reluctant Captive	*Joyce Jackson*	*$8.95*
The Missing Link	*Charlyne Dickerson*	*$8.95*
Truly Inseparable	*Wanda Y. Thomas*	*$8.95*
Unconditional Love	*Alicia Wiggins*	*$8.95*
Whispers in the Night	*Dorothy Love*	*$8.95*
Whispers in the Sand	*LaFlorya Gauthier*	*$10.95*
Yesterday is Gone	*Beverly Clark*	*$8.95*
Yesterday's Dreams, Tomorrow's Promises	*Reon Laudat*	*$8.95*
Your Precious Love	*Sinclair LeBeau*	*$8.95*

*You may order on-line at www.genesis-press.com, by phone at
1-888-463-4461, or mail the order-form in the back of this book.*

Love Spectrum Romance

Romance across the culture lines

Indigo After Dark

erotica beyond sensuous

Indigo After Dark Vol. 1	$10.95
In Between the Night Angelique	
Midnight Erotic Fantasies Nia Dixon	
Indigo After Dark Vol. II	$10.95
The Forbidden Art of Desire Cole Riley	
Erotic Short Stories Dolores Bundy	
Indigo After Dark Vol. III	$10.95
Impulse Montana Blue	
Pant Coco Morena	

ORDER FORM

Mail to: Genesis Press, Inc.
315 3rd Avenue North
Columbus, MS 39701

Name _____

Address _____

City/State _____ Zip _____

Telephone _____

Ship to (if different from above)

Name _____

Address _____

City/State _____ Zip _____

Telephone _____

Qty	Author	Title	Price	Total

Use this order form, or
call
1-888-INDIGO-1

Total for books _____

Shipping and handling:
    $3 first book, $1 each
    additional book _____
Total S & H _____
Total amount enclosed _____
MS residents add 7% sales tax

ORDER FORM

Mail to: Genesis Press, Inc.
315 3rd Avenue North
Columbus, MS 39701

Name _____

Address _____

City/State _____ Zip _____

Telephone _____

Ship to (if different from above)

Name _____

Address _____

City/State _____ Zip _____

Telephone _____

Qty	Author	Title	Price	Total

Use this order form, or
call
1-888-INDIGO-1

ORDER FORM

Mail to: Genesis Press, Inc.
315 3rd Avenue North
Columbus, MS 39701

Name _____

Address _____

City/State _____ Zip _____

Telephone _____

Ship to (if different from above)

Name _____

Address _____

City/State _____ Zip _____

Telephone _____

Qty	Author	Title	Price	Total

Use this order form, or
call
1-888-INDIGO-1

Total for books _____

Shipping and handling:
  $3 first book, $1 each
  additional book _____

Total S & H _____

Total amount enclosed _____

MS residents add 7% sales tax